Heart of a Tiger

***Other Five Star Titles
by Marlys Rold:***

The Mercenary

Heart of a Tiger

Marlys Rold

Five Star • Waterville, Maine

This novel is a work of fiction. Names, characters, places and incidents are either the product of the author's imagination, or, if real, used fictitiously.

First Edition
First Printing: March 2004

Set in 11 pt. Plantin by Christina S. Huff.

Printed in the United States on permanent paper.

Library of Congress Cataloging-in-Publication Data

Rold, Marlys, 1943–
   Heart of a tiger / by Marlys Rold.—1st ed.
      p.   cm.
   ISBN 1-59414-113-4 (hc : alk. paper)
   1. Wildlife photographers—Fiction.   2. Americans—Asia—Fiction.   3. Missing persons—Fiction.   4. Asia—Fiction.
   I. Title.
   PS3618.O54H43 2004
   813'.6—dc22   2003064713

To my husband, Dick,
my daughter Kim,
and my son Jeff and his wife Cathy
for their support.

Author's Note

For those readers wishing to know more about the Man-
eating Tigers of the Sundarbans and their accomplishments,
a fund of information awaits at www.Discovery.com, or use
any search engine to bring up information on tigers or the
Man-eating Tigers of the Sundarbans.

"Tyger, Tyger, burning bright,
in the forests of the night.
What immortal hand or eye,
could frame thy fearful symmetry?"

by William Blake

Chapter One

The tall, lanky man dressed in black—jeans, shirt, and range boots—watched the diminutive blonde walk toward him and wondered where she got the guts to keep approaching. Unshaven and disheveled, his eyes, what could be seen of them, were red-rimmed, angry, and now honed to narrowed slits.

It should have been obvious to anyone at the neglected bar in the remote village of Kalgola that the sandy-haired guy slumped in his chair at the table littered with empty shot glasses had to be as nasty and dangerous as they came.

But the woman just kept walking, regardless of his appearance. She didn't even flinch when she got close enough to get a clear view. So close she could reach out and touch the dark stubble on his brooding face.

Too close, he decided.

"Mr. Tanner?" Standing near him, showing tension only in the set of her slim shoulders, she waited.

Ahhh shit, he thought, *Barbie Doll wants to play jungle games.*

"Who wants ta know?" he snarled.

Signaling the bartender for another drink, with a flick of one large hand, he hoped she'd leave him alone, but knew she probably wouldn't—not until she said her piece.

What the hell could she want from him? And how in hell did she manage to step hatbox fresh into a smelly bar in the middle of this godforsaken land?

Unfortunately, even damn-near blitzed, his body tightened as the woman came to an abrupt halt directly in front of him.

His obvious anger appeared to have no tangible effect on her. Taking a deep breath, she seemed to stifle the urge to retaliate in kind and answered evenly. "My name's Kelly Griffin, and I'd like to know if you are Sam Tanner?"

In spite of a raging headache, Sam managed to make a thorough inspection of the lovely woman who stood so resolutely before him. He figured her for no more than five-two, and although she appeared delicate, the body under the khaki slacks and shirt was lush. Tempting. She wore her blonde, shiny hair in a no-nonsense ponytail, but her eyes were what commanded his attention. Wide, clear, and azure blue, they resembled a tropical sky before the arrival of a killer storm. Eyes that said don't mess with me.

For the first time in one hell of a long time Sam felt a simultaneous stirring in both his mind and body.

"Okay, blue eyes, I'll play along. The name's Tanner, so what?"

Kelly Griffin didn't seem to know whether to be relieved or disappointed. She'd found the man she'd come looking for, the man Louie Dupree, from the hotel, said might help—which should have been a good start—but he'd turned out to be a surly, drunken bully, and she felt shaken.

She sighed. She'd traveled a great distance.

"May I sit, please?" Guardedly, she watched the brooding giant with the craggy face as she placed a tentative hand on the chair across the small rattan table he was sprawled behind.

"Help yourself." He picked up the shot glass the bartender had just placed before him, guzzled the amber liquid in one smooth motion, slammed the glass back down on the table, and waited.

He might have been drinking water for all the effect the whiskey seemed to have. He didn't grimace or change expression, simply stared at her with the same hard glint in those arresting light-blue eyes—young Clint Eastwood eyes. However, when his gaze descended to her mouth and slowly inched back up to her eyes, a flicker of something predatory lurking in their depths, simultaneous heat and fear spun through her.

Kelly fought the sudden urge to flee for her life.

It took an effort to keep her voice steady. "I'd like to talk to you," she said.

"So talk. Who's stopping ya?" He canted his gaze to her lips again.

Hopeless depression settled over Kelly. He wasn't going to help. He was just another misbegotten drunken derelict.

Drawing a deep breath, gathering herself, she asked, "Will it do any good to tell you about my problem?"

He crooked one sandy eyebrow. "How the hell would I know?"

"You'll listen then?" She held her breath and suddenly wondered why.

"You're wasting my time. Spit it out or get your ass off my chair."

"Your chair?" Her frown denied the claim.

"You're running out of time." His bloodshot eyes were still full of malice. But his mouth, when he wasn't snarling, was somehow sexy and inviting, completely at odds with the rest of him.

"I need your help," she said swiftly, in an effort to overcome her demure stature.

"No shit! I didn't figure you looked me up to tell me I'd won the lottery, blue eyes. Two minutes."

"What?"

"You've got two minutes to get to the point or I pick that sweet little ass up and toss you out of here myself."

Crude. "I need you to help me find someone in the Sundarbans," she said.

The sound that escaped him resembled more of a grunt than a laugh. "What's the joke, lady?"

"It's no joke. A man's life is at stake, and I need you to help me find him."

"In the Sundarbans? Is that what you're saying?" He snapped the words off one after the other, like rounds from an automatic pistol.

She nodded. The pony tail flailed behind her. "Yes."

"Listen, sweetheart, I don't know who's been pulling your leg or why, and I don't care, but you can forget that little fairy tale."

The empty feeling that had filled Kelly's chest since her brother turned up missing enveloped her again. "What do you mean . . . fairy tale?"

"If some misguided bastard tried to spend more than an hour or two in any part of that uninhabited maze, he's already dead. Take my word for it."

Tears threatening, she shook her head. "No. Jeff's not dead. I'd . . . I'd know if he were dead." They'd been close since childhood. Even now as adults they had a way of reading each other's minds, finishing each other's sentences. If he was dead, she was certain she would know.

Well hell, figures it'd be a man she's looking for. A wave of inexplicable disappointment washed through Sam. She loved the guy, whoever he was. *Was*—that was the operative word, although it shouldn't matter a damn one way or the other. If

12

the crazy bastard had gone to stay for any length of time on the island, it didn't take a triple digit IQ to know his fate. There wouldn't be much left to identify, maybe a few scraps of clothing and a wristwatch.

The tigers in the Sundarbans were killing machines. Precise, relentless, and always hungry. They got their man every damn time.

Sam's expression softened. He recognized her pain, tainted by the same inexplicable despair as his own.

"Go back where you came from, blue eyes. He's gone. You can't help him now." He raised two fingers to the bartender and seconds later two shot glasses filled with dark whiskey arrived, so full they slopped over when the man plunked them down.

Holding one of the murky glasses out to Kelly, Tanner said, "This should help some. Drink up."

She gazed with disgust at the grimy shot glass he'd extended. "No, thank you. *I* don't need a crutch."

Son of a bitch! She had guts, he'd give her that.

"You've led a sheltered life, haven't ya, sweetheart?" He tossed down both drinks, one right after the other and stared at her, daring her to comment.

Kelly stared back, her gaze just as relentless.

Minutes ticked by.

You arrogant bastard! she thought.

But despite the anguish that threatened to overwhelm her, she wasn't ready to give up, and certainly not because some drunken lout in ragged jeans had just spewed his obviously prejudiced opinions.

No! Absolutely not. Her brother Jeff was alive. She knew. She could feel him out there somewhere. And she'd find him if it meant meeting all the drunken derelicts in Kalgola until she could hire one she could sober up long enough to help.

Scraping back the straight-backed rattan chair, she stood up. Reaching into her slacks' pocket, she retrieved a card and dropped it onto the table in front of Sam Tanner. Valiantly biting her tongue as the words, "eat dirt and die" narrowly failed to escape, she said, "That's where I'm staying if you sober up and change your mind. Otherwise, I'm sure I can find someone else . . . someone who isn't afraid of his own shadow. Good day, Mr. Tanner."

Along with every other man in the room, Sam watched her slacks ride up and cup one high, rounded cheek, then the other, as she strode away. Sam even scrutinized the spot where she disappeared through the doorway for several reverent minutes before he could tear his gaze away. When he did, he looked at the card she'd dropped in front of him. Picking it up, he read her name, address, telephone number, the company he assumed she worked for—Interior Designs—and at the bottom of the card, written in a lacy scrawl, the name of the only decent local hotel.

Even greener then I figured. Swearing under his breath, he wondered who else she'd given the card to, and who among them could read English and consider her fair game.

Shaking his head at her foolishness proved to be a major mistake. Dizziness swamped him, turning his stomach. *Maybe not all bad,* he decided, his expression rueful. It had quickly put an end to the uncomfortable tightness in his groin.

He could stand. Well, *maybe* he could stand. The question was, should he bother? Or should he just have another drink and forget Kelly Griffin and her tight little ass?

Of course, that would mean he'd also have to forget the poor bastard lost in the Sundarbans. *By some miracle could he still be alive? And if he was, could Sam rescue him?* His conscience flayed him mercilessly.

In less than a minute, he decided. Cursing himself for a fool, he ordered the bar's one and only food offering, a spicy stew-like conglomeration, made of only God knew what, hot and filling, and a pot of tar-black coffee, the house specialty.

After the hurried meal, he was full and more alert, but still slightly logy from all the whiskey he'd consumed. Sam left the bar and ambled toward the hotel, hoping the exercise would chase away the last of the hangover that still hammered away at the inside of his skull like a tiny angry carpenter plying his trade.

He'd been a fool to wallow in self-pity and regret. It hadn't solved anything. John was just as dead. Whiskey wouldn't bring him back. Nothing would.

"I'm getting out of this godforsaken country," he muttered. Kicking up dust, he strode purposefully down the baked-dirt track that could almost be mistaken for a road in the tiny village.

He was getting out, going back to civilization. He'd had a bellyful of adventure. "The hell with it! It's time to grow up. I just wish to hell I'd smartened up before John pulled that damn fool stunt."

As far as Sam was concerned, it was at least seventy-five percent his fault that John died. At this moment he chose to forget they had both wanted to come to the Sundarbans. Both had longed for that last great adventure. And he hadn't twisted John's arm. It had been his best friend's idea to challenge the tigers by getting close enough to them to take photographs without the use of a telephoto lens. To cheat death one last time. Couldn't see it, because of what had happened.

John had made a fatal error. John had died.

And Sam couldn't stop blaming himself. Surely there must have been something he could have done, some way to save his oldest friend.

Shit! If he let himself dwell on John's death another second, he'd reverse his course and go back to the bar and wallow in booze to try to extinguish the blinding pain. Still, he kept on walking, arguing with himself. Why should he stick his neck out for someone he didn't even know? It wouldn't bring John back. But *dammit,* he'd died a horrible death.

Well hell, it wouldn't hurt to talk to the woman about it, would it?

Sam consciously turned his thoughts to the luscious blonde, using her image to drive away his grief. It enabled him to reach the flat-roofed, two-story wooden dwelling that was the Benston Hotel. Four crude wooden posts held up the sagging tin roof over a splinter-filled, weather-beaten, plank decking that fronted the narrow, dusty street.

He took the six warped stairs that led to the rickety verandah two at a time and walked through the hotel's door. A spring loaded bell chimed as he entered, and in seconds a bespectacled, balding gnome of a man appeared behind the registry desk. Squinting up at Sam, he reached behind him to a pegboard where keys hung on hooks.

Sam took the extended key. "Which room is the Griffin woman's?" He didn't know whether to call her Miss or Mrs.; didn't even know whether she was single or married and the lack of knowledge irritated him. She hadn't worn a ring, he'd noticed, but out here that didn't mean anything. All travelers were warned about wearing jewelry, and unless they were looking to get mugged, they took the advice.

Apparently, Sam's scowl intimidated Louie Dupree, the hotel's manager. "Ms. Griffin is in room 6, Mr. Tanner, and I believe she's in at the moment," Louie answered quickly. "Would you like me to call and tell her you're on your way?"

"No, thanks. I'll just surprise her." Sam sent Dupree a

wicked grin, aware that the diminutive man considered him ill-mannered, at the very least. Still, he knew Louie wouldn't consider him a threat to a woman, although Louie had witnessed Sam in rare form when a burly waterfront lout tried to start a fight in the bar. Sam's hands had blurred and the larger man had hit the floor in a matter of seconds, startling the hotelman as well as everyone else nearby.

"Very well." Louie blinked hard several times, failing to conceal his disapproval, but he didn't do anything as foolish as to interfere.

The loud knock on her door startled Kelly. Shaken, she got up from the bed where she'd been resting, and called out, "Who is it?"

"Tanner."

She sucked in a breath. A confrontation with a drunken Sam Tanner in a crowded bar was a far cry from one with a blitzed Tanner in a small, cramped hotel room.

"What do you want?" Her voice tense, she stared at the door and the flimsy chain bolt that was supposed to protect her from intruders. Despite her trepidation, she couldn't help thinking about Sam Tanner's powerhouse build and remembering his hungry gaze on her mouth earlier, and she fought to steady her nerves.

"I thought *you* were the one who wanted something." He still sounded surly.

Suddenly hopeful, Kelly took a cautious step toward the door. "Are you offering to help?"

"Did I say that?" he growled.

Confusion stopped her hand on its way to release the chain. A tremor tingled up her spine. "Then what *do* you want?"

In a voice tinged with heavy sarcasm, he answered,

"You're gonna have to open the door to find out, now aren't ya, blue eyes?"

There's always a catch. Kelly sighed, turned the knob, opened the door as far as the chain would allow, and peered out.

Ohhh boy! He had a gun in a holster at his hip.

"Well?" Her cool voice belied her true condition—almost overwhelming fear.

"Open the damn door and let me in. I don't bite!"

He looked to her as though he might do worse than bite.

"You can tell me what you want standing there," she said.

Sam sighed and swore under his breath. "Look, I'm not here to harm you, but I don't intend to broadcast your business all over this damn hotel, either. It isn't half smart."

She considered this, then asked, "Why should I believe you?"

Shaking his head, he said, "Damned if I know."

She hesitated.

"Listen, sweetheart, if I were foolish enough to attack you, who in hell do you think would come to your rescue?"

Kelly peered out the slit in the door and saw no one. Come to that, she had a feeling the hotel was very nearly empty except for the few men she'd seen in the lobby from time to time.

"Just give me a clue as to why you're here," she said.

"I think you need help getting out of the country."

"I just got here!" she snapped.

"Do you want to hear me out, or should I just leave?" He turned away.

Intellect told her he was quite capable of kicking the door open, regardless of the chain, so she closed the door, lifted the chain, and flung the door open.

With a flourish she waved him in. "Be my guest."

Be bold and he might not figure that he scares hell out of me, she thought.

Her compliance sent a curious feeling of disappointment through Sam. He had to admit he'd wanted to use force on the door, and her. That wasn't like him. He might look like all kinds of a bully, but he'd never bullied a woman. Until now. So why was he so ready to have a confrontation with this one?

Because he itched to touch that velvet-like skin. And he knew damn well she wouldn't offer. She didn't know him and he'd acted like a complete fool since he'd met her. *Hell!* There had always been plenty of willing women, so why was this one getting under his skin? Sam didn't like the rash, out of control feelings she roused in him.

Tell her what's what and get the hell out!

He flicked a resentful gaze over her, as he stepped into the room and closed the door. She looked as good as she had earlier, maybe even better.

"I'm gonna give you some excellent advice, lady, free of charge. Get out of this fleabag hotel and out of the country. There's no one in this hellhole who's worth the powder to blow them to kingdom come. If anyone offers to help you, it will be for one thing and one thing only, to get into your cute little pants. You understand what I'm saying?" He glared at her, his eyes boring into her.

Kelly had been anything but happy when he closed the door, and now quivers of both apprehension and anticipation pulsed through her. Instinct warned her it wouldn't do to let her anxiety show, not to this guy. It would be like throwing flowers to stop a charging bull. Hopeless.

Hardening her voice, she managed to snap, "Thanks for sharing, but if you're trying to scare me off, you're wasting

19

your time. I can take care of myself. I intend to rescue Jeff with or without your help."

His eyebrows came together in a fierce scowl. "You have no idea what you're up against, lady."

If Sam Tanner represented the type of man she had to deal with and rely on, she was beginning to get a terrifying idea of just what she *was* up against. But that really didn't matter. She had no choice.

Holding her dread in check, her pulse escalating, she responded, "Thank you for the warning. But as I said, I'm quite capable of taking care of myself."

Her smug response goaded Sam. She was as vulnerable as a woman could be, just by being where she had no business being. Hell, he could take her right here—*right now*—and no one would try to stop him.

Lust swept away the last of his hangover. He stared at her, undressing her feverishly in his mind, unable to take his own advice and leave.

Kelly could accurately read the hunger in his gaze. Her pounding heart started to hopscotch. She slipped around him to open the door. Before she could get a grip on the door-knob, he struck with a mongoose's swiftness.

Grabbing her, he pulled her up into his arms, so close their faces were separated by mere inches. His breath, smelling of whiskey but strangely inviting, warmed her face.

The natural rasp in his voice deepened to a smoky growl as it escaped his clenched teeth. "You push a man too far, blue eyes, and you're gonna get in real deep trouble one of these days. You understand me?" He cocked his head.

Sam had convinced himself he only meant to frighten her, to scare her into leaving for her own good. But from the first touch of her soft flesh under his hands, he knew he had been lying to himself.

Passion flared, hot and consuming. The desire to kiss and taste that tempting mouth nearly overwhelmed him.

The swiftness of his attack had obviously stunned Kelly. Her first instinct might have been to fight him tooth and nail, but she didn't, probably realizing that against his superior strength her attempts would be futile.

He had her tightly against him, tight enough to feel the hard length of his arousal against her suddenly sensitive body. Her breathing quickened.

They stared into each other's eyes.

Her eyes widened as if she struggled to hold back an advancing blink with sheer determination, withholding a small weakness, giving him no encouragement.

His gaze dropped to her mouth and stalled. *Hell!*

"Put me down!" she snapped.

He blinked, abruptly put her down, and stepped back, scowling.

Drawing as deep a breath as she could summon, she opened her mouth and screamed.

The shrill shriek echoing in Sam's head brought his hangover headache back with a vengeance, a throbbing ache that hurt like the devil, all the way to his toenails.

In self-defense, he clapped his hands over his ears.

Man, his head was going to explode. "What in the name of hell do you think you're doing?" he said.

Eyes snapping, she pulled her leg back and slammed her foot into his shin, and they both grunted with pain. His muscled legs had the give of tree trunks.

She recovered first, darted around him, opened the door, and dashed into the hallway.

Sam watched her go with a sheepish look plastered on his face. When he got himself together, he held out his hands, palms up. "Hey, listen, I'm sorry. You don't have to run away. Let's start over and just change places. I'll stand in the hall and you can stand in your room. We'll keep the door open and talk. Deal?"

She continued to maintain a sprinter's stance. "I don't think so."

"Okay, you move down the hall toward the stairs and I'll come out and walk down to the other end. Will that work?"

As he spoke, he started through the door and she hurried toward the stairs. But he didn't follow her. Instead, he moved toward the opposite end of the hallway.

She stopped at the head of the stairs, turned, and glared at him. "Haven't you said what you came to say?"

He glanced down at his boots, back at her, and then sighed. "Yeah, I did, but you don't listen well."

Huffing, she snapped, "That's my problem and one I can't do anything about."

He mumbled something she couldn't possibly hear and leaned against the wall.

"Are you leaving?" Kelly sharply asked.

Sam crossed his legs and arms and lowered his head, still leaning against the wall at the far end of the corridor. "Just as soon as I figure out why I came over here in the first place."

Kelly, still perched at the head of the stairs, just shook her head. She waited, but he didn't move. Finally, slowly easing along the wall, she made her way back to her open doorway.

Sam didn't even lift his head as she dashed inside and closed and locked the door.

Minutes later, he pushed away from the wall and headed toward the stairs. He'd tried to warn her, he told himself, hoping to alleviate guilt.

Just as he reached the head of the stairs, the earth moved.

The movement shook the walls of the hotel, escalating to such frightening proportions that Sam could, in good conscience, no longer continue down the stairs. He swung swiftly around, sprinted down the hallway, and kicked Kelly's door open.

She was standing in the center of the room, frozen in terror. He dashed inside, grabbed her, and headed toward the door, just as the walls swayed in toward them from the top.

In the next moment, a crack streaked across the rough plaster ceiling. The hazy, spotted mirror over the dresser fell to the floor and shattered with a thunderous crash. Simultaneously, the only chair in the room, a cane rocker, danced its way across the floor towards them.

The earthquake grew stronger. Sounds of splintering wood littered the air. Outside, trees crashed to the ground, their death songs echoing long after they'd passed. Still, the shaking went on and on, as if the world were tearing apart at the seams.

Aware that the hotel was going to collapse at any second, Sam lurched toward the door, dragging Kelly with him. He stopped in the doorway, sheltering her in his arms under the archway as chunks of lath and plaster fell from the ceiling into the room they'd just left, splattering the threadbare rug where they'd been standing only seconds earlier.

The jungle's already stifling, moist air grew dense with dust, threatening to choke them.

Kelly clung to Sam.

They remained in the doorway, Sam covering her head by huddling over her, protecting her from falling debris as much as possible.

Seconds later, the fates threw them another nasty curve.

The lights flickered, and then went out. Darkness and dust engulfed them.

After what had seemed an eternity, but was probably no more than a minute, the shaking stopped. Dust continued to sift down all around them. Then, invoking deeper anxiety, the building trembled, as if trying to decide whether to stand or fall.

Sam tightened his grip on Kelly and pulled her with him down the hallway. Stumbling, barely able to see in the choking cloud of dust, they scrambled over piles of rubble that littered the passageway and eventually reached the shattered lobby.

There, chaos reigned. The wooden floor had buckled near the door, leaving broken planks that resembled a ragged pyramid, its apex pointing to what was left of the ceiling. Dust clouded the air here, too, making it difficult to breathe or see clearly. Fortunately, the front door stood wide open, hanging crookedly from its lower hinges, allowing a beacon of sunlight to angle its way inside.

Gingerly sidestepping loose boards and rubble, Sam and Kelly made it to the door.

The porch appeared to be nearly intact, but Sam, suspecting the steps were undermined, lifted Kelly into his arms and leaped to the street. When he reached solid ground and put a safe distance between them and the other swaying buildings, he stood Kelly on her feet.

"Thank God!" Eyes glazed with fear and shock, Kelly took in the devastation surrounding them. "I . . . I've never se . . . seen anything like this . . . it's dreadful. And it only took seconds . . . just seconds," she finished with appalled awe.

Sam grunted and gazed around with a fierce scowl. "Yeah, it just takes a few seconds. Then it's all over and these poor bastards are left with the nasty aftermath for years to come."

Several of the closest buildings were nothing but ruins, while, surprisingly, others nearby looked as though they had sustained little or no damage. But the inside of those buildings would be another matter. Given the magnitude of the quake, Sam figured none of the structures escaped un-scathed.

"Had to have been a six point something." He seemed to be muttering more to himself than Kelly.

Squinting at a store that appeared to be about to collapse, Sam turned to Kelly. "Stay put. I'm gonna see if there's anyone alive inside."

"Don't leave me!" Kelly cried, still totally shaken by their narrow escape.

Sam lifted her chin with his hand and studied her eyes for signs of shock. "You'll be all right, just stay put."

When she responded by squeezing her eyes shut, he gave her a little shake. Bending low, he got in her face. "Don't move from here. I'm going to see if I can help. Do you understand me?"

Staring at him, eyes filled with unparalleled terror, she finally nodded, but a sob escaped.

Sam didn't want to leave her anymore than she wanted him to go. Finally conquering the newly formed, rapidly growing fear of losing her, he started across the street.

He'd taken only a few steps when he had a sudden terrible visual that chilled him; Kelly lost and wandering in the jungle. He could almost hear the tiger's triumphant roar, see her body torn, mutilated, and lifeless, after the animal had feasted, and for a moment he couldn't move.

Then, the many pitiful cries for help from the injured penetrated his psyche and he reluctantly walked away.

A second later he stopped short, turned, and shouted. "Don't make me have to come looking for you, Kelly Griffin!"

Chapter Two

Kelly, shocked by the devastation surrounding her, didn't even think of rebelling against Sam's orders. Later she'd remember and be grateful she hadn't tried to disobey him. The aftermath of a catastrophe wasn't the time for dissension. Especially not with a virtual stranger whose very size intimidated her.

Ultimately, she realized that there would probably never be a good time to thwart the likes of Sam Tanner.

As she watched, he vanished from view. Dashing into the general store next to the hotel, he reappeared moments later, a frail, elderly woman cradled in his arms. Placing the sobbing woman gently down on the ground by Kelly, he headed back toward the store.

This time he didn't come right back.

Kelly's anxiety grew with every minute that passed without Sam's return. To distract herself, she attempted to focus her attention on the sobbing woman beside her. Kneeling, she scrutinized her closely for signs of physical trauma.

Relieved to find no obvious injuries, she asked, "Are you hurt?"

The woman sat straddled in a fetal position, head in hands, rocking back and forth and occasionally moaning. Her unresponsiveness led Kelly to believe she probably didn't understand English, and Kelly's attention wandered between the store front and the weeping woman.

Tanner . . . where are you?

There was absolutely no reason for Kelly to care what happened to a drunken lout like Sam Tanner. For starters, he'd turned her job offer down flat. Then he'd insisted she go home and forget her brother—even insisted Jeff was dead. All of which gave her every reason to hate this loathsome derelict.

So why was she so afraid for him? It didn't make sense.

Dammit, get out here—now, Tanner!

Suddenly, from the end of the street, an ominous cloud of smoke rose from one of the shattered structures. Within breathtaking seconds, angry flames shot through the thatched roof, leaping high into the air.

The stunned and injured villagers turned collectively to stare in horror at this new threat to their humble community. A murmur swept through the tattered survivors and the less injured began chattering excitedly among themselves. They dispersed, running and stumbling in different directions and returning with dilapidated buckets. Filling them from the well in the center of town, a brigade of disheveled villagers formed a line to fight the fire.

The straining bucket brigade toiled on, seemingly committed to the hopeless exertion—even as sparks from the fierce blaze drifted to other structures, igniting more lethal fires.

Feeling utterly helpless, Kelly watched as the hungry blaze spread at a frightening pace, engulfing each primitive thatched building in its path with a *whoosh*, then a crackling roar that almost sounded gleeful. For a moment, the fire's ferocity drove back the inept bucket brigade, but then the wind shifted, blowing back on itself, enabling the villagers to save the east end of the small hapless community.

The old woman beside Kelly began to moan louder, keening a steady sing-song lament that sent Kelly's jangled nerves closer to the edge.

Sam Tanner, get out here!

Her mind, feverish with fear, fabricated a terrifying scenario with little to no trouble. She envisioned something heavy pinning Sam down so he couldn't escape the building. She saw the insatiable flames reaching out for him. Saw him burning to death.

Unable to stand by and watch the inferno envelop the store with Sam inside, she gathered her courage, dashed across the street, and vaulted onto the porch.

A burst of wind blew intense heat from the nearby fire to Kelly, slowing her steps for a moment. Clenching her teeth, she made for the door. She nearly bumped into Sam as he emerged, carrying a man who must have been the old woman's husband.

Perspiring and flushed from the heat and exertion, he snarled, "Didn't I tell you to wait across the street. Get over there, *now.*"

Stung by his wrath, *she'd* cared enough to be worried, she turned and fled. But not before snapping back, "I shouldn't have worried. You're too damn mean to die."

Sam followed, easing the injured man down beside the woman he'd rescued earlier. Unburdened, he appeared to notice the fire for the first time as his penetrating gaze drifted from the advancing inferno to Kelly and back again.

Seeming to relax ever so slightly, he growled, "This isn't the time or the place to get into it, but next time I give an order, you might consider following it."

She just stared at him.

Shifting his attention to the injured man before she could defend herself, he said, "His leg's broken. We'll have to try to set and splint it."

Kelly's stomach lurched. She wanted to say: not we, *you.* However, she took the set of Sam's jaw as a warning and remained mute.

Addressing the man's wife, Sam continued his orders, "Try to keep him quiet, while I find something that'll work as a splint."

Not even waiting to see if the distraught old woman understood, he left again, leaving Kelly to deal with the problem of explaining. Fortunately, for all of them, the injured man remained motionless. His wife, however, never stopped. Clucking over him, she was like the head chicken in the hen house, scratching around in the dirt, making absolutely no impact on the rest of the flock—in this case, her husband.

Numbly, Kelly watched Sam move among the ruins, picking up and discarding several different length boards until he seemed satisfied with two short straight slats. Grabbing a coiled length of rope as well, he ran back to them and knelt down beside the injured man. Kelly tensed as he slit the man's pant leg with a Bowie knife he drew from a sheath on his belt. Pulling the two pieces of cloth back from the leg, he stared down at the bruised and broken limb. She swallowed hard as she watched him gingerly feel along the break, mumbling to himself. As he gripped the old man's foot and gave it a quick jerk, setting the leg with a grinding crack, a wave of nausea and dizziness sent Kelly to her knees.

Sam cut her a granite-faced glance, and then, muttering something unintelligible, he went back to working on the leg. As luck would have it, the injured man was no longer in pain. He'd fainted dead away. Placing the boards along both sides of the limb, Sam lashed them securely with twine he'd gathered while collecting the splints, effectively immobilizing the leg.

"That should minimize further damage." He spoke to the old woman who stared at him with gratitude.

Straightening, Sam switched his attention to the fire behind him, which still wasn't completely under control. It turned their faces red from the reflected glow.

He sighed, scooped the injured man into his arms, and addressed Kelly. "Hell and damnation. It looks like we'll have to move him whether we want to or not. Let's go, blue eyes."

Kelly struggled to her feet and followed, as he led the way down the smoke-filled street.

When they were safely away from the village, having made their way slowly to the Bay of Bengal on the Arabian Sea—a good quarter mile from the reach of the voracious fire—Sam lowered the shop owner, carefully leaning him against a boulder on the sandy beach. Then, standing tall, Sam silently surveyed their surroundings. The beach wasn't as safe as he'd have liked; tigers were excellent swimmers and over the years had killed hundreds of villagers. But with dozens of other survivors huddled around them, it would have to do. At least here the predators would lack the element of surprise. It wasn't like being in the jungle where one could see no more than a few feet in any direction.

"I've got to go back and see if I can help. Take my gun, and stay here. Don't go wandering off. And *don't*, under any circumstances, come looking for me." Sam's scowl could intimidate grown men, but he could only hope it would dissuade Kelly long enough to keep her out of harm's way. Apparently, she already knew him too well, he thought. She knew he wouldn't harm her. On the contrary, she had to know he'd

30

protect her with his life. He'd already exhibited that foolish behavior in her hotel room.

"You understand me?" He hunched his shoulders when she didn't immediately respond.

She gingerly took the gun, and glared back at him with a sullen frown. "I understand the language," she muttered. "It's just . . . well, I don't know who put you in command."

He stared down at her with his fiercest killer squint.

"I don't have time for this bullshit," he said, then turned on his heel and stalked away.

That last small act of defiance had drained what was left of Kelly's energy, and fatigue won out. Sinking to the sand, she gave thanks for the chance to rest legs that had been threatening to fail her in those last few minutes.

Watching Sam stride away, in spite of what she personally thought of him—it wasn't good—she marveled at his strength and stamina and wondered if anything would ever defeat him. Surprisingly, she found herself hoping that nothing ever would, even knowing he could intimidate her without half trying. One thing she knew for certain. She'd fight like the devil to keep that knowledge from him, because once he got hold of it, he would plow over her resistance until her backbone was putty.

Sheltered under a stand of mangrove trees, with the sun no longer overhead—it had set a good hour before—Kelly gazed at the moon. Hanging low in the sky, it shimmered across the water, fanning rays of light across the tranquil bay and cooling sand. If she'd been somewhere safe she'd have thought it a romantic picture. As it was, her imagination had her seeing tigers paddling with sinister stealth toward the shore in the moonlight.

Kelly gave up watching for predators, and listened as the

waves lapped in and out softly. However, there was no peace in the sound.

She and the old couple had been joined by refugees from the village, but as evening settled over the bay and the night deepened, the villagers in large groups silently abandoned them, heading back toward town. Every time another group left, Kelly felt more vulnerable, more exposed.

Sam had yet to come back, and she began to worry that he wouldn't return at all. He could have decided, she reasoned, that she was just too much trouble and abandoned her. I can't really blame him, she thought. All the same, the idea cut her to the quick and if she'd had the strength she'd have shed a few tears.

A half hour later, like a silent stalker, a cloud drifted across the moon, turning the already deep night even blacker.

The shopkeeper's wife, already nervous, started to chatter at Kelly in rapid Hindustani, growing more excited and agitated by the second. And when Kelly didn't understand her, she began to fling her hands into the air, as if she were shouting at the heavens for help. Then, apparently giving up on Kelly and heaven, she turned and pulled at her husband's arm, attempting to raise the injured man to his feet.

Tugging violently, she only managed to jerk him onto his side, where he sprawled awkwardly. Moaning from the added pain the movement cost him, he resisted her with what little strength he had left, slapping her arm with his free hand.

Kelly, fearing that the poor man would be more seriously injured, stepped in to try to dissuade his wife. "Please don't do this, he shouldn't be moved. You'll only injure him more."

The woman stopped tugging at her husband long enough to point at him and then at Kelly. Then she waved a hand toward the village, indicating that Kelly should help her move him.

Kelly shook her head. They'd never make it to town. Although frail, the shopkeeper would be too heavy for the two small women to manage on their own. "No. We can't do that. He's too heavy. Besides, it will only cause him more pain."

Abruptly the woman dropped her husband's arm. Still ranting, she grabbed Kelly by the wrist, shaking and scolding her all the while. Obviously motivated by fear, the woman constantly glanced over her shoulder as if expecting a vicious predator to leap upon her bowed back at any moment.

Then the moon completely disappeared behind the cloud, allowing the darkness to close in around them.

Kelly felt the woman's fear through the tension in her fingers as they squeezed her wrist. Insidiously, the old woman's fear turned contagious; Kelly felt the hairs on her neck twitch, her nerves ratcheting up in response.

On the verge of panic now, the old man's wife glanced behind her again. Appearing frightened enough to consider abandoning her husband, she again tried to lift the wounded man by yanking on his arm, and managed to elicit nothing but more anguished groans.

A muffled animal roar off in the distance froze the woman in mid-yank. Her face became a mask, depicting indescribable terror. The whites of her eyes grew prominent, her mouth became an elongated oval, and her body stiffened. When she could move again, she dropped her husband's arm, turned, and fled toward town without a backward glance.

The terrified old woman had covered no more than a hundred yards, head swinging from left to right, obviously searching for danger, when a large shadow emerged from the darkness and loomed over her. Throwing her arms up in supplication, the woman fell to the sand and pleaded with the shadow in rapid-fire Hindi.

Kelly's sudden shriek of fright never escaped. It died in

her throat. A low murmur came from the shadow hovering over the old woman. Then it began walking towards her. Sam materialized from the gloom. With one hand on the old woman's arm, he pulled her to her feet and led her firmly back to her husband and Kelly.

"She just ran off and left me with him," Kelly muttered, frustrated by the unexpected turn of events that had left her alone and responsible for the injured man.

Sam signed. "Yeah, I know."

Kelly, thoroughly outraged, snapped, "He's her *husband* . . . and he's injured."

"Simmer down. If you'd seen the carnage she's seen, you might have run too."

All of the recent tension, the fear, and uncertainty caught up with Kelly, and she exploded. "Damn you! You don't *understand* me. You don't have the faintest idea what I would or wouldn't do in any given situation."

Sam had bent down, apparently preparing to pick up the stricken man, but after Kelly's eruption, he straightened, his gaze narrowing on her face.

"You can have a temper tantrum some other time. Right now we're going to get our butts outta here and into town. You got anything else to get off your chest before we get started?"

He was undoubtedly the rudest, surliest, orneriest man she'd ever had the misfortune to meet. "It would be a waste of time and effort!"

Sam's deadly gaze pierced her and it looked for a moment as if he couldn't decide whether to pick the injured man up or come around him and get his hands on Kelly.

Finally, he gave her a tight grimace that might have barely passed for a smile but which she read as a near threat.

"We'll sure as hell hash this over later, Kelly Griffin." He lifted the old man easily, and led the way back toward town, with the two women trailing not far behind.

As they trudged through the sand toward the road, they were treated to repeats of the harrowing beastly roar that had panicked the old woman earlier. To Kelly's dismay the roars grew louder each time, sending a chill careening along her spine. There was no doubt in her mind as to the nature of the tiger who seemed to be narrowing the gap. It had to be one of the man-eaters Sam had told her about. She was sure of it.

What was it doing so close to the village? It had been Kelly's understanding that the man-eaters stayed on the islands, at least most of the time. If they did venture across, it was just to the beach to look for dead bodies.

She was on the mainland. She should have been safe. At least, that's what she'd been led to believe from talking to the so-called experts at the State Department back home in Los Angeles.

Sam's hurry-up gesture ended Kelly's ruminations. They hadn't trekked far along the road to the village when the old woman stopped and plucked at Sam's sleeve. Pointing east, using sign language, she indicated he should follow as she began to lead them off the road, down a path, away from the village.

"Why did we leave the road?" Kelly asked. "Where are we going?"

Sam stopped for only a moment, shifting his burden from one shoulder to the other. "Apparently, she wants to take her husband home."

"Wouldn't town be safer?" Already uneasy, Kelly eyed the dense, encroaching jungle.

"She indicated otherwise, and I tend to believe her since she abandoned him back at the beach when she felt threatened."

Kelly nodded, reluctant. "I suppose you're right. How far away is it?"

"She indicated that we're close. Let's get moving before we drop in our tracks."

The peasant woman, who had been disinclined to stop, halted when they paused to talk and moved forward again as soon as possible. She followed the narrow path with little trouble, for it was clearly distinct at night, even with the thickening vegetation on both sides. The drawback was that it seemed to go on forever, taking them farther away from Kalgola and what Kelly thought of as their only haven.

It felt as if they were walking for miles. She stumbled along, every muscle aching, her feet plodding one after the other. The impenetrable jungle seemed to be closing in on them more with every step they took, throwing them into a dark, threatening world.

If she'd had the strength to complain, she would have. She might even have begged for a rest stop. The occasional tiger's roar now sounded distant, but, ironically, she had enough faith in Sam to know he'd get them wherever they were going as fast as humanly possible.

Just when she was about to drop from exhaustion, a clearing opened directly in front of them. A small circle of bamboo huts, thatched with thick, dried grass, suddenly emerged in the eerie moonlight. Surprisingly, the tiny huts appeared to have fared better in the earthquake than the sup-posedly more solid buildings in town.

The old woman stopped before one of the dwellings and pulled aside a blanket covering the entrance. Chattering softy, she motioned for Sam to take her husband inside, then followed him. She indicated where she wanted him placed, and fussed about until she appeared satisfied her husband was as comfortable as possible. Then she followed Sam back outside and squatted near a circle of stones to the right of the hut. Using tiny pieces of kindling stored beside the door, she started a fire and, when it was burning brightly, placed a badly dented teakettle over the flames.

Then she gestured for Sam and Kelly to sit beside her.

Kelly dropped gratefully to the ground and watched as Sam lowered his big body to sit across from her. Too tired to speak, even with a world of questions eating away at her, she closed her eyes and just rested.

The old woman slipped back into the hut. Soon she returned with a teapot and a flower decorated tin of loose-leaf tea. With great precision she measured the leaves into the pot, added hot water when the kettle hissed steam, replaced the lid, and placed the pot carefully on a grill she'd positioned near the fire. She then patted the pot with a gnarled hand, and murmured as if to coax the tea into hurrying.

While the leaves steeped, she tottered back into the hut again, and this time returned with three battered tin mugs. Minutes later, she lifted the lid to the pot, smiled with satisfaction, and poured black tea into the mugs. Then, with great ceremony, she offered the steaming mugs of tea to her two guests.

Sam received his mug first and thanked her, his face solemn.

Kelly, realizing the significance of the offer, followed suit. The old woman, generously sharing her meager supplies, was thanking them in a way words never could.

Humbled, grateful, and utterly exhausted, Kelly sipped the pungent tea. But even strong black tea couldn't keep her eyelids from drooping. It had been a long, torturous day and there was still no end in sight. Earlier in the evening, while she waited for Sam on the beach, with fear her close companion, she wondered where she would be spending the night.

Even if the hotel had gone untouched by the fire, there was no way she could even think about sleeping there. Another quake, even a small aftershock, could collapse the building with little effort. And clearly the old couple's hut wasn't large enough to accommodate visitors. Kelly had peered in when Sam entered with the woman's husband and had seen the tiny interior. Concentrating on her mug of hot tea, she waited patiently for Sam to speak, to tell her when they'd be leaving. Then she realized, with a jolt, that she'd placed her safety and life completely in his hands, in spite of everything that had happened between them.

But *really*, what else could she do? The immediate world as she knew it had disappeared, and *it* hadn't been easy. Not in Bangladesh.

If a small voice in her head asked why Sam should bother with her, she ignored it, deciding this was no time for logic that could only succeed in making her feel worse. He could at least get her back to Kalgola. Once there, she'd decide on a plan. If there was no one capable left in Kalgola, she'd catch the boat back to Calcutta and dig up someone willing to help. It would take time, but she had no choice.

The old woman rose stiffly and entered the hut to check on her husband, leaving Sam and Kelly alone. He swiveled his shaggy head in her direction, and asked, in a voice grainy from fatigue, "Are you ready to get the hell out of Asia now, blue eyes?"

She hadn't expected that particular question, perhaps because she thought she'd emphasized her decision to stay and hunt for Jeff no matter what the odds. If she'd somewhat bonded to Sam during the night's events, it obviously hadn't affected Sam.

It pained her to have to admit that her little inner voice

had been right on target; he hadn't changed his mind about helping her. Silently, she contemplated the fire and wondered how she'd ever be able to rescue Jeff. She ignored Sam's question about leaving, which she considered unworthy of an answer.

"You busy tying a knot in a cherry stem with your tongue?" Sam drawled, as she sat silently brooding.

Kelly glared back at him, wondering why she couldn't just let his sniping bounce off. She'd let a drunken derelict lead her around by the nose for hours and foolishly believed they'd somehow bonded in that time—it was all too much. She ignited with fury. "Apparently it wasn't enough to have to live through a terrifying earthquake and a fire. I had to meet up with the world's surliest bum, as well. I don't know what your problem is and I don't *care*. I do thank you for saving me back there at the hotel, but that doesn't change the fact that I never want to deal with you again. A gorilla would be easier to get along with."

He opened his mouth, but she cut him off. "No, do *not* say a word. I couldn't stand it."

No more. It was past time to pull herself together, to find a place to spend the night. Actually, the next few nights. However much time it takes to find Jeff, she amended. She had no intention of letting her only brother down. She'd find him if it took all of her money and the last breath of her life.

She'd mulled the problem over enough times to have come up with a scenario she could accept as a reasonable possibility. Jeff had obviously been injured and could no longer get off the island on his own. That meant he was holed up somewhere, waiting to be rescued. And, somehow, whatever it took, she'd find a way to do just that. And the hell with Sam Tanner.

Coaxing stiff, sore muscles into action, she rose just as the old woman came out of the hut. Kelly handed the mug back with her profuse thanks. Then, giving the old crone a reassuring pat on the shoulder, she turned, ignoring Sam, and started to make her way back down to the path.

Before she'd traveled ten steps, Sam caught her arm, stopping her. "You tired of living?" He spoke sternly, his fingers pressing into her flesh.

Yanking her arm from his grasp, she continued walking. "I'm a hell of a lot more tired of you."

"So tired you plan on feeding the tigers that tempting body?"

"Don't worry about me. I can take care of myself." She walked faster.

He caught her arm again, and this time spun her around to face him. Taking her chin in his hand, he pointed her head to the side.

"Look over there . . . *real* close." He spoke through clenched teeth. "You see what I'm pointing at?"

Reluctantly, she looked. "You mean those little strands of wire?"

"Yeah, those *little* strands of wire. For your information that's a fence . . . an electric fence. Goes all the way around the encampment. But, hey, I guess you didn't notice, right?"

"It wasn't there earlier."

"It was, but the path was open. While we were resting, some of the natives closed it."

Even though she was furious with him, her body betrayed her by reacting to his masculine touch. A stab of heat sliced through her, from her chin all the way to her sensitive center. Disgusted with him and with her body's unwanted response, she jerked her chin from his hand. "Does that mean I can't get out?" she asked. Two strands of wire held by spindly poles didn't appear to be much of a deterrent.

"It means you don't *want* to get out," he replied, trying to keep his voice even, but shaking his head in obvious frustration.

"I see." Of course she did—the jungle wasn't safe. That was obvious and no surprise.

"Wonderful," he muttered.

She glared up at him with eyes as blue as hidden forest lakes. "Okay, they electrify that wire every night to keep out the predators." She became aware of a humming noise she'd been too distracted to acknowledge before.

"Yeah, the man-eaters." He shot her a slanted smile.

She paled in the moonlight. "You said the tigers stayed mainly on the islands."

He grunted. "Yeah. But they visit the mainland when they don't get enough to eat out there."

Kelly's gaze swept the enclosure, moving from the silent huts, to the wire fence, to the darkened, silently waiting jungle, and finally back on Sam.

"Well . . . so . . . where am I supposed to spend the night?"

A glint of what she took as malice flickered in his sharpened gaze. Then he turned and pointed back to the ring of stones, where the fire still glowed against the velvety blackness.

"Reckon that's as good a spot as any," he said.

"I'm supposed to sleep on the ground . . . is that what you're saying?" She viewed the fire warily, then turned to him, hoping to see something in his face that told her she was mistaken, that he just wanted to give her a hard time before he came up with a real solution.

His answer killed all hope. "Looks like it."

The thin smile he gave her made her want to hit him—hard. Reminding herself it wouldn't help the situation any—although she suspected she'd feel a lot better—she stomped back to the ring of fire and sat down cross-legged. It was doubtful she could stay in that position throughout the night, but she certainly wasn't going to complain to Sam. He'd only enjoy her discomfort.

He followed her back.

"Tell me," she fumed, "do you make an effort to be obnoxious or is it a gift?"

He actually grinned at her question, the first real smile she'd ever seen on his face. "Just born with it, sweetheart."

Frowning, Kelly watched him lie down, curl up next to the fire, and shut his eyes. She studied the holstered gun on his hip and wished she had something similar. Still, she knew better than to risk taking his. Feeling abandoned—Sam was asleep and the old couple had retired for the night—her anger melted into loneliness. No one stirred in any of the huts.

Suddenly a shiver of dread hit her and she glanced over her shoulder, checking the electric fence, wondering how well it really worked.

After a few minutes of watching Sam sleep, she grew too tired to care about the fence. With her eyes too heavy to hold open, she followed Sam's lead and curled into a fetal position, nodding off in seconds.

Kelly didn't hear Sam sit up. She wasn't aware that he kept watch throughout the rest of the night. That he stoked the fire, keeping it warm for her, as well as high for their protection.

Sam knew all too well that the fences frequently failed to protect the enclaves. There were many causes. The power might fail for one reason or another—the generator was old, the maintenance nonexistent—or a tree limb might fall on the wire and short out the whole system. And when the fences failed, a predator often found an easy meal. Man, woman, or child. The tigers didn't discriminate.

Sam was thoroughly pissed, but mostly at himself. He would have given almost anything for his old Enfield .303 bolt-action rifle, but he'd left it back on the rental boat he and John had anchored up the coast in the Bay of Bengal. Like a damn fool he'd left it behind, taken only the Webley .38 revolver when he'd gone into town to get plastered out of his head. He hadn't wanted to lose the prized rifle Grandfather Tanner had given him for his tenth birthday.

If he'd brought the Enfield, he damn well wouldn't be spending the night sitting in the dirt. He'd have been in his bunk on the boat, comfortable, safe, and warm. It was late, dark, and without the rifle he wasn't foolish enough to brave a jungle where tigers prowled. Tigers craved human flesh. As a food source, they'd come to prefer humans over almost everything else the jungle had to offer. Earlier, he'd had no choice but to get the old couple and Kelly to safety, so he'd braved the jungle without the rifle. Now he had a choice.

Sam understood what had happened to turn the tigers into man-eaters.

It wasn't a pleasant story.

Mother Nature was to blame. That was Sam's opinion. Every time she sent a cyclone to sweep through the territory, it killed dozens of natives. Bodies would litter the area and some would be stuck in the mud at low tide—a feast for the taking. Others lay on the ground, readily available.

Who could blame the tigers for enjoying an effortless, tasty meal? They would eat their fill after each storm. Then, not too strangely, they began to prefer the taste of man. To appreciate how easily a man could be taken down, even if he was still alive.

That's when the tigers started actively hunting men.

The long, hushed night gave Sam plenty of time to reflect on the day's happenings; on Kelly and her search. She had tenacity, he'd give her that, but not a clue as to how impossible it would be to find one man in thousands of miles of swamp land and small islands. She must really love the guy, he thought, which left him out in the cold. So why in hell should he even be contemplating helping her find him?

But he was. *Hell!* Maybe it would help to ease the pain of the loss of John if he helped find the man she'd come looking for.

He wanted to know about the guy—all about him—and why she'd risk her life to find him.

Kelly just didn't seem like the kind of woman who would chase after a man unless she had a damn good reason. Sam wanted to know what that reason was, and everything else about Kelly Griffin. Curiosity, he told himself. But his gaze never strayed far from her lovely face the entire night, and possessiveness sprouted roots deep within him, a new and savage feeling so strong it shook him to the very core of his being.

Chapter Three

A brilliant sun slipped over the horizon, lighting the sky with varying yellow and orange hues before it rose high enough to clear the edge of the earth. When it did, it turned into a blinding, virulent, golden orb that infiltrated every corner of the immediate world, waking the villagers.

Kelly stirred, stretched, and immediately wished she hadn't. She was stiff and sore all over, and cold in spite of the fire that still glowed within the ring of blackened stones.

Extending her hands toward the warmth, she realized dully that she was very much alone. Tanner was nowhere in sight. To make matters worse, she didn't know how long he'd been gone. For all she knew, she might have spent the entire night alone, oblivious prey for any hungry predator who breached the fence.

Hopelessness settled over her like jungle mist. The bitterness of defeat filled her empty tummy. For the first time she could be honest and admit that, without Tanner, she didn't have a hope of finding Jeff. She also finally acknowledged that she'd been a fool to come all the way out here by herself. She should have listened to those who had advised her to hire someone from the States to look into his disappearance, let them come out and investigate first, then follow. But she'd given in to a headstrong streak that had plagued her since childhood. She had wanted to see for herself and not trust a second party to tell her whether or not her brother was still alive.

All alone now, in a devastated, unfamiliar country, she wondered what her own chances were of getting out of here alive.

The jungle and its foliage around the small settlement came to life with the sounds of wild monkeys and birds. Although she didn't hear any tiger roars, Kelly knew that didn't necessarily mean there weren't a few lurking nearby, and that single thought sent a ripple of fear resonating up her spine.

Soft, stirring sounds escaped from the hut, reassuring her that she wasn't entirely alone, but any feeling of comfort quickly faded. She couldn't count on the old woman for help because she'd be preoccupied with caring for her disabled husband. Then, too, there was the shortage of food. Kelly had to leave before she undermined the couple's meager supplies.

Hell! Why did Tanner have to sneak off? He could have at least taken her back to town before abandoning her.

It hurt to realize he'd skulked off when she was asleep and vulnerable. Maybe she couldn't blame him for wanting to rid himself of the excess baggage, but he could have told her first. And if an ache stabbed near the heart area, she sure as hell wouldn't admit that it was because she missed him.

No way.

What she needed to do now was decide what to do, and quickly. If Sam had left for town, she reasoned, he might not have started until after sunrise. A glance at her watch told her that could mean he had left just minutes earlier, which also meant she might catch him if she hustled.

Rising stiffly, she admitted to feeling shaky and uncertain about following him into the jungle. Before she could dwell very long on the current predicament, she caught movement in her peripheral vision. Remembering the tigers, her head snapped around, fear rising like trout to a fly.

Sam Tanner, moving with the grace of a panther, sauntered toward her from behind the last hut, hat in hand.

Sighing with relief, Kelly relaxed. He hadn't abandoned her.

Seconds later, when the distance closed enough that she could see clearly, doubt surfaced. His hair was wet and it looked as if he'd finger combed it, but the two-day-old whiskers and dark shadows under his eyes gave him a more rugged appearance than the day before. Unfortunately, Kelly still found him devastatingly handsome.

Without a bit of help her mind shifted back to what the Clint Eastwood double had done to save her and some of the helpless villagers, and her doubts fled.

She finally managed to murmur, "I thought you'd abandoned me."

He squatted down and began to expertly place branches on the dying fire, encouraging it back to life. Glancing up, he acknowledged her comment with his death-ray squint, then went back to patiently feeding the fire.

Humbled, she added, "Thank you for staying."

Having nursed the fire to blazing life, he stood. "You're a pain in the butt, but I could hardly leave you for the tigers, now could I?" He canted his head to the side, sounding angry, but something warm crept into those light eyes, taking the sting out of his biting words.

Maybe it is possible to soften up a hard-ass, she thought.

"I love it when you sweet-talk me," she said, sarcasm edging every word.

A flicker of emotion glinted in and out of his extraordinary eyes so fast, she wondered if she had imagined it.

Quickly, not giving him time to respond, she asked, "Do

47

you think the boat from Calcutta will arrive on schedule today?"

Kelly had come to Kalgola on the daily boat and had decided to leave today on its return trip, to search for a guide from Calcutta—something she should have done in the first place. Unfortunately, she had no way of knowing what devastation the larger town had sustained, or whether it would affect the sailing schedule of the ferry.

"You planning on leaving this here jungle paradise?" Sam craned his neck around to take in the oppressive, surrounding forest.

Kelly stifled the irritation that sprang from his flippancy over circumstances she considered devastating. Striving for patience, she repeated, "Do you think the ferry will run today?"

Appearing languid, gazing out at the forest of trees and meandering vines, he murmured, "Haven't a clue."

And guess what? He doesn't give a damn, either. Just because he'd stayed beside her during the night, it didn't mean he'd help her get back to town, she realized. He could be toying with her for the hell of it. In spite of her concerns about his intentions, she continued the painstaking process of trying to extract information from him.

Worn nerves had turned her testy. "Are *you* going back to town anytime today?" she snapped.

He glowered. "Not much percentage in sticking around here, now is there?"

Deciding his question was probably all the answer she'd receive, and painfully aware she couldn't assume anything with this difficult man, she continued. "If you're going back, may I tag along?"

He let his narrowed gaze roam her body. "What's in it for me, sweetheart?"

Embarrassment, anticipation and anger merged in Kelly, coloring her cheeks a vibrant pink. *The bastard!*

Lowering her head, she stared into the flames. "Forget I asked. I can get along without *your* kind of help."

"You got a hell of a lot of attitude for such a *little* girl," he rasped.

She slanted him a gaze heavy with venom, got up, brushed off her slacks, turned her back, and started to walk away. Her tone waspish, she suggested, "Go harass someone else."

The village wasn't *that* far away. Besides there were other people stirring now, leaving their huts, getting on with their day. Some of them might even be going into Kalgola. She would move about among them and try to assimilate.

A part of her expected Sam to intervene and stop her, as he had the night before. He didn't, but she could feel his glare penetrate her back. Feel the waves of heat escalate up and down her spine as his burning gaze drifted up and down.

Furious with him, and absolutely unwilling to feel anything at all for a lecherous derelict, she moved away. If she could somehow stop him from stirring her in any way, she'd be a grateful woman. If denial was the way, then she'd deny, over and over. Until she got it right. *Dammit!*

The physical attraction she felt would dissipate, then vanish, she assured herself. She'd survive without him *very* well, thank you. All she had to do was pretend he didn't exist. Then she could go back to relying on her own instincts to pull her through. They'd gotten her this far.

Yeah . . . right into Sam Tanner's ruthless hands.

Fighting the urge to cover her ears with her hands, to still her own traitorous thoughts, she continued toward the center of the huts where the most occupants were milling about.

Childishly, she had the bizarre urge to turn around and

shoot Sam a raspberry. But she wasn't foolish enough to succumb to the impulse.

Kelly just kept walking.

Two men wearing the traditional long sarong skirts were working barefoot, removing part of the electric fence that enclosed the settlement, creating a gateway. She veered in their direction.

She observed them a few minutes before asking, "Are you gentlemen going into town by any chance?" She directed her attention to the younger of the two, thinking someone of his generation would be more likely to understand and speak English.

He hadn't acknowledged her presence earlier, but now he gazed directly at her, and nodded shyly. "Yes, Miss, soon we go into the village."

Kelly relaxed and smiled. Here was salvation.

The young man, perhaps anticipating her desire to accompany them, shifted his gaze beyond her. A quizzical expression formed on his thin face, as if he puzzled over why she wasn't asking Sam, a man with a gun, to accompany her.

Feeling no need to explain—all she wanted to do was tag along when they went—she expanded her most enticing smile and asked, "Would you mind if I walked along with you?"

She had their undivided attention now. The older man seemed to have understood her request, as well, for he looked nervous as he started jabbering rapidly in his native tongue. Occasionally, he swiveled his head to frown at Sam.

Very quickly, Kelly came to understand that she wasn't the only one Sam unsettled. It was clear the older gentleman feared Sam, or his wrath, should Sam perceive an insult. Apparently, taking Sam's woman with them *certainly* appeared to top the list of insults in this man's mind.

When the old gentleman stopped yammering, the younger

one cautiously asked, "Your tall friend, is he not going into the village?"

"He's *not* my friend," Kelly snapped, impatient now. "And I don't want to go with him, even if he is going."

Her answer brought on another rush of words and arm waving from the old man, and this time the younger one appeared to be losing confidence.

Eyeing her doubtfully, he said, "You slept at the tall man's fire, so Father believes he *is* your friend and that you have had a quarrel. Is that not true?"

Kelly sighed. She hadn't meant to cause a problem between the two men. If she continued trying to enlist their aid, that's exactly what would happen. They were already quarreling.

She gave up and spread her hands, palms up in front of her. "Look, just forget I asked. It isn't that important." Then, giving them a gallant smile, she stepped through the opening they'd created and began to move briskly down the path, demonstrating to them that she wasn't afraid to go by herself.

The young man called after her, tension raising the pitch of his voice. "Wait . . . do not go alone."

She whirled around, forced herself to smile, and waved. "Don't worry. I'll be fine."

That bastard Sam will come after me, she decided.

As she walked away, the two men resumed their argument, both talking at once, each obviously trying to swamp the other's opinion with a flood of words.

Fear that had been dormant awakened low in Kelly's spine the second she stepped into the dense, verdant jungle. She scanned her immediate surroundings with a twitchy eye, hating the fear, knowing she had to get back to Kalgola as fast as humanly possible.

If you had just half the guts Jeff has, you wouldn't let a little old jaunt in the jungle deter you, she thought. *Yeah, but if he hadn't gone tiger hunting with that darn camera of his, we'd both be safe at home.*

It startled her to realize she could even think of censuring her older brother when she was clearly scared to death for him. He'd always been the one to come running the minute she got into trouble as a child, ready and willing to bail her out.

So now it's your turn. Quit grumbling!

The narrow footpath led deeper into the jungle and Kelly followed it, confident it was the way they'd come. She recalled veering off the main path to reach the tiny gathering of huts, but couldn't recall how far back they'd changed directions, or, if they had traversed other crossing paths. It had been hauntingly dark during the night and she'd been too exhausted to notice much of her surroundings. Most of the time she'd been so fatigued, all she'd noticed were the feet directly in front of hers, Sam's. Truthfully, she wished they were still in front of her.

They weren't, so she'd make the best of a dire situation. One goal at a time would be her motto. First, she had to reach Kalgola. Second, she had to find out if the boat to Calcutta was expected. Third, if it was, she had to buy a ticket. Fortunately, she still had money in her small backpack. Then, while she waited for the boat to leave, she might even be able to scavenge some of her personal belongings from the hotel. That is, if the building still stood and hadn't been destroyed by the fire.

She'd been too tired the night before to ask Sam what had survived in the village, if anything. He certainly hadn't volunteered any information, either.

Damn his hide!

Hating Sam Tanner could be a satisfying pastime, she decided, if she could only work up the effort. A distraction from the eclectic sounds of the jungle—the chirps and warble of birds; the snapping of underbrush as animals moved about; and the buzz of insects crawling over and under the deep green vines and multi-colored debris covering the ground— would be a welcome intervention.

Ruefully, she admitted *that* type of concentration just wasn't possible.

The sudden screech of a rhesus monkey, high in the canopy of tall trees blocking the sun, had her jumping nearly a foot off the ground.

"It's okay," she whispered to herself when her heart resumed pumping. "It was just a monkey."

Still twitchy, she found herself straining her ears for the roar of distant tigers.

Twenty-five minutes later, having distanced herself from the huts without coming under attack, she convinced herself there was nothing to worry about. It still didn't feel like a walk in the park, for she vividly recalled the spooky discordant sounds from the previous night—shrill squeals as predators preyed on the vulnerable—but it was doable.

Before she could get truly comfortable, the underbrush thickened and seemed to target her. Tree branches reached out to tangle her hair and slap at her face. Vines seemed to wait in ambush just to tangle her feet in an attempt to throw her to the littered ground.

Then the narrow path shrank even more, threatening her from every side. After another half-hour of struggling, she gazed around and decided nothing looked the least bit familiar. Oh, sure, the jungle was still a jungle. But it felt different, somehow.

"I'm lost," she conceded, feeling convinced they hadn't come so far the night before.

No, I'm not lost! Denial kept her from panicking. But it

wouldn't last long if the path continued in no way to resemble the trail she remembered from the previous evening.

Kelly battled sudden debilitating claustrophobia. The sense of being swallowed alive by the encroaching vegetation nearly sent her mind reeling. She felt herself in the middle of a giant Venus flytrap!

"Stay calm. You've just taken a wrong turn," she reasoned. The question of where and how far back spooked her. Unsure whether she should turn back or continue to move forward, she stopped and gazed behind her, searching for something familiar to soothe her nerves.

There was nothing. It all looked frighteningly the same in every direction. Except it felt denser, somehow, and just not right.

"If I turn back, it could be a mistake. I could unknowingly veer off and miss the circle of huts where Sam and I spent the night."

The idea that she could wander endlessly, until something got her—thirst, hunger, or a wild animal—brought tears to her eyes. She would never be able to save Jeff. She couldn't even save herself.

Before she could even begin to reach a decision and move, she detected a new sound in the jungle. It rattled her. Clearly something was moving down the path toward her from the direction she'd come. Something stealthy. Something that made the tiny hairs on her nape quiver.

Then, abruptly, before she could decide how to proceed, the furtive noises ceased, as though the stalker had also stopped to listen.

In spite of the oppressive heat, goose bumps appeared on her arms and a chill shimmied through her. Downright appalled now, Kelly wheeled around, searching frantically for a place to hide.

Desperate, she caught a fleeting glimpse through the foliage of a large mangrove tree that looked promising, about twenty-five feet to the left of the path.

Did she dare leave the relative safety of the path to venture across the jungle terrain? She'd read that the area harbored 200 species of snakes, poisonous and non-lethal alike. The deadliest of them was the king cobra who could rear up to three feet in the air before striking, and whose bite killed within minutes.

She shuddered, remembering what she'd read about what to do if bitten. The article had quoted a man advising, "The only thing to do is find a big tree, sit down under it, and wait to die." There were no other options, apparently.

Indecision held her captive for seconds. Then, realizing she needed to be quick if she hoped to escape the stalker, she took one tentative step off the path. Her feet sank into the dense undergrowth, bringing a grimace to her face, along with a sharp yearning for the firmness of the path.

She thought of the snakes, knowing they slithered freely and silently under and over the rotting vegetation. Also remembered the article said that the smaller snakes struck before you had a chance to spot them.

The mangrove tree's branches hung low to the ground, beckoning, offering the promise of safety.

Realizing if something was truly stalking her, it could be a man-eater, she whispered encouragingly, "Don't think about snakes . . . just move."

Kelly took another shaky step away from the path. The sinking feeling had her shuddering with fear, but she toughened her resolve, forcing herself to take her chances with the jungle denizens.

Ten feet from the path and committed, a malevolent-looking lizard head, complete with flicking tongue, emerged in front of her. With waddling slowness, six feet of monitor lizard crossed in front of a frozen and terrified Kelly, then disappeared into the undergrowth. It completely dismissed her presence, but even so it was several moments before her limbs began to function.

On the move again, as fast as the tangled bottom of the forest permitted, Kelly reached the mangrove tree without further incident. Unfortunately, the lowest branch hung higher off the ground than it had appeared from a distance.

Grunting with the effort, she jumped, caught the limb, and barely managed to pull herself with a struggle onto the top of the branch. Still not feeling entirely safe, she shinnied up higher, until she reached an elbow where another thick branch split off the main trunk. Resting in the vee, she wiped perspiration from her brow and caught her breath.

Once again breathing freely, she turned to study what she could see of the jungle path. Her limited view allowed nothing more than a couple of inches of space four feet or so off the ground in one small clearing. As far as she could tell, at that moment, nothing was moving along the trail.

"Damn." Her palm smarted from an abrasion and her slacks were torn at one knee. The thought that it might have been for nothing stung almost as badly as her hand.

Realizing she couldn't afford to rest in the tree for long and still expect to reach Kalgola before the ferry departed, she peered down, trying to decide how best to lower herself back to the jungle floor.

Then, as luck would have it, she caught a glimpse of something large, dark, and most likely sinister moving cautiously along the path. Freezing in place on the limb, she inhaled nervously, her heart pounding like a trip-hammer.

Kelly focused in on a flash of blue.

Her stalker wasn't a tiger after all.

Sam?

Maybe, but she couldn't be certain.

The person moved swiftly down the path, past the section where she had detoured, and kept going. Unhappily, she realized that if he were indeed following her, it wouldn't take him long to realize she was no longer leading the way. When that happened, undoubtedly he'd turn, retrace his steps, and try to find where she'd separated from the trail. It wouldn't be that difficult. When he discovered where she'd left the trail, it wouldn't be long before he found her.

Hopefully, she thought, *it is Sam.*

But what if it isn't?

Thoroughly shaken, she clung to the branch, loathe to exit her temporary haven and equally afraid to stay put.

Agonizing minutes ticked by.

"What the hell you doing up there?"

The suddenness of the growled question coming out of nowhere startled her so badly she nearly lost her grip on the tree limb. Kelly hadn't heard or seen Sam, but somehow he'd managed to sneak up on her until he stood right under the damn tree.

"What the hell do you think I'm doing?" she exploded. When he just stared up at her, she said, "What are you doing, sneaking up on people, anyway? You nearly scared me out of my wits."

"Wouldn't take much of a scare, I reckon," he replied. Then he had the effrontery to grin up at her. And, slowly, he allowed his quizzical light-blue eyes to move with lackadaisical ease from her face to her butt, where it straddled the branch.

To Kelly, he appeared to be having one hell of a good time at her expense. *The wicked bastard!*

Decidedly out of sorts, she asked, "Are you going to just stand there or are you going to help me down?"

His grin deepened. "You got up there by yourself, so I figure you should be able to get down the same way." The look on his face told her he certainly was enjoying the situation. She waited for him to do something, but he just stood there, relishing the view.

A string of obscenities flew to Kelly's tongue, but she held them back, pursing her lips, not wanting to give him the satisfaction. Concentrating instead on slipping one leg off the branch, she found a purchase with her toes and slid down the steepest section of the limb until she reached the horizontal section she'd first hoisted herself onto. It wasn't easy, but she made it. Without his help.

All she had to do was drop to the ground.

Suddenly, a movement overhead caught her attention.

Straining her neck, she gazed skyward.

Just above her, a slithering green snake hung upside down, its languid head a couple of feet higher than hers. Unhappily, it was uncoiling and dropping fast.

Frozen with fright and unable to move, Kelly managed no more than a strangled shriek.

A deafening explosion drowned out her scream.

The sound of the pistol shot reverberated throughout the forest, creating frenzy, as creatures large and small fled in terror.

Above her, the snake's head disintegrated into the moist air.

Kelly lost her grip on the tree.

She fell.

Sam caught her before she hit the ground. She landed in his arms with a jolt that would have sent a lesser man to his knees.

Shuddering from fright, she grabbed him around the neck and buried her face in the warm, tender place under his ear. Feeling safe, she gave in to tears.

"I hate snakes, dammit! Even *more* than tigers," she said between sobs.

After a few minutes, Kelly's tears were gone, replaced by a subtle sexual awareness that sprang up between her and Sam. There'd been no physical contact since the earthquake and she was acutely aware of the pressure of his muscled arms on her body. The place where one bulging bicep pressed against her breast. The texture of his skin, smooth, but hard and corded with muscle. She found herself wondering if the torso under the shirt he wore was toasted the same golden brown as his exposed limbs. She hoped it was.

Pressed so closely against him, Kelly felt Sam's heart rate accelerate, and the knowledge that he was becoming aroused brought reality rushing back. This was the same guy she'd walked away from back at the huts. The same arrogant bastard who'd bargained for her body. He was also the reason she'd climbed the damn tree in the first place.

He's just as dangerous as your run-of-the-mill boa constrictor. Remember that, she told herself.

Pulling her arms from around his neck, she muttered, "You can put me down now."

Sam was smiling in spite of the scare Kelly had given him. Holding her close, he'd allowed her time for tears. Surprising himself, he had voiced no recriminations, uttered no smart-ass remarks, because she felt good in his arms. Too damned good.

When she spoke to him, it hit him like a fist in the gut. Sam didn't want to put her down, now or ever. He'd come so damn close to losing her, he couldn't think straight.

The snake was a poisonous green tree snake, and it had been ready to strike. He'd been an idiot to follow so far behind. Anything could have happened and it would have been his fault. Wondering what type of crazy fool he'd become, he acknowledged the stunning fact that a slip of a girl had turned him into someone barely recognizable.

Even so, he definitely didn't want to put her down. He liked the feel of her soft curves pressed against him and he wanted to fill his senses with the essence of her, to taste that tempting mouth.

Nope. Putting Kelly down hadn't even made it to his "tough stuff to do" list. *Maybe later.*

The last thought barely registered before he pulled his arm out from under her legs and allowed them to drop. Then he shifted her around to face him. *So damn beautiful.*

It was impossible for Sam to take his hands off Kelly. He wanted, no *needed,* to keep touching her anywhere he could. Anywhere she'd allow, he amended. Because she'd gotten so deep into him, he wasn't completely sane. But he would be. Soon. All he needed were a few wet kisses to cool the fire.

He allowed his gaze to descend to her mouth.

His mouth followed, while he tried to convince himself that if he kissed her long enough he'd get over her.

He certainly didn't want to admit she made his life worth living. That she set his blood on fire as no woman ever had. He especially didn't want to entertain the idea that he needed her in some fundamental way that couldn't be explained logically.

Not now.

Maybe never.

Chapter Four

Animal sounds began to trickle through to the jungle surrounding Kelly and Sam, breaking the silence that followed the great exodus caused by Sam's gunshot. For long seconds, neither of the two people clinging together noticed.

With a will of its own, Sam's tongue went on a scavenger hunt inside Kelly's mouth, searching out all her luscious hidden treasures.

Kelly stopped thinking at all. What happened to her when Sam touched her was totally unlike anything she'd ever experienced. Until now, no man had ever made her forget herself or her surroundings.

Several of Sam Tanner's heart-stopping kisses made her forget who he was.

Stunned by this sudden unwelcome reaction, her brain cells struggled to come back on line, to aid in her efforts to release her mouth from Sam's. When she did manage to pull away, he groaned, as if he were in physical pain. Too clearly, she knew exactly what he felt. The bereavement over the loss of his mouth was just as keen. That couldn't stop her, however, not if she wanted to survive him.

She reminded herself that Sam was a sexual predator. No matter what else he might be, she knew, with certainty, that he was a love 'em and leave 'em kind of guy.

And Kelly wasn't buying. No, sir. No way.

Sam cradled the back of her head with one hand and again pulled her within an inch of his mouth.

Then, surprisingly, Kelly's lips opened invitingly, showing not a trace of respect for her mind's resolve. What could one do when there were traitors among the ranks?

Sam didn't hesitate. Dipping his tongue into her tiny mouth, the kiss deepened into something so intimate that the blood pounded fiercely in her head and heated up her most private places.

The sensations he invoked were so intense, Kelly felt dizzy. Fortunately, she was still alert enough to realize she was in big trouble. If he could do this to her with mere kisses—okay, so they aren't even close to mere—she'd never survive if he made love to her. *Never.*

A sudden fluttering of wings high in the trees near the trail was the beginning of a warning by the jungle's exotic inhabitants. Squawks of alarm soon followed.

Sam, apparently instantly aware of what was happening, ended the kiss well before Kelly regrouped. For a moment she clung to him, not interested in standing on her own, grateful for the support of his arms. Then he slowly released her and stepped back, forcing her to face the jungle's harsh reality—stay alert or die.

"Something's moving our way." He pointed to the trail.

Thoroughly intoxicated by his torrid kisses, it took Kelly precious seconds to process this new and unwelcome information. When she finally managed to do so, she had to stifle a strong urge to jump back into Sam's protective arms.

She slowly regained perspective. "What do you think it is?" she whispered.

He shook his head. "Most likely villagers. But until we're sure, it pays to be cautious." As he spoke he maneuvered behind the tree, pulling her with him, effectively shielding them from view.

Why hadn't I thought of hiding behind the damn tree before I skinned my knee climbing the darn thing? she wondered. Then she remembered the creepy crawly creatures that populated the jungle floor and knew why. Shuddering, she glanced down and scrutinized the area around her feet. Nothing moved, thankfully, and she sighed with relief. In her mind, the only good creepy crawly was a dead creepy crawly.

Sam handed her his canteen while they waited, and she drank greedily before handing it back.

Completely hidden behind the tree, she had no view of the trail. But Sam had stationed himself in such a way that he would be able to recognize advancing predators. She felt his tension ease, and knew the moment he recognized the intruder wasn't a predator.

"Who is it?" she whispered, still tense.

"Looks like the two men you were teasing this morning," he muttered. "Probably out looking for you."

She took exception. Miffed, she snapped, "I wasn't *teasing* them, I was simply asking them if I could accompany them if they were going into town. And they were, so obviously they aren't looking for me. *You* weren't exactly cooperative, as I recall."

He sent her a wicked grin. "You must have forgiven me, 'cause you were downright friendly a few minutes ago."

The nervy bastard!

She stepped back. "That was sleep deprivation. I haven't slept fifteen whole minutes since I got here."

Sam finally admitted to himself how much he'd missed her softness, the feel of her in his arms. For a moment he'd lost himself in sensations that were exciting and too enjoyable to even think of relinquishing, and then their situation had forced him to put her down. And now she seemed to hate him.

His expression sobered. Regarding her closely, he said, "You have a sharp tongue, blue eyes."

As she elbowed her way by him and headed for the trail, she said, "Never forget it."

"No problem. You can count on me to remember *everything*, sweetheart."

The way he said it, softly with a hint of gravel in his voice, made the nerve endings in her stomach quiver. Sam Tanner was a handful, and the more distance she kept between them, the better off she'd be.

Sam caught up and grabbed her arm. "Slow down and watch where the hell you're stepping. The jungle floor is teeming with vermin."

"You're just trying to cheer me up, right?" she snapped. All the same, her gaze dropped to the ground in front of her and she took her next few steps with more caution.

As Sam watched her pick her way forward, he sighed.

When they continued down the trail the same way Kelly had been advancing, she realized she hadn't been lost. Still, nothing looked the least bit familiar and *everything* looked familiar. To Kelly, the jungle was a deadly enigma.

They hadn't trekked far when Sam abruptly stopped and squatted. Kelly just barely saved herself from running into him by coming to a screeching halt. Peering over his shoulder, ready to question him, she suddenly saw what had grabbed his attention.

Paw tracks were clearly evident in a patch of mud next to the trail. *Large* paw tracks. *Fresh* paw tracks.

"Is that what I think it is?" Her breathing sounded labored.

Sam stood and scanned the jungle. "Afraid so. Stay close."

She'd have climbed into his back pocket if she thought she could manage it. Short of that maneuver, she followed so closely behind him that she trod on his heels a time or two. They hadn't traveled far when she asked in a voice that noticeably trembled, "Are the tracks from last night or this morning? Can you tell?"

"They look fresh," he hissed. "Don't talk."

Earlier, he'd had his gun holstered, but now he carried it in his right hand as they slowly resumed walking. Then, as if a sixth sense warned him of the onset of disaster, Sam picked up the pace.

"Stay with me," he ordered in a harsh whisper.

Kelly had to jog to keep up with his longer strides and was breathing heavily when they heard the first terrified scream.

The shriek came from directly ahead, but by the time it was repeated, it had a different tone. One drenched in agony.

"Son of a bitch!" Sam broke into a dead run. "Keep up!" he snapped.

They rounded a bend and he drew to another abrupt halt. In front of them, the young man from the huts was caught up in grief. Kneeling in the dirt, he pulled his hair and moaned.

Dread dried Kelly's mouth. Fear grabbed her.

"Where's the old guy?" Sam addressed the boy as he searched the area for a sign the man might be near, hoping the worst hadn't happened.

The young man ignored them and continued to moan pitifully.

Sam dropped to one knee and pulled the kid's hands from his head. "Listen to me!" He spoke sharply. "Are they still on the trail?"

His eyes brimming over with tears, the young man pointed with a shaking finger into the jungle off to the right of the trail.

Sam nodded, stood abruptly, and told Kelly to stay put. He plunged into the nearly impenetrable jungle and was immediately swallowed up by the dense foliage.

Sam easily followed the tiger's trail, trampled vegetation and spattered blood. But all too soon the dribbled splashes turned into gory puddles and Sam knew it was too late. The old man had met his fate from lack of blood, if he hadn't already been killed. Tigers had a penchant for snapping the neck of their prey and, in this case, Sam hoped that was what had happened, that the old man died quickly.

Further pursuit would be pointless. There was no way to save the ravaged villager. Sam regretfully turned back.

He'd hated leaving Kelly behind, but had rationalized that the tiger already had his meal for the day. She would be safe unless another tiger was nearby, an unlikely event since tigers were known to be territorial.

Unless, however, it had a mate that it shared its area with. That thought had Sam moving faster to reach her, taking risks that bordered on foolish, even when he couldn't see more than a few feet in front of him.

The realization that only a few minutes, one way or the other, could have placed Kelly in danger shook him badly. And the hell of it was, he could and did blame himself. If he hadn't been playing stupid mind games, letting Kelly go off alone—just to give her a scare—he could have thwarted a tragic outcome involving her. But he had. And he wouldn't forgive himself anytime soon.

His heart lurched at his first sight of Kelly unharmed. She and the young man were right where he'd left them. His strong response told him he already cared too much, and the news wasn't welcome. Not when he knew deep down she'd never consider *him* marriage material.

Marriage?

Now where in hell did that idea come from?

When Sam emerged on the trail in front of Kelly, she felt relief flood her face. It turned to despair when she registered the fact that he was very much alone.

"You couldn't find him?" she whispered.

Sam's jaw tightened and he shook his head. "No." He studied the boy's tortured face. "We'll have to take him back to his village." It would take much longer to get back to Kalgola if they had to cover the same territory twice, but there was nothing else to do. The boy needed emotional support and would be better off in his own small encampment.

Kelly nodded.

Sam helped the devastated young man to his feet, and gesturing for Kelly to lead the way down the path, started the return trip. It was clear they were all uneasy about turning their collective backs on the tiger, but they had no choice.

Following at the rear, gun holstered, Sam calculated their odds. The tiger that had attacked the old man was somewhere behind them. True. But clearly, it was occupied. At least for a while. *And full,* Sam thought with disgust, giving the three humans a good chance of making it back to the boy's tiny encampment alive.

When they finally reached the circled huts, the natives appeared to know instinctively that they'd lost one of their own. Surrounding the boy, they offered the comfort and support he would need to recover.

Realizing they could do nothing else to ease the young man's pain and knowing that time was wasting, Sam and Kelly said their good-byes. Saddened, they both headed back toward the trail.

When they were out of earshot, Sam alerted Kelly. "We're going to move fast now, so hang tight. If there's a boat from Calcutta today, I want you on it for the return trip."

Kelly, already exhausted, only nodded to conserve energy. She'd begun to agree with Sam. She wasn't cut out for this kind of exercise or trauma. Apparently, adventure wasn't her forte.

They'd covered no more than a few hundred yards when Sam glanced behind him and noticed Kelly had fallen several yards back.

"Don't lag behind, Kelly. I know you think the tiger's occupied, but you never know. There may be more than one tiger in the area. And even if it's just the one, that devil may enjoy killing for its own sake."

Fatigue didn't keep Kelly from shuddering. The old man's blood she'd gingerly avoided on the trail was planted firmly in her mind's eye and seemed to fill her senses. She could see it, smell it, and almost taste the metallic tang. As hard as she tried, it was impossible to think of anything else. Had the poor man died instantly? She prayed he had.

Or, horror of horrors, had he died an agonizing death inch by inch as the tiger began to devour him?

That distressing thought had sudden nausea dropping Kelly to her knees. If she'd had anything in her stomach to purge, it would have emptied right then. But all she could produce were a few painful dry heaves.

Sam instantly jerked around. Quickly kneeling beside her, he slipped an arm around her quaking shoulders to steady her small frame.

"Take some deep breaths, blue eyes. You'll be okay."

She shook her head. Then the tears came. Like a flood, they sluiced down her cheeks in twin tracks of pain and dropped to the ground.

When she was finally reduced to hiccups, Sam drew her to her feet, tipped her head up with a hand under her chin, and dried her tears with his own leathery palm.

"Hey, where's my tough guy? You know, the gal who could whither me with a look?"

Embarrassed by her sudden collapse, Kelly sniffed. "She's missing in action."

"Well, get her back, pronto. This is no place for wimps."

Her spine stiffened. "I'm *not* a wimp." But deep inside she worried that maybe he was right.

No! She'd made some mistakes, granted, but who wouldn't, broadsided by something like this, and given no time to think. She'd come good as soon as humanly possible and she'd save her brother or die trying.

"This really isn't the place to debate whether you are or aren't a cream puff, sweetheart. This is a place to get the hell out of. Right now." He turned her, coaxing her along the trail with a hand to her backside.

It didn't take long for Kelly to decide to move without prodding. Even under such adverse conditions, his touch still affected her more than she cared to admit.

When they'd traveled what seemed like forever, Kelly stopped dead in her tracks. "I can't move another step without something to eat. I swear, I'm going to die right here on the spot from low blood sugar."

Sam pushed his hat back, revealing narrowed eyes. "Trust me. Hunger isn't what's gonna get ya."

Kelly's head snapped up and she immediately began to search the jungle for signs of the tiger. However, when nothing disturbed her more than the usual jungle, jungle, and more jungle, she glared at Sam.

"Gee, thanks for sharing," she said. "I appreciate how encouraging you are. It's always nice to know I'm potentially on someone's menu. Keeps me nice and relaxed."

Sam's eyebrows did a dance toward his hairline. Then he grinned. "Hey, Sassy's back. Great. Let's get a move on."

69

"Told you. I'm not moving until I get something to eat!"
His grin vanished. "You can hold out a little longer."

"No!" To emphasize her determination, she sat squarely down on the path.

He observed her for several tense seconds, studying her mutinous chin. Finally, with a sigh, he fished in his shirt pocket, and, in seconds, like magic, produced a protein bar.

The sight of the bar had Kelly's breath *whooshing* out. When she could speak, she shouted at him, totally outraged and indifferent to the danger. "Damn you! You've had that all along, haven't you?"

He grinned and nodded. "You'll have to get up and start walking before I share, though."

"You bastard! I've been starving all day. And you've been munching on protein bars." She got up and made a valiant effort to grab the bar.

Sam snatched it away. "Hold on. This is *it* . . . I only have this one left."

"I'll just bet!" She couldn't remember being more furious with anyone.

He shoved the bar back into his shirt pocket and grabbed her wrists. "You're gonna have to start believing me, blue eyes. I don't lie, even when it might be easier. Especially with someone like you."

"Someone like *me?*"

"Yeah, you, the queen of skeptics."

She pulled away. His touch always affected her, even made her forget hunger and anger for about half a second.

"Whatever you say . . . just share before I faint," she muttered.

He produced and unwrapped the bar, took one bite, and handed it to Kelly, who proceeded to nibble on the end he'd bitten into. As ravenous as she was, her senses tingled when she took the first bite, placing her mouth where his had been moments earlier. She proceeded to nibble away, savoring each bite until she neared the end. Then, feeling guilty—after all, it *was* his protein bar—she offered to hand it back.

He shook his head. "Go ahead, finish it."

"Are you sure?" *She* had a conscience.

"Yeah, finish it," he growled.

Kelly didn't argue, but she turned away, sparing him from having to watch as she devoured what was left. When she'd eaten the last bite, she licked the few remaining crumbs from her fingers.

Sam had shifted his position enough to get a load of her licking her fingers with her small pointed tongue. His crotch tightened. What she could do to him without half trying made him wonder what would happen if she *meant* to turn him on. Irritated with himself, as well as her, he started down the trail, ordering her to follow and to stay close. All he wanted to do, he decided, was get her back to Kalgola, onto the boat to Calcutta, and out of his life. Then he'd take the next day's boat, and from Calcutta, go all the way home to the States.

It would have been more expedient to take the boat with her, but he didn't trust himself. More time in her company just gave him more time to act like a fool. To want what he knew wasn't possible. The two of them together were oil and water. Until he touched her. And then all hell broke loose. But he'd be damned if he'd willingly get on that kind of roller coaster. He'd seen what sexual chemistry could do to a man. First it teased him, then it drove him crazy, and finally it all blew up in his face when the woman turned out to be the opposite of what he'd perceived, leaving him singed and wounded. Then, ironically, after the pain dwindled down to a dull ache and he looked back, the poor sucker couldn't figure out what in hell had attracted him in the first place.

"I can't keep up this pace," Kelly wheezed, interrupting Sam's dreary thoughts.

"Shit!" He slowed, then stopped. "What's the matter now?"

"You can walk faster because your legs are longer. I practically have to run to keep up with you. Give me a break. Slow down." She bent over, breathing heavily. Then she placed her hands on her knees and let her head hang down, obviously hoping to garner some much needed strength. And time.

"You got asthma or some damn thing?" Sam scowled at her.

"No. I'm just out of breath from trying to keep up with someone who has legs as long as a damn giraffe."

Sam's lips twitched. "Why didn't you say something sooner?"

She gave a humorless laugh and peered up at him. "Because I didn't think it would make a difference."

Sam's lips flattened out and his eyes narrowed even more than usual as he studied her. "You trying to tell me I'm mistreating you?"

"I'm trying to tell you you'll have to slow down. That's *it!* Plain and simple. Even you should be able to understand the concept that we're built differently."

Shaking his head, Sam managed a low mutter. "Oh, yeah, that's a concept I understand *all* too well."

Kelly obviously knew what he implied with the remark, for her cheeks grow hot along with the rest of her.

"I thought you were in a hurry," she said, straightening. "Shouldn't we get moving?"

He gestured with his head. "You first. That way I won't be

running those sexy little legs off." He allowed himself a good, long look at her butt as she turned, enjoying the fact that he could look all he wanted with her leading.

Sexy legs? If Sam was mentioning body parts, she was probably in more trouble than she'd be able to handle.

Turning back around to face him, she asked, "What about the tiger?" If she could redirect his cerebral cortex, she might survive.

He shook his head. "There you go again . . . bringing up the bad stuff."

"I thought you were worried."

"Yeah, well, maybe, a little," he conceded. The corners of his mouth lifted.

Huffing, Kelly turned her back on him and stomped down the trail.

"You might try to be quiet. Damn tigers have ears, ya know," Sam complained. His voice came from close behind her.

He had a natural ability to rile her and he used it well, she decided, as she began to walk with increasing care.

She could feel him watching her for some time, apparently enjoying the view before he commented dryly, "Hey, you wanna get there today or next week?"

"I guess that's your quaint little way of telling me to walk faster, huh?"

"You nailed it dead center, blue eyes. Haul ass."

Kelly shook her head in annoyance. But she moved faster, knowing that his gaze was probably glued to her butt when he wasn't looking for tigers.

Myriad small animal sounds accompanied them through the verdant jungle, so when the noises ceased suddenly, Kelly quickly noticed and came to an abrupt standstill.

"What is it? What's wrong?" she asked Sam in a whisper.

He'd gone as still as the jungle, his senses alerted even before hers. As an answer, he just shook his head and continued scrutinizing their immediate area while he listened for unusual sounds.

In hushed seconds they heard the sound that had terrified the jungle inhabitants and sent them fleeing. The whack of a machete against solid wood. One of the jungle's precious trees was being hacked down.

"I've gotta check that out," Sam whispered.

"And I suppose you want me to wait right here until you get back?" she dryly uttered.

He nodded and canted his head. "Damn good idea. Wish I'd thought of it."

"No," she said.

Sam's chin rose in arrogance. "Say what?"

She sniffed, looking all high and mighty. "No."

His teeth ground together. His eyes squinted. "Dammit, I said you'd have to take orders if you were with me."

She folded her arms across her chest and held her ground. "Not this time."

Women . . . they're always unreasonable, he thought. He figured it must be in the genes. He hadn't liked the idea of leaving her alone, but he'd thought it safer. Now she was going all stubborn on him, again. Hadn't she been bad enough about the damned protein bar?

"They could be cannibals, you know," he whispered low.

She cocked her head and bug-eyed him. "I don't think cannibals live in Asia."

"Could be they imported 'em," he said.

"Dammit, Sam, I'm coming along!"

He shook his head as if she were the most impossible person he'd ever run across. "Fine. Just watch your ass."

"I thought *you* were doing that," she muttered as he turned away.

He stopped in mid-stride and whipped around, a fierce expression on his rugged face. "The fun and games are over, sweetheart. So watch the hell where you step."

Chastised, she followed him as quietly as she could. Sam made virtually no noise as he left the trail and moved silently through the debris on the vine-tangled jungle floor.

It wasn't as easy for Kelly. At first, she tried to walk in his steps. But soon the unnatural leg extensions wore on her and she took to a shorter gait. And then, of course, she managed to occasionally step on and snap a twig. Each time, Sam turned and glared at her, accusing her with a look, telling her that *she* was the one putting them in jeopardy.

She'd just shake her head and hiss that she was doing her best, dammit.

Thanks to the repeated resounding whack of the machete biting into bark—a sound that shook the jungle inhabitants, sending them fleeing—the noise Sam and Kelly made didn't reach whomever was intent on destroying the tree.

Shortly, Sam stopped and held a hand up. Then he bent forward, parted the foliage directly in front of him, and studied what he could see through the fronds of a large stand of ferns. He remained a still-life study for minutes as he took in the scene before him. Slowly, he turned to Kelly, and with a finger to his lips indicated for her to backtrack.

When they reached the trail where they'd left it, Kelly turned to Sam. "Well, are you going to tell me what was going on?"

"It appears a couple of tough guys from Kalgola are trying to build a cage out of mangrove branches. Probably think they can lure a tiger into the trap and earn some easy big bucks."

She sputtered with exasperation. "If that's all it was, why didn't you just ask them how far we are from Kalgola?"

He moved his lecherous, green-eyed gaze deliberately over her body. "I didn't know 'em, but they sure as hell looked like opportunists to me. And well, it's just my opinion, of course, but they might have decided you represented more opportunity than the tiger."

The heat in Sam's stare made her muscles bunch in intimate places. It also turned her weary. At least that's what she called the sudden tension that filled her body.

What she refused to admit to, however, was feeling aroused or anxious.

Chapter Five

When Kelly could pull her gaze away, she held up an accusatory finger. "You made that last part up just to try to frighten me, didn't you?"

"Did it work?" he drawled.

"Damn you!" It infuriated her that he would try to make her more fearful than she already was. "Isn't the situation bad enough?"

"Keep your voice down," he whispered. "I don't know who they are or what they're capable of, but, personally, I believe it's easier to stay out of trouble than to get out of it. You understand me?"

She understood, but she'd never let him know that. She rolled her eyes heavenward. "Shall we move on then?" she asked in a waspish tone.

"Just waiting for you, sweetheart," he rasped.

Kelly had the violent urge to strike at him or scream at the top of her lungs, but because the situation demanded prudence, she decided to be reasonable. Huffing, she resumed trudging down the trail as harrowing jungle noises began to return.

In minutes Sam impatiently took the lead. "Stick close," he ordered.

As they neared the shattered village of Kalgola, a subtle

change overtook the jungle. The animal sounds slowly diminished until there were only a few chirping birds. Everything else had been replaced by the sounds of civilization.

The sounds of a society, even a primitive, devastated one, brought Kelly comfort and an end to the nagging fear that had haunted her the night before, when they'd heard the tiger's roar—the real fear of being overwhelmed and dragged to her death by one of the ferocious felines.

"I don't see the boat," Kelly said. She'd just gotten her first view of the dock.

She stopped on a small rise and, shielding her eyes from the sun, studied the water in front of them. Then her eyes followed it all the way to the distant horizon.

At this point, Sam wasn't sure how he felt about *anything.* Earlier he'd decided to put Kelly on the boat to Calcutta, come hell or high water. But now that they'd reached Kalgola, his gut was telling him he didn't want to let her go, no matter how much grief she might cause him. And that made him edgy. Worse than edgy.

Sam's gut unclenched. He checked his watch. "Might be late," he muttered. *Or not coming.*

Looking thoroughly dejected, she grumbled, "More than likely, it's not coming."

Sam allowed his gaze to wander over her arm to her shoulder, then down to her breast. He found himself wanting to follow the same route with his hand, his mouth, his body. He wanted her *real* bad.

To distract himself, he strode down toward the ticket office on the land side of the dock. "Come on. Before you jump to conclusions, let's ask the ticket agent."

Kelly followed, but when they were close enough to see the window, they could clearly see it was closed. A sign hung from the door.

It read: THE BOAT FROM CALCUTTA WILL NOT BE HERE UNTIL TOMORROW. CHECK BACK TOMORROW TO SEE IF IT WILL BE HERE THEN. THE MANAGEMENT.

Kelly sighed. "Swell."

Sam grunted, then turned his attention to what was left of the village. What hadn't been destroyed outright by the quake had been burned to the ground by the fire. Only a few buildings looked habitable and the villagers were busily shoring those up with lumber salvaged from other destroyed buildings.

Here and there, open stands had sprung up with entrepreneurs selling everything from fresh fruit, vegetables, fish, and any useful objects salvaged from some of the ruined buildings. As he watched, at one of the stands an argument broke out over a dented coffeepot. Obviously found among the ruins, it was now being claimed by the rightful owner, over the protests of the finder.

Sam could almost see Kelly's already dampened spirits plummet when she realized the boat to Calcutta wouldn't be taking her back. Not today, anyway. And maybe not tomorrow. She had nowhere to stay. Nowhere to turn. No one but Sam to take care of her.

"What am I going to do?" She whispered the question aloud.

"What's that?" Sam responded to the tone of despair because he hadn't heard the words.

Kelly blinked hard and stared into the distance.

"I'm just not certain what I'll do next," she murmured, gazing at the blackened ruins.

Sam had come to the conclusion that he'd have to look out for her a while longer. This also meant he had more time to get to know her. *Oh, yeah . . . sure!*

"Well now," he said, "I don't think you have much choice in the matter. Obviously, you'll have to come with me."

The realization that she'd be totally under Sam's control threw Kelly. Any relief she felt about not being alone was quickly wiped out by a myriad of emotions.

"Just where are you going?" she asked.

He slanted her a hard look. "Does it matter?"

Her stomach quivered. She bit her lip. "It might."

His mouth quirked for a nanosecond. "Look, trust me, it'll be okay. I'll keep you safe." He took hold of her arm and steered her to one of the newly formed fruit and vegetable stands.

Picking up a banana, he handed it to her. "Here, eat this. It'll make you feel better."

She might have wanted to protest, to make him give her a definitive answer before she went anywhere with him. But one glance at the devastation surrounding them silenced her. It would be difficult to complain when so many others were dealing with worse circumstances.

She devoured the banana.

Sam purchased a wide selection of what the shopkeeper had to offer. Then, with Kelly following along like a lost puppy, he moved on to the next stall. There he purchased more, some which he handed to Kelly. When they were both loaded down, he continued down the road in the opposite direction from the night before, toward where the fire had started, leaving the devastated town behind.

"Do you mind telling me where we're taking all of this stuff?" Kelly finally asked. She had visions of another large mangrove tree in her future.

"I've got a boat docked about twenty minutes out of town."

She stopped and gaped at him, open-mouthed. "Twenty

minutes out of town? I don't understand. Why didn't you dock it in town where it would be handy?"

He stopped when she did, but only for a moment. " 'Cause I didn't want to have the damn thing jacked out from under me, that's why."

Kelly watched him move off, knowing he'd quickly outdistance her. Running to catch up, she imagined she'd never met anyone so suspicious in her life.

"Does that kind of thing happen a lot?" Her tone indicated she doubted it happened at all.

The lines in his face hardened. "Too damned often, if you ask me. It might be hard for you to believe, but pirates still ply their trade in remote areas of the world."

His formidable expression convinced her. "Pirates?"

"Yeah, pirates."

"Has something like that happened to you?"

"Hell, no! And I don't expect it will. Not if I use my head and continue to take precautions."

The way he said it, she had to wonder just what precautions he'd taken. Certainly he hadn't left the boat unattended, which meant he had deckhands. Would they be natives? Or crew he'd brought along from the States?

"Did you sail the boat from home?" she asked, in a quest for knowledge.

"You're just full of questions, aren't ya?" His mouth curled up real slow at the edges.

She hated it when he patronized her. "Questions you're not going to answer, right?"

"Maybe later. For now, I'd like you to keep that cute little trap latched."

Kelly's lips pursed with annoyance. Even his use of the descriptive "cute" didn't make her feel any better. He always treated her like a witless child and she didn't appreciate the slight in the least. Still, since he wanted her to stay quiet, she would, simply because she wasn't interested in attracting anything even remotely carnivorous. *If* that was what he was worried about. But, hell, who knew? He was so damned secretive, she wondered if *he* even knew what he was thinking.

Sam veered from the dirt road to take a trampled path that Kelly assumed would eventually lead to the boat, and darn, she hoped they'd get there soon. For most of the day they'd trekked through a jungle teeming with all kinds of vermin. And she felt hot, tired, and dirty. Praying the boat had a shower, she fantasized about washing her hair, scrubbing her body, and changing into clean clothes. Unfortunately, all she'd managed to salvage from her room had been her small backpack. Everything else had been left behind to burn. The hotel now consisted of nothing but charred, useless rubble.

Almost too tired to think, she made a conscious decision to worry about one thing at a time. Right now, all she would allow herself to think about was getting clean. If she accomplished that, she'd worry about clothes.

They reached a length of debris-littered beach. Jutting out from it was a small, dilapidated dock that stretched fifteen feet into the water. Tied up to the dock was the sweetest sight Kelly had seen in many a day.

A large, gleaming-white cabin cruiser rocked gently in the ocean swell, kissing the dock with the delicacy of a maiden.

Sam placed his packages on the first of several steps that led to the dock and drew the gun from his waistband. "Stay here until I make sure everything's cool," he ordered.

Kelly sighed softly and nodded. The thought that anything would keep her from the cold shower she felt certain awaited her brought a decided ache to her bones. Still, as a belated invited guest, there was nothing to do but wait and watch him mount the last few steps to the dock and cautiously advance toward the cruiser.

Before he'd made it halfway down the dock, a tiny brown-skinned man appeared on the boat's deck. He held a malevolent-looking rifle in his small hands and quickly pointed the business end of it at Sam's midsection.

Fear for Sam froze Kelly in place. She couldn't catch a breath. Words of warning stuck in her throat. Unable to move, she wouldn't be able to save Sam or herself. Clearly, there was nowhere to hide. The little man had the advantage. After he gunned down Sam, she'd be completely visible. And standing like a stone statue, she'd be an easy target.

Kelly finally managed a strangled whisper. "Sam!" She had no idea whether he heard.

Obviously, Sam didn't need a warning from her. There was no way on earth he could miss spotting the danger. It was *right* there in front of him. God help them.

Kelly's heart stuttered when she saw Sam begin to raise his gun. It was evident he didn't stand a chance of getting a shot off first.

He'll be killed!

She couldn't stand to watch. But she couldn't disconnect her gaze, either. Horrified, she stood there as the terrible drama played out.

Sam's gun seemed to move in slow motion as he raised it to shoulder level, his finger clearly not on the trigger, his aim wide of the mark.

The native didn't fire, just continued to hold Sam in the crosshairs of his rifle, his eyes resembling twin flames.

Suddenly, Sam yelled, "Bang, bang, you're dead!"

The little man shrieked. "Too late! Too late. I already kill you. Besides you miss by a mile." Then a grin broke over his face and he started to dance a wild jig of glee.

"Didn't hear ya say bang, bang," Sam grunted in denial.

The little man shouted, "Doesn't matter, you dead anyway."

"Well, hell." Sam shook his head. Sounding disappointed, he holstered his gun.

"Just so." The little man flashed a toothless grin.

Sam took off his hat, slapped his knee with it, and nodded. "Okay, you win, I guess."

Gleeful now, the native said, "Of course."

After this little ritual, Sam turned to Kelly, who stood open-mouthed. "Come on, let's get on board."

She'd jumped a foot into the air when Sam shouted the first "bang" and had felt her heart skip in fright. Now, fully recovered, she sputtered furiously. "How could you let me th-think he was going to k-k-kill you? What's the matter with you?"

Sam cocked his head at her and dryly asked, "You gonna let a little playacting throw ya?"

Stung, Kelly stalked over to him and slapped him hard on the arm. "I should punch you in the nose. Dammit, you scared me out of a year's worth of life, at the very least."

Appearing weary, he muttered, "Don't let nothin' but fear hold ya back."

Kelly growled and stalked past him, only to stop when she neared the little man who'd ceased dancing to stare at her.

Sam advised his brown friend, as he came up behind her. "Appears she's a mite touchy, Pele. Better steer clear."

Kelly swung around and glared at him. "Trust me, it's only the company I keep."

Sam grunted, then took Kelly by the arm and helped her onto the boat. "Keep a lookout, little friend, 'til I get our jumpy guest settled."

The little man nodded, then saluted. He planted his feet

apart, rested the rifle butt on the planking, one hand supporting it around the barrel, and scrutinized the jungle beyond the dock, apparently treating Sam's command with the utmost seriousness.

When Sam opened the door to a small neat stateroom and ushered Kelly inside, the prospect of a tepid shower had her considering forgiving him for the thoughtless joke.

"The head's through there." He pointed, indicating a small pocket door across from the bunk bed. "Help yourself to a shower and I'll try to find something that might come close to fitting you." He narrowed his gaze as he scanned her small body. "Won't be easy," he muttered, more to himself than her. Then he was gone before she could thank him.

Her first inclination was to wait until he brought her something to wear, but the lure of the shower was too great. She locked the adjoining door—it was a shared bathroom—and showered using what she presumed was his bar of Zest. She washed her hair with his shampoo, geared to the male gender, which gave her a strange feeling of shared intimacy. Afterward, she combed her hair and wrapped the oversize towel around her body before venturing out into the cabin. She was relieved to find he'd left her an oversized man's shirt, more than likely his, and a smaller pair of faded jeans, which she quickly donned, rolling up the bottoms several inches. That accomplished, she brushed out the tangles in her hair and began to feel almost human.

By the time she'd touched mascara to her lashes and dusted her cheeks with blush, her hair had partly dried and curled around her face. Then, barefoot, hungry, and unsure what to do with herself, she left her cabin and wandered down the passageway to the main salon. The galley lay just beyond, and remembering the fruit Sam had purchased, she headed that way.

A large wooden bowl, holding a variety of the fruit, sat on the small table surrounded by a tiny railing. Kelly helped herself to a ripe, delicious-looking plum, tore a paper towel off the roll hooked under a cabinet, and made herself comfortable near a window on the side exposed to the tiny beach and jungle. From where she sat she couldn't see their small sentry, but she felt confident he still stood guard on the dock. He'd seemed so happy to accommodate Sam.

Idly, she wondered just who Sam thought might commandeer the boat. Then she realized most anyone from Kalgola might feel justified in taking the boat if they'd lost their home. And she couldn't really blame them. It felt wonderful to know she had a clean place to lay her head for the evening, even while she wondered what price Sam might attempt to elicit for the privilege.

After finishing the plum, she stood. The boat rocked as if it had been boarded. Instantly on the alert, her gaze riveted on the salon entrance, she waited for whoever it was to enter. A trapped feeling overcame her, especially since she hadn't taken the time to explore the ship for other exits.

When Sam, ducking his head, came through the door, her relief was unmistakable.

Voice tight with tension, she asked, "Where did you go? I thought you were still on the boat."

She watched him stare at her as she stood there in his over-size denim shirt covering all but a few inches of rolled up jeans, her small bare feet planted slightly apart on the floor for support against the pitch and roll of the boat.

Muttering something unintelligible, he brushed past her.

"I didn't hear what you said," she cried, exasperated.

"Lucky you," he shot back.

"Now just a minute. . . ."

He stopped, swung around toward her, and gave her a look that told her just how much of a threat he was at that moment.

Breathing fast, Kelly took a quick step backward. Then she sat down and stared out the window at the jungle that now appeared tame by comparison. Her heart thudded in her ears like a sky diver on her maiden jump.

Shit! Growling under his breath, Sam strode by her before he lost control and damn well grabbed her and had her the way he wanted her. Flat on her back on a bed.

Sam, eyes glinting dangerously, left the salon. As he stepped into the stateroom adjoining the tiny head she'd used, he softly closed the door. It took him several long beats to unclench the jaw that had begun to twitch from tension. It would take a long cold shower to unclench the rest of him. If *that* even worked.

Showered and dressed, his mind and body once again under control, Sam strode back into the salon in search of food. That was a hunger he could assuage. Ignoring Kelly, he opened one of the cabinets and extracted two large cans of Dinty Moore stew. He opened the cans, scooped the contents into a sauce pan, and began to heat the lot on the tiny gas range.

She watched him. "Is that lunch?"

"Right."

"Is there something I can do?" she asked, appetite obviously stirring.

"You can set the table and cut a few slices of the bread we bought in the village."

The unwrapped loaf was still sitting out on the counter and she found the silverware easily enough. The bowls were overhead in a cabinet.

"Placemats?" she inquired.

He shot her a look. "This isn't the Four Seasons. Just put the stuff on the table."

"Do I set it for three?" she asked.

"Get three of everything out, but leave one set on the counter. Pele won't leave his post to eat. I'll take it out to him."

She nodded. "What do you want to drink?"

"I'll have a beer. Get an orange soda out for Pele . . . he's addicted."

Kelly managed a smile, even though it was obvious she was still leery of the little man. "How long have you known Pele?"

"Five or six weeks. Since we've been out here." *Damn.* He still expected to have John appear any minute when he was on the boat, and the loss of his friend pained him every time he had to face harsh reality. He needed to get back to the States where he had a chance of getting beyond the grief.

"We?" Kelly asked.

"There's just me now." He scowled as he stirred the stew.

"Why is that?"

"You don't wanna know," he snapped, then busied himself pouring steaming stew into the three bowls.

Immediately, Kelly decided there'd been a woman along and her stomach gave a disquieting flutter for no reason she could fathom. After all, Sam was nothing to her beyond the fact that she needed him to find Jeff. Still, she couldn't help wondering what had happened. She realized that, whatever it was, it was undoubtedly the reason behind his getting blind drunk in the disreputable bar where she'd found him.

"Did you have a falling out with your friend?" she persisted. Somehow, it was easier to say friend than lover. But that didn't mean anything, she assured herself.

He turned off the water he'd been running into the pot to

soak it, picked up a bowl of stew, a couple of slices of bread, and the orange soda. Ignoring her, he headed out of the salon. Just before he got out of sight, he shot a mean glance over his shoulder.

"No. He's dead! Just like your guy. Happy now?" he growled.

Stunned, Kelly quickly sat at the table to keep her knees from letting her down. She even managed to eat her stew and a piece of bread after he returned, his face devoid of expression, except for tautness around his eyes.

She waited until he'd finished taking a swallow of beer, then raised her gaze to his face, her eyes steady on his. "Jeff isn't dead. He's out there somewhere. Maybe your friend isn't dead, either."

Sam shook his head, his eyes as shiny and hard as agates. "Oh, he's dead all right. We buried him . . . what was left."

Chapter Six

Kelly's hand flew to her mouth. Eyes wide and unblinking, she whispered, "I'm so sorry. I shouldn't have pried. Please forgive me."

He stared back, his expression unreadable. Finally he muttered, "Sometimes you're better off not knowing the gory details."

Realizing she'd blundered, badly, Kelly kept her head down and didn't say anything. After hearing the fate of Sam's friend, all her worries for Jeff had flown back to the forefront of her mind, sending her into a tailspin of doubt.

Slowly, her anxiety eased. That inner sense of enlightenment, an indefinable sense, ESP, or whatever one called it, had never let her down. And she knew, without a doubt, that she'd have a terrible feeling of loss in her gut if Jeff were dead. That didn't mean she wasn't worried about him, but *that* anxiety wasn't the same as the painful void she'd be feeling if he'd been killed. *Yes,* she assured herself, *I'd know.* And that knowledge alone was her salvation. The one thing that kept her sane when anxiety threatened to overwhelm her.

Having emptied her bowl and finished two large slices of bread, she dared to level her gaze on Sam's face. Now he was the one intent on the bowl before him, seemingly unaware she existed.

She murmured, "Excuse me," stood up, and took her dishes to the sink, where she proceeded to wash them and everything else Sam had used to prepare their meal. Finished with the task at hand, she turned to see if she could collect his dishes.

He was close behind her. So close, she brushed his flat stomach with one hand as she swung around.

Kelly's instant response was to back away. But, already up against the sink, she had nowhere to go.

Sam reached around her and deposited his dishes on the counter beside her, his arm brushing hers. The same arm took a detour on the way back and settled around Kelly's waist.

Sam had finished his meal, kicking himself all the while for deliberately hurting Kelly. It wasn't her fault John had died. The truth was, Sam was damn certain no matter who the guy was she came to search for, she loved him, and it had been eating away at Sam, turning him sour. But when he saw the hurt flash across her face, after his devastating reply, he felt as guilt-ridden as a kid who'd been caught sneaking a reefer.

"I'm sorry," he murmured softly. "Sometimes I'm too damn blunt." With his other hand he tilted her chin so he could gaze into her eyes. "You feel up to telling me about this Jeff?" he asked. He tried to steel himself against the pain that would inevitably flood his emotions when she told him about her lover, and he failed miserably.

"Why? What does it matter? You're not interested in helping me find him."

"Tell me about him, Kelly," Sam gently urged.

She studied him a moment, then took a deep breath. Tears deepening the color of her irises, she began to tell the story.

"Jeff came out here to make a documentary about the tigers for the television station he works for," she said. Her voice trembled. "Then . . . he just vanished."

Sam's heart constricted. Just like John. But worse. She might never find out what really happened to the guy.

"When did you hear from him last?" Sam asked.

"A week ago."

"How often did he call up until then?"

"Every other day. He knew the shoot was dangerous, so I was his backup if anything went wrong."

He felt her tremble and nodded in sympathy. "A week is a hell of a long time to be out of touch here. You made good time, though." What he couldn't bring himself to tell her was that she was almost certainly a week late. The Sundarbans' only inhabitants were animals, and most of those were maneating tigers. You got off the island quickly or you didn't survive. This Jeff, whoever he was, evidently hadn't gotten off.

She closed her eyes and a tear worked its way out from under her lashes and down her cheek. "A lot of good it did me," she whispered.

Sam melted. He wanted to kiss away her tears, to hold her so nothing would ever hurt her again. But he couldn't do that until he'd convinced her that her lover was dead. And that was a damn big hitch. When he had proved the guy was dead, she'd hate him for sure. He was damned if he did and damned it he didn't. *What the hell!*

With a thumb, he caught the tear and lifted it to his mouth. It tasted salty and delicious because it was hers, and he savored that infinitesimal part of her.

With the bittersweet taste of her tears still on his tongue, he made his offer. "I'll try to help you find him."

I should definitely have my head examined, if I survive this, he thought, after he'd made his offer.

Kelly's stomach fluttered the moment he touched her

cheek. Her senses told her the fate of her tear and her eyes popped open in response. Her heart stuttered, as well, and she could barely utter the word. "Really?"

The sigh came from deep down. He nodded. "Really."

"Why?" She didn't quite fathom her sudden good fortune.

"Because it's important to you."

She was confused, unsure of what he was implying, and she turned uneasy. Then, after a few tense moments, unable to think of anything but the slim chance to save her brother, she simply said, "Thank you."

"Hold the thanks until I get back. If I get back," Sam muttered.

His last words galvanized Kelly. "You're not leaving me behind. I'm going along." She was sick to death of wondering what was happening. And she wanted to be there, in the thick of it, whatever *it* was.

He dropped her chin. "Not a chance!"

She didn't care how stubborn *he* was, *she* was going. "If you don't let me go with you, I'll just follow you."

He grabbed her shoulders, obviously wanting to shake some sense into her, but the feel of her delicate bones and warm flesh apparently calmed him. His voice stern, he said, "I told you it's deadly over there. If the tigers don't get you, the crocodiles or snakes will give it a damn good try."

Crocodiles? She knew about the tigers and snakes. Were there really crocodiles, or was he just trying to scare her? *Don't be silly. Why would he bother when I'm already terrified?*

Forcing a shrug, she asked, "Will I be safe *here*, without you to protect me?" She knew he'd have to take the boat to the islands. That meant leaving her in town or sending her back on the boat to Calcutta tomorrow, if there was a boat.

"If the boat comes from Calcutta tomorrow, you're on it,"

Sam replied. "Then I'll try to find the guy. Right now, I want you to tell me who this Jeff is and what he is to you."

Somehow, she thought she'd told him already, but events had unfolded so quickly she had obviously been remiss. "Jeff is my brother. My only sibling."

Ninety-nine percent of Sam's tension immediately expunged itself from his body. Feeling almost light-hearted, he glanced down at her.

"Your brother?" Sounded too good to be true. But, hell, he was due a break. Wasn't he?

She nodded. "My older brother."

He placed his hands on her shoulders and searched her face for dishonesty. Finding none, he said, "I promise you, as soon as I see you safely onto the ferry, I'll start looking for him."

Sam thought that should be good enough for anyone, but she challenged him anyway.

"If you insist on putting me on the ferry, I assure you I won't feel compelled to stay there. I'll get off around the first bend of the river, even if I have to swim. I'm not going back to Calcutta until I know Jeff is safe."

Dammit, why can't her attitude be as soft as she looks and feels?

His fingers tightened on those soft shoulders of hers. "If you knew how unreasonable you sound, you'd bite your tongue."

"I don't care how I sound. I'm tired of wondering and waiting for someone else to do something. I'm going with you. Or if you insist on denying my right to go along, I'll go by myself, no matter what you say."

It had been downright wrenching for Sam to come to the decision to put Kelly on the boat for Calcutta, knowing he might never see her again if he didn't find her brother. Or, even if he found him as he expected—just bits of clothing, boots, and maybe some camera equipment. After that, she'd be too devastated by grief to give him the time of day. He understood all too well. He was still experiencing that kind of pain first hand. And it was numbing, a real spirit killer.

"Look, it's just too damn dangerous for you to go onto the islands. Just going there, you risk your life in the mud. Hell, there are places where the mud is so deep it can suck a man down like a Slurpee."

She glared at him. "Just keep right on going."

He stared at her. "Keep right on with what?"

"Now it's mud! Enough already. You've thrown tigers, snakes, and crocodiles at me. Give it a rest."

"I'm telling you the truth," he snarled.

"Okay, I believe you. So I'll stay on the boat, out of the mud, where it's safe."

"The hell you will!"

She smiled and placed a palm against his wide, warm chest. "I promise to follow orders and stay on the boat. Please, will you take me?"

All she had to do was touch him and his body fired up, hotter than hell. Taking her was a glorious fantasy never far from the forefront of his mind. How in hell was he supposed to resist? Especially when she looked like an angel, even in the mammoth clothes that swamped her. Groaning, realizing he'd undoubtedly regret his decision, Sam relented.

"You damn well *will* stay on the boat or I'll feed you to a predator myself," he snapped. Then, as difficult as it was to walk away without stealing the kisses he hungered for, he turned and stomped out of the room.

"We leave at first light," he muttered, just before disappearing around the corner.

Trembling from both the argument and close contact with

Sam, Kelly turned back to the sink and washed the rest of the dirty dishes. She blamed her shakiness on overwhelming fatigue, instead of the fact that Sam had had her pinned in place and left her vulnerable and yearning.

Yearning?

"I'm tired, that's all," she grumbled. Her feelings for Sam had to be an aberration due to the extreme stress she'd been under, she decided, pulling the plug on the dishwater, watching it swirl down the drain, gone forever.

Will that happen to me? she wondered, mesmerized by the small whirlpool. Once she ventured into that haunted place where the tigers reigned, would she disappear? Eaten by the man-eaters?

What a way to go.

She prayed her fears wouldn't become reality, because, if they did, Jeff might never be found. And that would be a tragedy. He was so talented. So young. So lost. The last thought came unbidden and she shivered, remembering the spine-tingling tiger's roar of the night before.

A sudden, not so farfetched fear that Jeff could indeed have been prey for the tigers shattered her hopes and she abruptly dissolved into tears.

The tears, she assured herself, had nothing to do with the fact that Sam hadn't kissed her, or that he'd stalked away angry. Absolutely nothing.

Kelly took refuge in her tiny cabin. She curled up on the bunk and cried herself into an exhausted slumber.

Without locks on the inside of the cabin doors, it presented no problem for Sam to look in on Kelly later. Finding her sleeping in a protective fetal position tugged at his heart. She looked so vulnerable, he wanted to pick her up and cradle her in his arms. But the danger in that action was all too obvious. If just gazing at her could excite him, it would be downright hazardous to touch her. He knew that, but it still took a concentrated effort to step back outside and close the cabin door, then proceed to his cabin and attempt to get some rest.

Unable to sleep, Sam relieved Pele and stood the early evening watch.

Sam surveyed the dense jungle and tiny littered beach. With his keen eyesight he searched for any signs of predators, either man or beast.

Kelly awoke with a start. It took her a moment to realize why. Then the knowledge penetrated her sleep-dulled brain and she realized, without peering out the porthole, that the cruiser was underway. The only question in her mind was: which direction was it moving? To Kalgola to catch the ferry? Or were they headed for the islands? In which case, Sam had truly capitulated.

She had to know. Fighting the lure of the rumpled bunk, she crawled out and stepped to the porthole. And then she sighed with relief. The boat was moving at a good clip, far from the shore on the port side, which meant they weren't headed toward the devastated village.

Sam was taking her to the islands.

Showered and dressed in the same jeans, Kelly opened the tiny closet and borrowed another shirt, a colorful Hawaiian patterned with flying fish. She knotted it in tails at her waist. She supposed the man who'd worn such bright shirts was Sam's missing friend, but wasn't certain. She just knew they weren't Sam's; they were too out of character for him.

Sam had implied his friend was killed by a tiger, but he hadn't come right out and confirmed it, so she wasn't one hundred percent certain. Afraid to ask for clarification, it didn't stop her from wondering what Sam and his friend were doing in this exotic part of the world. Did Sam think he was responsible for his friend's death? If so, that would explain many things. The drinking. The surliness. The belief that they'd never find her brother alive. All of that, plus his grudging respect for the tigers.

Kelly wandered into the galley in search of breakfast. After helping herself to coffee from a carafe on a burner of the stove, mug in hand, she perused the tiny refrigerator. She finally settled for a hefty wedge of cheese and crunchy bread torn from the loaf they'd dined on the previous evening. She finished her breakfast by enjoying a ripe mango. At least she thought it was a mango, even thought it looked different from what she usually purchased at the grocery store. It tasted slightly different, too, but what the heck. It satisfied.

After refilling her cup, Kelly made her way up on deck.

The cabin cruiser was moving at a fast enough pace to make her sway. Although cooler here, she lost her breath as the moist heat hit her, forcing her to swing toward the rear of the boat to catch a breath.

Gazing aft, the cruiser's wake caught her attention. It flowed out behind the boat like a rippling fan, expanding until, some distance off, it lapped onto the shore on the side of the bay Kalgola was on. She began to think how one small event in another person's life could extend to those around them and change their lives forever.

Jeff going missing wasn't a small happening, but the ripples of his disappearance would probably affect her forever, she decided, thinking about Sam's appearance—wanted or not—in her life.

Moments later, a slight movement in her peripheral vision caught her attention. She turned and, due to the glare of the sea, squinted as long, muscular legs descended the ladder from the wheel house, accompanied by a body that could make her forget most everything else.

She watched as Sam advanced toward her, wondering what his mood would be this morning, hoping for something better than the night before. Her expectation died quickly when she saw his fierce expression. Disappointment engulfed her as she quickly realized she'd been waiting to see that devastating pirate's smile he used all too rarely. At least with her.

"Good morning. Could I get a cup of coffee for you?" she asked, flashing her most enchanting smile. *At least I will be gracious*, she thought.

"What the hell are you doing on deck?" he snarled. He stopped two feet away, so she had to crane her neck way up to look him in the eye. When she did, and saw his fury, her mouth felt as if it was stuffed with cotton batting and her pulse skittered.

Great, Mr. Charm is back.

Kelly battled to control the panic he could spur. She turned away to gaze at the distant shore until she could regroup. Finally she said, "To answer your 'oh-so-polite' question, I needed some fresh air. Okay?"

"It damn well isn't okay. Get below and stay there. Now!" He appeared angry enough to spit nails.

Damn him! Tears building, she brushed by him and rushed to the hatch. Halfway down the steps, the boat hit a wake from other water traffic and her coffee slopped over the side of the mug and landed on the deck of the salon below.

"Just swell," she grumbled. Aggravation dried her tears before they could build enough to spill over.

Placing her half-full mug in the sink, she tore paper towels off the roller and headed back to the stairs. She didn't get far, because Sam had followed and stood, hands on hips, at the bottom of the ladder, glaring at her.

"It looks like I can't count on you to use good old-fashioned, common sense, so I'm laying down the law here and now." He jabbed a finger at her. "You stay below, unless I tell you it's okay to come on deck. You don't even show that pretty head of yours above deck by so much as peeking out the door. Got that?"

Kelly, always the rebel, just naturally questioned dictatorial orders. "Tell me why I can't be on deck."

"Because this area is full of desperate people who might try anything to get out."

"The boat is moving," she protested.

He seemed to swell in size. "That won't keep a bullet from hitting its target."

"They'd be more apt to shoot you," she snapped.

He was on her so fast she barely had time to blink. His intentions may have been punitive, but his actions didn't respond that way. Instead of shaking sense into her, he shook her to the core by punishing her with his mouth. By invading her with his tongue, molding her body to his, and pushing his steel-hard erection savagely against her.

Dragging his mouth from hers, he shoved her away. "If you want this to go farther, keep pushing. And remember, I won't be the one responsible for what happens."

Her heart pounded. She took deep breaths to clear her head. She'd been his, her need as great. But thinking he'd just threatened her with rape fueled her temper.

"If you even *think* about forcing sex on me, I'll shoot you myself."

His tone, acid with sarcasm, broke over her. "You're a little late with that one, sweetheart. I've already thought about it," he snapped.

Stunned by this admission, Kelly stumbled backward, prepared to turn and flee.

He stopped her by saying, "When I take you, blue eyes, you'll want me as badly as I want you. So relax."

She breathed the denial. "Never!"

His grin was more wicked than that of any black-hearted devil who'd ever lived. "Oh, absolutely, sweetheart. And at the rate you're going, it will be sooner rather than later. To tell you the truth, I can hardly wait."

Then he left her with her mouth hanging open and her knees threatening to buckle onto the floor.

When she could move, she stumbled to her cabin, closed the door, and collapsed onto the bunk.

It took her nearly fifteen minutes to question how he dared speak to her in such a manner.

And, unfortunately, no possible answers satisfied her. They only raised more questions. Why could Sam Tanner turn her into a weak-kneed teenybopper? That was the biggest question. Did her hormones need a major realignment? Or was it the steamy, hot climate?

When he reached the wheel house, Sam was still needy and rock hard and damned happy Kelly didn't know how the encounter had affected him. He also knew one glance warned Pele that now wasn't the time for fun and games. And if the little man had had any doubt about the relationship between Kelly and Sam before, he most certainly knew how the land lay now. Sam was a desperate man. A man unable to take this particular woman lightly. A man in love, whether he would admit it or not.

Unfortunately, that little encounter below deck had also told Sam more than he wanted to know. That he couldn't touch her without losing control. That he couldn't kiss her without needing to have her. That it was difficult as hell to keep his hands to himself. He wondered why he had lied to her, and why he continued to taunt her when what he wanted, desperately, was to make love to her.

Sam had never had a struggle with his libido anywhere close to this conflict. Oh, sure, he'd been in lust from time to time, but he'd always been able to play it cool and allow the woman to come to him. Now it was different. So damn different, he almost didn't recognize himself. He'd wanted Kelly from minute one. Had to battle instincts that urged him to hunt her down and take her from the moment she walked out of the bar in Kalgola. And that desire hadn't faded. It had grown. Grown to such proportions that he found it difficult to think of anything else but having her.

Shaking his head, he swore violently. The man-eaters would sure as hell have the edge when he ventured onto the islands in search of Kelly's brother.

Sam knew damn well his concentration should be totally on the tigers. And he knew it wouldn't be. He hadn't been able to get Kelly out of his mind for half a second, let alone long enough to survive in the jungle for as long as it would take to find a sign of the man he'd come to rescue—given the remote possibility that a man could survive for a week in that killing field.

"I'll take the helm," Sam told Pele. "You get some rest. We'll need all of our energy when we drop anchor."

"No worry, sahib. Pele not afraid of tigers."

Sam didn't miss the sudden widening of eyes that accompanied the bold statement from Pele, and he didn't blame his small friend. A genuine lack of fear regarding the man-eaters would point to stupidity or an arrogance that could get a man killed. Pele had neither fault. Sam knew he simply wanted to make his boss feel better about a venture that was fraught with risk. And it did help. Just knowing Pele was accompanying him gave Sam a lift. The little man was invaluable.

★ ★ ★ ★ ★

The water traffic thinned and finally turned nonexistent as the cruiser neared its destination. Sam navigated gingerly among the many sandbars that lurked in the waterway waiting to ground unobservant sailors. He finally shut down the throttle and dropped anchor.

Before the anchor hit bottom, Pele appeared on deck. "We there, huh, sahib?"

"Afraid so, my friend. Keep a sharp eye out while I go below."

"I do that, sahib, no worry."

Sam patted Pele on the shoulder and went below. He was more than worried, damn close to paranoid. And for that he had only himself to blame. If anything happened to Kelly on the heels of John's loss, it would finish him. Before he could rap on her cabin door, Kelly opened it and stepped into the narrow hallway.

Sounding anxious, she asked, "Why have we stopped?"

"We're stopping for a rest."

"Oh. I wondered when the engines shut down. . . ." Her voice trailed off.

In a voice raspy from lack of sleep, Sam said, "I thought you might want to come up on deck and see what we're up against."

"Yes, of course." Like a puppy, she followed him through the salon, up the ladder, and onto the deck. Then, watching her face, he could almost see her heart sink as she got a clear view of the tightly woven jungle beyond the sandbars; a green mélange that stretched as far as the eye could see in both directions.

Her voice soft with confusion, she said, "I didn't realize it was such a large area."

His demeanor on the cold side, he replied, "Yeah, well, it *is*. Any suggestions?"

Mute with disappointment, Kelly shook her head.

"That's what I thought," he growled.

As they stood, staring at the dense jungle, Kelly said, "A boat. Jeff hired a boat to bring him down here. Maybe it's still here, anchored off the area where he went ashore to make the film."

Sam bit out his words. "More than likely the skipper dropped him, then took off and left him."

"You don't know that. Shouldn't we sail around the islands and see if we can spot a boat first? At least that would give us a clearer starting point." A sudden blush of excitement painted her cheeks.

He hated to see her get her hopes up, then have them dashed. "Your brother couldn't pay the skipper enough to wait around for a week," he insisted.

"How do you know? You don't know who brought him out here. It could be someone who cared, someone he could trust."

"There's a short supply of altruistic skippers in this part of the world, blue eyes. But hell, if it'll delay going ashore into that—" he nodded his head toward the green maze "—we'll have a look-see."

Sam called for Pele to weigh anchor, as he headed to the wheel house. "Come with me," he ordered Kelly.

The wheel house was surrounded by a Plexiglas shield to protect the captain from spray, but it gave a clear view of the water surrounding the cruiser. Although the wheel house was small on this particular cabin cruiser, there was enough room for Kelly to stand behind Sam, where he indicated, before he fired the engines.

"Keep your eyes open. Tell me if you see anything, even debris that could come from a boat." Sam also scoured the shoreline, but it all looked the same—dense foliage, sand bars, and waterways that entered the jungle on a regular basis, some shallow, some so deep into the island he couldn't see where they ended.

Kelly nodded, shielding her eyes with one hand. "Could you take a boat up one of those waterways?" she asked, pointing out the closest one.

"No way. Too shallow."

She nodded again. "Well . . . I guess we don't have to search them, then."

"Yeah, that's a real break."

His sarcasm turned her ears red. But she kept on squinting into the harsh brightness, searching for any signs of life or a boat.

Fifteen minutes later, she inhaled sharply.

"Oh, my God!"

Chapter Seven

"Look . . . there." In her excitement Kelly pointed rapidly several times. "A tiger!"

Sam throttled back, and spotted the enormous cat prowling a particularly large sandbar. "He must not have scored last night."

The tiger lifted its head and stared directly into Kelly's surprised eyes.

"He's beautiful," she breathed. "Those magnificent, yellow eyes. I've never seen anything like them. They're extraordinary. I feel as if he can read my mind."

Sam uttered a harsh laugh. "If you could read *his* mind, you'd know he was considering having you for his next meal and wondering how he could make that happen."

It was still difficult for Kelly to think of the dazzling-looking beast with its beautiful tawny fur coat and silky black stripes as the enemy, even while she knew it was the harsh reality. The urge to touch its fur—which appeared soft as velvet—drew her attention, even while she knew such a thing would never be possible. Not with a live tiger. Especially if he truly was a man-eater. Even so, the sighting was an astounding experience.

Sam engaged the throttle and the cabin cruiser left the prowling predator safely behind, staring hungrily after them.

For Kelly, the deceptively calm waters lent an air of peacefulness to a scene that Sam would tell her was wholly unrealistic; a mirage of the lulling, deadly kind. One she'd better be as wary of as tigers.

She wasn't deceived for long by the peaceful scene. In fact, just being in close proximity to Sam made her feel anything but tranquil. Her pulse quickened around him, advancing to erratic every time he glanced her way. And if her face didn't stop flushing, she feared she'd stay a permanent reddish hue.

The day wore on to dusk, when they had to give up the search.

Dropping anchor, they settled in for the long night. Sam handed Kelly a can of bug spray as they retired for the night. "Use it liberally. You'll need it."

She thanked him and retired, her eyes weary from straining to spot anything that wasn't a natural part of the jungle. She felt disheartened that they'd found no sign.

The following day dragged by in the same dreary manner.

"We don't even know if he's still out here," Sam grumbled as they prepared to retire for the night.

"Where else would he be?" Kelly asked.

"He might have made it back to Kalgola."

"You don't believe that," she snapped. "You just want to give up."

He swore. "Two more days," he warned.

She fled to her cabin.

Early the next morning, as they cruised the islands, Sam muttered more to himself than to her. "What's this?"

Kelly had seen the boat-like shape almost at the same time, but disbelief stayed her tongue for the second it took Sam to speak. As determined as she'd been that they look for another craft, it had been more of a dim hope than a true belief that they'd find one.

"It's a boat." She whispered, afraid the image would disappear if she spoke louder.

"Sure as hell looks like one," Sam admitted, showing genuine surprise.

"Do you think it's Jeff's?" Her eyes turned luminous at the prospect.

"Only one way to find out." Sam pulled his gaze from her face, and opened the throttle.

The cruiser flew over the water, quickly closing the distance. In minutes they pulled parallel with the unidentified boat, about twenty-five feet away. Pele dropped anchor.

"I don't see anyone." Fear shadowed Kelly's voice. "Shouldn't someone on board have heard our motor and come topside to investigate?"

Sam's manner had swiftly shifted from one of surprised optimism to cautious concern. "They should have, if they left someone on watch, but who knows, they might not have." What he didn't say was that they damn well should have had someone on watch twenty-four hours a day. He refrained, because there was no point in upsetting Kelly prematurely.

"Pele, let's get the dinghy into the water. I'm gonna row over and take a look."

In an aside to Pele, before he pushed off, Sam alerted the little man to be prepared for anything. He cautioned him to have his rifle at his side every minute, and to get the hell out of there if Sam didn't get back in ten minutes from the time he boarded the other cruiser.

"Yes, sahib, but you come back, okay?" Pele pleaded.

"I will, but remember what I said . . . just in case." He shoved off in the dinghy.

"Yes, sahib," Pele replied.

Kelly and her small protector watched anxiously as Sam rowed across to the other boat and secured the dinghy to the ladder. She and Pele held their collective breaths as Sam climbed the ladder and went over the side onto the deck. They observed silently as Sam inspected the starboard side of the boat, and inhaled sharply, as one, when Sam disappeared into the belly of the boat.

In less than five minutes Sam emerged alone and started forward on the port side, out of their line of vision. He reappeared on the prow. Looking grim, he inspected something on the deck below their line of sight.

"Something's wrong . . . I can feel it," Kelly whispered.

Pele shrugged several times, his bony shoulders rising and falling like pistons.

"Look like nobody on board, I think," he cautiously ventured.

"Why would they *all* leave?" Kelly pondered aloud, not really expecting an answer.

"Not know, but think maybe bad reason," the little man whispered.

Kelly felt the hairs on her nape twitch. Did he mean the tigers? Was that even possible? Could they actually get on deck?

Sam came aft and they thought he'd return, but he passed the ladder and disappeared as he again entered the salon.

"Why do you think he went back inside?" Kelly asked Pele. Her hands were tightly gripping the rail, her knuckles white.

Again the shoulder pistons. "Do not know, Missy. But, Sam, he a brave man."

She nodded in agreement, but that didn't stop her from worrying.

Moments later Sam appeared on deck and headed for the ladder. Kelly watched him descend, enter the dinghy, and rapidly row back. Pele helped him stow the small boat, with

Kelly hovering in the background, anxiously awaiting answers.

When Sam didn't offer news fast enough, she said, "Was anyone on board?"

Sam just shook his head.

"What were you looking at for so long on the deck?" she wanted to know.

"Nothing important," Sam responded.

"Then why'd you spend so much time up there?" She turned to Pele for confirmation. "He spent a lot of time up there, didn't he?"

The little man's eyes widened. He cocked his head at Sam, but remained silent.

Huffing, giving up on getting confirmation from Pele, she attacked Sam again. "Tell me what you saw."

The skin seemed to tighten over Sam's features. "Let it lie. You'll be better off not knowing."

Transfixed with fear, she grabbed his arm. Now she had to know. "*Tell* me what you saw."

"Let it alone," Sam warned, shaking her off.

"Tell me or I'm rowing over myself," she threatened.

He squinted down at her, his anger obviously bubbling just below the surface. "I found a hell of a lot of blood. Happy now?"

Kelly stumbled backward a couple of steps before stopping. "Whose blood?" she whispered.

Pushed once too often, Sam turned nasty. "Well, hell, sweetheart, I don't know. It wasn't labeled, ya see?"

A split-second later he swore, reached out, and grabbed Kelly as her knees buckled. Cradling her in his arms, he carried her until he could settle her on the padded bench that ran the length of the stern.

He couldn't sustain the anger. "Just once," he whispered,

"I wish you'd listen when I tell you something that's for your own good."

She drew a wobbly breath. "I need to know the truth. Why can't you understand that?"

"I should tell you the truth so you can faint on me?" he asked, rubbing the circulation back into her hands.

"I didn't faint," she protested, dragging her hands away.

"It looked like you were damn close," he insisted, wanting to hold and comfort her.

"Close only counts in horseshoes." She tried to smile, but it came out lopsided and sad.

Sam sighed. He hurt for her, but what could he do with harsh reality staring them in the face?

"There's no telling whose blood it was, but I suspect it was your brother's boat and he probably left one man on board to keep watch. The guy might have been foolish enough to fall asleep. Then, who knows what happened?" Sam figured he knew—tigers or pirates—but he wasn't sharing that particular bit of news with Kelly. Not unless forced.

"What did you find below?" she asked, holding her breath.

"Nothing unusual, except for some camera equipment," he replied softly.

She winced. "Then it probably *is* Jeff's boat."

"Appears that way, unless there's some other photo-fool out there," Sam agreed. "Which seems unlikely."

Kelly sank back against the cushions, unable to speak.

"I'll be going ashore as soon as you pull yourself together," he informed her.

Kelly straightened, squared her shoulders, and tightened her ponytail. "I'm going with you."

Sam's voice came out sounding choked from between clenched back teeth. "What we've been through so far has been easy. But that's *over* now. From here on out it's high stakes. Hell, you saw that tiger back there." He jerked a thumb over his shoulder. "He wasn't just out taking a casual stroll. He was looking for a body or an easy kill. And when he saw you, he was imagining how tasty you'd be and if he had a chance to snatch your ass for dinner."

As terrifying as that sounded, Kelly stood her ground.

"From what you saw over there—" she nodded toward the other cruiser "—can you honestly tell me it's safer to stay on board?"

"You'll have Pele with you."

She smiled apologetically at their small companion. Then she said, "Thank you, but no thank you. I'm going along."

Kelly thought she heard Sam's teeth grind before he rasped a command to Pele to go below for a couple of minutes. She tensed as the little man disappeared.

Sam stepped closer. "I warned you about pushing a man too far. You're staying behind if I have to use force."

Her stomach fluttered. He was frustrated and angry. She knew it would be safer on the cruiser, but her brother was out there, maybe not far away. She had to go. Had to see for herself.

"I can't stay behind." She glanced from him to the other boat. They were so close.

Stiffening her spine, she lifted her chin and squarely met his glare. "You'll *have* to use force to keep me behind, so do your worst!"

His expression of astonishment turned quickly to rage. Cursing a blue streak, he stomped away, mumbling to himself incoherently.

And in spite of the suffocating surroundings, dire circumstances and an uncertain future, a smile touched the corners of her mouth. For a moment she felt so darn good she could have crowed. She'd bamboozled Sam Tanner.

Too soon, he reappeared, replacing her joy with unmistakable fear. He carried a rifle and an uncompromising expression. He was going ashore without her, and if it was really as dangerous as he indicated, she might never see him again.

He spared her a mere glance. "Pele will keep watch until I get back. In the meantime, the best thing you can do is go below and say a prayer."

"You're just going to disregard my wishes?" She crossed her arms over her chest.

"You got it." He didn't even turn her way, just retrieved the dinghy and began to descend the ladder. Before he rowed away, he called, "If you don't have sense enough to go below, help Pele stand watch."

"I love that mushy good-bye," she snapped. She felt bereft and wanted to burst from frustration.

Sam just cocked one eyebrow and continued to work the oars.

Kelly knew better than to scream at him. A shriek might attract the tigers. And if that happened, Martha Stewart's "It's a good thing" definitely wouldn't apply.

Sam beached the boat on what appeared, from a distance, to be wet sand. But when he stepped onto shore, she saw his boots sink into mud.

He swiveled his head around for half a second, as if to say "I told you so."

Retracting a breath, she held it as he pulled one boot after the other out of the deep mud and made his way to the first mangrove trees without sinking out of sight.

He appeared to reach solid ground, and she whispered, "Thank you, God."

But all too soon, a hollow feeling settled in Kelly's chest. She blamed it on seeing Sam melt into the jungle like a large, loose-jointed spirit.

★ ★ ★ ★ ★

For Sam, the world quite literally darkened as he moved into a jungle so dense that someone—undoubtedly someone from the empty cruiser—had hacked a narrow trail. A trail that, for the moment, was easy to follow. The unknown individual had cleared a path wide enough for one man to move forward without shifting sideways through the foliage, but he must have tired after 500 yards or so; wielding a machete wasn't easy. Soon the path narrowed and Sam had to turn sideways to slip through tight areas.

Uncertain how many people had passed over the path the machete wielder cleared, Sam decided, from the look of the trail, that there had to have been at least two men passing through, possibly four. Unfortunately, he knew numbers wouldn't save them. The tigers would stalk silently, hanging back until they could strike quickly, picking off the last man if he lagged even a few paces behind.

At times Sam could almost feel the fetid breath of a tiger on his neck as he paused to rest. Those times, he'd take a long look behind him before he started out again, and even that precaution didn't reassure him.

Sam's heart stalled.

Suddenly from behind, he heard the faint sounds of gunfire. Gunfire that could only be coming from the boat. And it wasn't the signal—three shots in rapid succession—that he and Pepe had worked out before he left, in case there was trouble. Stricken, realizing he was too damned far away to do more than observe the aftermath of whatever was going down, Sam lurched around and charged back the way he'd come, seized by blood-chilling dread.

Abandoning caution, he broke through the vegetation when it couldn't be quickly pushed aside, and in doing so, he made noise. Noise that could attract predators. But Sam was beyond caring about his own safety. Sweat cascaded down his face, and the shirt that was already soggy clung to his body like a wet rag.

Kelly was all he could think about. In his arrogance, he'd insisted she stay behind. He'd left her and now he wasn't there to protect her from being kidnapped, raped, or eaten alive. It was *his* fault. She'd pleaded to come along and he'd been too pig-headed to let her. Too afraid he couldn't protect her on an island teaming with man-eaters, snakes, and crocodiles.

Now, thanks to a hasty decision, she could be dead or dying that very minute. And there was nothing he could do about it. Except pay for a lifetime.

The same helplessness he'd felt when he'd been unable to find John nearly engulfed him. Was he doomed to lose those he cared about most? Had he been that rotten? Somehow pissed off the "powers that be" to such an extent he'd be doomed by karma to lose those he loved?

Fighting the jungle and his own despondency didn't stop Sam from moving like the wind back down the trail. But even moving with the speed of sound couldn't help him save Kelly. The shooting had stopped. Whatever happened was over. And he hadn't been able to lift a finger to help. He was just too damn far away.

By the time he reached the edge of the jungle, the sounds of firing had long since ceased.

It was too late.

Now all he could do was pray, so he offered up every prayer he could remember. Then promised God everything he could think of, if he'd just let Kelly live.

Sam's safety was secondary. In fact it hardly mattered. If Kelly died, he might as well die, too. The realization that he didn't want to go on without her, that life held no meaning without her, took possession of him.

But until he knew with certainty that she no longer lived, he struggled to hold onto hope. Knowing every incautious step he took led him that much closer to his own death, he plunged out of the jungle onto the muddy beach, thankful he didn't come face to face with a tiger out to soak up some sun.

The cruiser was right where he'd left it, still firmly anchored, rocking gently in the bay's current.

"Couldn't have been pirates then," he muttered, plowing swiftly through the mud, stepping in his earlier footsteps to keep from being sucked deep into the muck. A pirate's goal was to grab a ship and sell her as quickly as possible, and pirates weren't fussy about how they got a ship. They'd murder the owners if that's what it took.

His breathing labored, Sam muttered, "Damn thing looks deserted."

Just like the other one, his mind screamed, remembering the blood on the boat he'd boarded earlier.

The deck appeared empty.

Pele should be on watch, if he's alive.

Nothing moved.

The slim hope Sam clung to dimmed even more.

Almost instantly, a new thought emerged to the surface of his mind. A tiger could have boarded and taken Pele, leaving Kelly to cower below deck. Breathing a little prayer, he crossed the final stretch of mud to where he'd left the dinghy beached. He boarded and paddled to the cruiser. Tied the dinghy to the ladder and began to climb, only stopping momentarily to drop the rifle from his shoulder into his hand before boarding.

Sam landed with a muffled thud on the deck, causing the cruiser to rock harder.

If Kelly's below, she'll know someone boarded.

But she couldn't know whether it was man or beast. Which meant she probably wouldn't surface on her own.

The sound of a nearby voice brought Sam to a standstill.

Could pirates have left a crew aboard, then taken off in their own ship for some unknown reason?

Old habits die hard it seemed, for instantly Sam became a soldier. With stealthy haste, he moved toward the prow of the cruiser, his weapon cocked and ready to fire. The pirates would have felt the sway as he boarded and would be hunting him, as well.

When Sam was halfway to the prow, a head popped around the corner, then ducked quickly back out of sight.

Sam went still. He caught only a glimpse, but there'd been something strikingly familiar about it.

His heart racing, he took a deep breath. "Pele?"

The little man's head reappeared. "That you, sahib?"

Sam rubbed the sweat out of his eyes. "What in hell's going on? Why weren't you keeping watch? Where's Kelly?"

"Here I am." The taut voice came from behind him.

Sam swung around to find Kelly holding a handgun. It was pointed in the general vicinity of his heart.

"What are you doing back so soon?" The strain in her voice clearly betrayed the dread that he had found something terrible on the island.

He struggled to come to grips with a situation that was the reverse of what he'd feared. Kelly hadn't been mauled, killed, or kidnapped. She had a gun on *him*.

"You think you could lower the gun?" he asked, his voice wary. He shouldered his own weapon as a surge of relief turned to such intense anger it threatened to choke him.

"What in hell were you shooting at?" he demanded to know.

Before Kelly could respond, Pele said, "I not know Missy decide to practice shooting gun."

Turning on Pele with teeth-clenching fury, Sam snapped. "How'd she get hold of the damn thing anyway?"

Chagrined, Pele looked down. "I sorry, sahib. She offered to stand watch. She want to hold gun, so I let her."

Sam shook his head. "Son-of-a-bitch!" He'd believed Pele would be impervious to Kelly's charms. And he'd been dead wrong. The mistake could have cost him everything, because he knew damn well she couldn't charm the man-eaters. *Maybe pirates,* he conceded grudgingly, *but not hungry tigers.*

Kelly deflated like a popped balloon. "You came back because you heard me practicing?"

Moments before she'd looked like a small avenging angel, with the gun ready for action, her knuckles whitened from the strain of a tight grip on a heavy weapon. Now her head hung as low as Pele's.

"Damn straight!" He still appeared angry, but part of that was to cover the profound relief he felt at finding her alive.

"What are you going to do now?" she asked, sounding dejected.

He shrugged. "I don't know." His heart was still in overdrive, his blood pressure soaring.

"You were gone a long time. Did you see any sign of Jeff or the men from the boat?" Kelly asked.

"Just their trail. Couldn't tell how many there were, though. Then I heard the shots." He scowled at Pele. "And I busted my hump getting back here."

"Don't blame Pele. It's my fault. I nagged until he gave in. I just . . . well . . . I thought I should know how to use this." She stared down at the gun hanging at her side. "In case something bad happened."

Sam ran a sweaty palm through his hair while a muscle in

his jaw twitched. He'd fought the desire to snatch her off her feet and hug Kelly to his chest the moment she appeared safe. Now all he could manage, battling a flood of emotions that threatened to overwhelm him, was to reach down and gently remove the gun from her hand.

"You won't be needing this right now. I'm going below." He eyed Pele. "I trust I can count on you to keep watch this time?"

"Yes, sahib. Not worry, sahib." The small man nodded, reminding Sam of those loose-headed dolls people attach to their dashboards or rear windows, constantly animated as long as the vehicle is in motion.

Sam wanted to drag Kelly below with him, but at that moment he didn't trust himself. He needed her too badly. Needed to know, somehow, that she'd be his no matter what happened.

Like hell!

Unfortunately, he knew damn well she was a long way from needing him for anything but finding her brother, so he left the two culprits on deck.

Instead of the drink he figured he deserved, Sam heated the leftover coffee and tried to decide how in hell he'd proceed from here. He'd managed to leave Kelly behind the last time, but after the fright she and Pele had just given him, he didn't believe he possessed the strength to do so again. If he took even one step into the jungle, with her behind on the boat, it would be like killing himself slowly. Hardly top form for a dangerous task. More like an accident waiting to happen.

Certainly, he'd be no match for a savvy tiger. Or tigers.

Yet, if he took her along, he'd worry about her safety so much he might be too distracted to think clearly and act coolly.

119

"You're doing a wonderful job of making yourself nuts," he hissed, raking back the hair that had fallen over his forehead with a shaky hand.

Well, hell. There was no use agonizing any longer. He'd known the outcome from the beginning. He just hadn't wanted to admit how emotionally tied up he'd become. He couldn't leave Kelly behind. Once had been torture. Twice just wasn't conceivable.

"Sam?" Kelly stood in the doorway, self-consciously shifting her weight from one foot to the other. "May I come in?"

He stared at her. "Sure. Why not?"

Her cheeks glowed pink. She drew a bracing breath. "I'm really sorry. Can we . . . just start over?"

Cocking his head, he said, "It's a far piece from the bar in Kalgola, don'cha think?"

A hiss of air escaped through her lips. "That's not what I meant."

With a sigh, he ran a hand over his stubbled cheek. "I know that. What did you mean?"

"Today. Could we just start over today?" Her feet shifting became more noticeable.

He watched her. "What'd ya have in mind?" He sure wasn't doing so well.

"I thought we could talk about this whole thing. You know . . . maybe change the plan a little?"

His narrowed vision pierced her. "*How* little?"

She spoke rapidly. "Well, I thought maybe I could go along, you know, to help out."

He'd bite. "Doing what?"

"I'd help you look for Jeff, and keep an eye out for tigers, snakes, crocodiles, you know, that kind of stuff." She sent him a big-eyed glance, then dropped her gaze to her toes.

His grim expression never altered. "Don't you mean give me more to worry about?"

"I won't be in the way," she declared. "Besides, you could use an extra pair of eyes."

He shook his head. "You won't be in the way? A fat lot you know."

"Please. . . . I just can't stay behind and worry anymore. It's too terrible."

If she knew how he felt about her and about leaving her behind, he figured, she wouldn't be begging for a chance to go along with him.

But, hell, she *didn't* know.

Chapter Eight

Sam scowled at Kelly. "And if I find your brother, how do I explain what happened to you, if you're carried off by a damn tiger, bitten by a poisonous snake, or eaten by a croc?"

A shiver tracked down Kelly's spine. "I know how to use a gun now. No animal will get me."

His mouth curved into a sexy grin. "Something else might," he said.

If Sam had wanted to put her off, thought Kelly, he had. For a millisecond. But the fact was, her nerves couldn't stand the strain of waiting and wondering, not for another day. Even another hour. Besides, she felt safer with Sam than without him, no matter what he threatened. Of course, she wasn't going to tell *him* that.

"I'm not worried. I want to go along," she insisted.

He shrugged. "Okay, fine, you can come along."

Her mouth gaped open in surprise.

A grin transformed his face from sullen to disarmingly boyish.

Kelly found her voice only after regrouping her thoughts. She'd been geared to argue and fight for what she wanted, and Sam knocked the wind out of her sails by agreeing so swiftly. She wondered if there wasn't something suspect about his quick capitulation. In the past he'd shown her just how difficult he could be when he wanted his own way. But after the surprise faded, all she felt was eminent relief.

"Great. What do I need to take along?" She wanted to be prepared and not be a burden.

His stare brushed her like a chill wind. "Keep the jeans and a couple pairs of socks so you can fill out the boots you'll find in the closet," he said, his voice cold and businesslike. "I've got a backpack you can put a change of clothes in. We'll have to carry rations for a couple of days, which means you'll have to carry your share."

"I'll manage," she said. Even to her own ears, she sounded downright optimistic.

"Yeah, well, we'll see. Get ready and we'll have something to eat before we take off."

"Won't it be too hot for such heavy clothing?" she asked.

"Yeah, but you need all the protection you can get. The insect population on the island is infinite."

Kelly squirmed. "Okay, I'll just be a few minutes. And I'll bring the bug spray." She dashed to her cabin to dress properly, trying to block snakes, insects, and other nasty creatures from entering her thoughts. With two pairs of socks, the boots stayed on, making her feel her feet were secure from nasty pests.

By the time she returned, having borrowed more of John's clothes, Sam had packed a large and a small backpack. He shoved the smaller one across the galley table toward her.

"There's room for spare clothing at the top. When you've got that stowed, there's a sandwich in the refrigerator. Eat it and we'll be on our way."

Sam watched out of the corner of his eyes as Kelly placed each carefully folded item inside the pack, and when she added a tiny, silky pair of underpants, he jerked as if bitten.

"I'm going up on deck," he snapped. "Call me when you're ready to leave."

I'm a damn fool, Sam thought as he went topside. *Preparing to risk my life for a scrap of a woman.*

A woman who he knew wouldn't give him what he wanted without a fight. Maybe not even then. Because he wanted more than her body. He wanted all of her. Every last thought in her head, along with the delicious flesh on her body. Wanted it so badly he'd go through hell to get it. Even when he knew he should know better.

He dug a cheroot out of his captain's bureau drawer. When he reached the deck, he lit up, the first time in a year. He knew better than to bring his cheroots along, but it wasn't the first time he'd used less than stellar judgment. And, he supposed, it wouldn't be the last. Not with the company he was keeping lately.

As Kelly came on deck, he took one last drag and tossed the cheroot overboard.

"I didn't know you smoked," she said.

"I don't."

Her head swiveled to where the cheroot was slowly sinking out of sight. "What was that, then?"

"A fantasy," he snapped. Then he stared intently into her eyes. "You ever fantasize, blue eyes?"

His tone was intimate and Kelly ducked her head to try to hide a deep pink blush. "Didn't look like a fantasy to me," she murmured.

He canted his head to the side. "Well, hell, I might just have to teach you the difference between fantasy and reality, huh, sweetheart?"

His sudden mood shift, new and unsettling, had Kelly wondering uneasily what he'd do next. Finally she blurted, "I thought we were leaving as soon as I finished eating."

He straightened and squinted at her. "You trying to take the fun out of this amazing adventure?"

"Just call me Ebenezer." She raised her chin high.

Sam's tightened lips lifted at the corners. "I think 'sassy' suits you better then Ebenezer." He eased around her. "I'll get the packs."

Kelly watched Sam disappear below deck. While she awaited his return, she struggled to quash the warm feelings his tiniest smile could manifest. Logically, there was no reason in the world why he could stimulate all of her senses to such a degree. But then, what did logic have to do with attraction? Because, face it, she was well and truly magnetized by nearly everything he did; good, bad, or indifferent. And that could give a woman a lot to think about.

Sam returned and held her pack out, indicating that she should slip into it. "Stop squirming and stand still," he commanded. He adjusted the straps on the smaller backpack to her body. When he seemed satisfied with the position of the pack, she felt his arms go around her and meet in the front.

She stiffened.

"Relax. I'm just hooking a belt around you to hold your holster."

Her voice squeaked, "Holster?"

He was bent over her, brushing her with his chest, touching her with his arms, feathering her hair with his breath.

Oh, my!

When he was this close, Kelly noticed his body reacted like a teenage boy's. It snapped to attention immediately.

He finished buckling the belt and backed away, but not before slipping a small automatic pistol out of his waistband and into her holster.

"Don't draw that thing unless you plan on killing something. You got that?"

He sounded bad-tempered as hell, but, instinctively, Kelly knew he'd been as affected by their closeness as she. Maybe even more so.

She whirled on Sam. "Don't worry. I've got it."

He relented, softening slightly. "I suppose Pele told you about the safety." He pointed to the button near the barrel. "It's on now. If you need to shoot, you have to slip it back like this." He moved the small lever back. Then he slipped it forward again. "Okay?"

"Okay."

"Swell. Let's get moving then. I've given Pele instructions, so we're all set."

Kelly's stomach somersaulted. She wasn't certain she'd ever be ready to face man-eating tigers, snakes, and crocodiles. Still, there wasn't much choice. She couldn't stay behind and worry. Not anymore. Not when Sam wouldn't be there with her. The knowledge that she only felt safe with him by her side wasn't new, and, thankfully, it no longer upset her. She'd finally managed to chalk her inappropriate feelings up to the region, the earthquake, and the harrowing circumstances. Nothing more.

Sure!

I need him for this, that's all.

Kelly quickly shut her mind to thoughts of sexual needs. They were off-limits.

Sam boarded the dinghy first and held out a hand to help Kelly. The touch of his strong, warm hand holding hers shot like fire up her arm. Thoroughly disgusted, she sat down hard and turned away to stare unblinkingly at the island with its many inlets. Fortunately, by the time Sam had the dinghy halfway to the largest sandbar, her thoughts had turned to

Jeff. Although her insides still churned with fear for him, she felt certain he was alive and on the island somewhere. Many questions still tormented her. Could they find him? And if they did, what condition would he be in? Would he even be alive?

"How large do you think this island is?" she asked, when Sam eased the dinghy onto the mud and carried her ashore.

"I don't know in square miles, but it's too damn big, that's for sure. It'll be like looking for a needle in a haystack. We're just about as likely to find your brother as we are to find Elvis."

"There's a difference. Elvis is dead. Jeff's alive."

"So you say." Sam dropped her feet on firm ground. At the same time, he watched the dense jungle's edge.

"What's wrong?" Kelly's hand strayed to her holster as she watched him study the mysterious dark foliage.

"Just about everything, I reckon. But hell's fire, I guess we'd better get a move on."

He led the way to the spot where Kelly had seen him disappear earlier, when he'd been alone. They entered the jungle, trampling the same vegetation he and others had beaten down before them on their way into the interior.

The noise of the jungle had been evident while they were on the mud bank. But the moment they stepped inside the misty, verdant forest, the sounds intensified. To Kelly, it seemed as if they were under attack from above in the trees, below on the jungle floor, and all the crowded foliage that surrounded them. She found herself wanting to grab onto Sam's belt and hold tight for her life. Jumping onto his back might be even more satisfying, but she didn't think he'd oblige.

Their progress seemed painfully slow to Kelly, but she knew why and appreciated Sam's caution. He frequently stopped to listen and check behind them for signs that they were being stalked.

She didn't know how much time had elapsed since they left the beach. But when they reached a wider trampled area, Sam tersely informed her that this was the spot when he'd heard her target practicing. The place where he'd turned back.

"Obviously, I haven't been beyond this point," he informed her in a brusque voice.

What he'd said earlier when he'd confronted her and Pele on the boat hung silently between them—that he'd busted his butt to get back to them. And now, as they cautiously progressed down the trail, Kelly realized that in doing so, he'd undoubtedly endangered himself to a significant degree. The thought that he could have been killed tightened the knot that had already formed in her stomach; a worry knot that wasn't likely to ease anytime soon, at least not until they found Jeff and got him safely off the island.

Sam came to a halt, unclipped the canteen from his belt, unscrewed the top, and offered it to Kelly. She took a drink, wiped the top, and handed the canteen back to Sam.

"How far do you think we've come?" she asked.

"No more than a mile or so."

"Are you sure?" she asked, disappointment shrouding her voice. "Seems as if we've been walking forever."

Sam glanced at his watch. "We left the boat an hour ago."

Kelly shook her head. "Seems like hours."

"Maybe you should have stayed on board." He mouthed the words, but there was no conviction behind them.

"You know I couldn't."

Sam just sighed, clipped the canteen to his belt, and moved ahead. Kelly knew he considered her an albatross around his neck, but it didn't much matter. It was too late to turn back now, even if she wanted to, which she didn't.

A screeching monkey caught her attention as it leapt from tree to tree beside them. Keeping pace, the animal sounded as if it were scolding, warning them to turn back. When it finally gave up and stayed behind on a high branch of a particularly tall tree, it continued to screech. But given the density of the foliage, she and Sam were soon out of view, if not earshot.

When Kelly could no longer hear the little imp, she felt a letdown, as if they'd left a caring friend behind. She knew it was a silly notion. The monkey had probably just been angered by their invasion of its territory. Still, the disappointment lingered.

The next time Sam stopped to listen intently, they heard a new faint but sporadic sound echoing through the jungle.

"What is it?" Kelly whispered.

"Shhhh," Sam cautioned. He turned around slowly, obviously attempting to pinpoint the origin of the sound. "Sounds as if it's coming from somewhere up ahead."

"I thought it was coming from over that way," Kelly whispered, pointing to her right.

Sam cocked his head. "It's damned difficult to tell which direction it's coming from."

"What do you think it is?"

"Sounds man-made." The puzzled expression on his face slowly gave way to a hopeful one. "I'll be damned if it doesn't sound like someone's blowing into an animal horn. The natives sometimes use them to communicate."

"It could be Jeff." Kelly's voice rose with excitement.

Obviously not wanting to raise her hopes, only to have them dashed, Sam cautioned, "I suppose that's possible, but it could be someone else from his party. Or natives over from the mainland, gathering wood or honey."

"They come here to gather wood and honey?" She sounded incredulous. The danger was so clearly obvious.

"The desperate ones do, even if it isn't the single desig-
nated time during the year when it's allowed," Sam responded. "And, unfortunately, a lot of them don't make it
home."

Kelly shivered. "It must be terrible to be that desperate."

Sam sent her a hard look. "You should know."

"It's not the same thing at all. Jeff is here, somewhere, and
it's my duty to find him. He's my brother."

Sam held up his hand for silence.

Kelly went mute as they listened to the repeating sounds.
When Sam lowered his hand, she whispered, "It does sound
as if it could be coming from ahead of us now."

He nodded.

She peered into the prolific vegetation to the right of the
barely-there trail and wondered how they'd ever get through
such a chaotic overgrown tangle if the sounds weren't coming
from close to the path.

"What are we going to do?" The task of finding someone
in the dense foliage seemed nearly impossible.

"We'll stick to the trail. It isn't much, but it's a damn-sight
better than hacking our way through that." Sam gestured
with his head toward the thick mass of growth beside them.

"But what if the trail takes us farther away from whoever is
making the noises?" She felt a sudden sense of urgency.

"Then we'll have to reconsider. For now, we'll forge
ahead." He started moving. "Don't lag behind."

Fat chance. Kelly wasn't about to let him get more than a
foot away from her.

Sam hadn't, even for a moment, really expected to find
anyone alive on the marshy island. But clearly the sounds
were man-made. They also seemed to be growing louder,
which meant he and Kelly had been right to stay on the trail.

Abruptly, he halted and Kelly slammed into his back with

an *ooff*. He shot her a questioning glance over his shoulder. "You having trouble staying on your feet, blue eyes?"

That frown he liked appeared on her face, the one that made her look both angry and beautiful at the same time. "You might signal when you're going to stop on a dime," she snapped.

"Signal?" He looked at her as if she were so stupid she had to be watered twice a week.

She shook a threatening finger in his face. "Don't *do* that!"

He cocked his head at her, and sounding innocent, asked, "Do what?"

"Look at me like I'm the village idiot!"

"I never—"

"Yes, you did! You *do* it *all* the time."

"You're making a lot of noise," he warned.

"*You're* changing the subject."

Suddenly, he had her in a vise grip. One hand was over her mouth, the other held her head so she couldn't get away. "I said hush," he hissed.

Kelly might have struggled, but Sam was insistent and kept her perfectly still. Then her eyes widened as she stared into the dense greenery with a worried frown.

Having drawn her attention to the problem, Sam removed his hands and stood quietly beside her.

"How long ago did it stop?" Kelly asked, in a whisper.

He spared her a squint. "It stopped, then I stopped."

Kelly nodded. "What do we do now?"

"The only thing we *can* do. Keep moving."

Sam hadn't gone far before he came to another abrupt halt. This time Kelly didn't run into him. And it was clear from the look on his face, when he turned toward her, that he'd come up with an idea he didn't much like.

Swearing softly, he snarled at Kelly. "Why in hell couldn't you have stayed behind?"

"Don't you think it's a little late to go over that again?"

He ground his teeth before drawing his revolver. Kelly lurched around, half expecting to be pounced on from behind.

He placed a hand on her shoulder. "Relax. I'm gonna fire into the air to get the attention of whoever's out there," he explained. "Hopefully, I can get him to respond by blowing into the horn again."

Relieved about not being at immediate risk, she smiled for the first time since they'd landed on shore. "That's a great idea."

"Yeah, great," Sam grunted. What he didn't say was that the shots would alert anyone else who might be on the island.

"Cover your ears," he advised before holding the gun in the air and firing two quick shots. The reverberating noise set off a flurry of animal sounds, and then to their relief, within seconds, another blast on the animal horn.

Kelly's hand flew to her mouth. "Oh, my. It's Jeff. I know it."

"We'll see."

Obviously understanding that there was help on the way, the person with the horn continued to blow into it at regular intervals. And, fortunately, Kelly and Sam were able to stay on the trail. It was difficult to decide how far sound traveled in the jungle, whether the dense foliage swallowed it quickly or let it echo, resounding off the trees like a ricochet. There was no way to tell how close she and Sam were getting. They might blunder right into the horn-blower on the trail. Chances were good that whoever blew the horn was still within a short distance of the path, if he or his companions were the ones who had done the trail blazing.

After a few minutes, the haunting sounds grew louder. Kelly fought the urge to protect her ears by covering them with her hands. She didn't because it would make her feel too vulnerable to attack.

Sam stopped again. They were very close now. "I think we're just about there."

"And I suppose you want me to wait right here while you go check?" she snapped.

"Damn good idea. Wish I'd thought of it."

"Nooo," she protested. Reaching out, she grabbed the back of his shirt. "It's probably Jeff."

He turned, breaking her grip. Whispered harshly, "What if it isn't? Here, take the rifle if it makes you feel better." He tried to hand her the gun.

Kelly pushed it away and shook her head violently, gazing frantically around. "I don't want it, and I don't want to be left alone."

All Sam wanted to do was crush her to him and never let go. But that wouldn't be productive at the moment. And it sure as hell wouldn't get them back to the boat where he might have a real chance of doing just that. Hoping he would have better luck with persuasion, he leaned down and grazed her mouth with his. "Be a good girl. Stay here for a minute."

One tiny touch of his mouth and she was apparently ready to do his bidding, whatever the results. "Well . . . okay . . . but just for a minute."

He sent her a warm smile. "That's my girl." Then he melted into the jungle and, in a second, was out of sight.

Dammit! Kelly wanted him back. Immediately, if not sooner. Every snapping twig, every swinging vine, sent her imagination to running wild. She could almost feel a tiger's breath on her neck. She swung wildly around, eyes wide, rifle raised. But there wasn't anything to see. Except jungle.

Terrified, she readily admitted that she wanted Sam beside her every minute, and a part of her feared it wasn't because of the tigers.

No.

It was something worse! She was truly afraid she wanted him because she'd fallen for him. Hook, line, and sinker. And dammit, she knew he wouldn't thank her if that was the case. Oh, sure, he'd like to have her body at least once, that much was obvious. How could she miss it? There was lust in his every glance. But was that all he wanted? Men like Sam didn't want commitment. They couldn't even acknowledge the word.

Get your act together. Firm up for heaven's sake.

Before she could do any more deep thinking, Sam reappeared as if by magic, without making a sound.

Kelly just barely refrained from throwing herself into his arms. "Did you find him? Did you find Jeff?"

His hooded gaze told her the story first. "It isn't Jeff. It's a native who was with your brother. Come on, I'll take you to him."

Disappointment dampened her spirits for only a moment. There was hope. If someone else had survived, Jeff could have too.

They reached an especially stout tree and Sam stopped, again. "Come on down," he called, looking up.

Kelly raised her head, as well, and watched a man slowly lower himself and drop to the ground, holding tight to a burlap bag. He was small, wiry, and appeared to have lost weight, for his clothes hung loosely on him. He also had a round spot of mud on his forehead, peeking through the black, roughly chopped hair that fell forward.

"This is all of your party?" the little man inquired with a deep frown and worried brown eyes.

"The crop." Sam nodded.

"But you do not have enough guns. The tigers will kill us all." He appeared ready to climb back into the tree.

"We'll be okay. Do you need food or water?"

The native slapped the burlap bag he carried over his shoulder. "I had food, but it is gone now."

"Do you want water?" Sam asked. "What's your name?"

"I am called Zayed. I do not need anything right now, thank you."

"Well, tell me, Zayed, where did you leave the man who hired you?" Sam asked.

"Off there." He pointed ahead. "Too far. We must go to the shore. You say you have a boat. We must go there immediately." He waved his hands for them to lead.

"We're not going back to the boat, not until we find your sahib," Sam said, standing firm.

"No, no, we must go to the shore." Zayed slipped around Sam and headed down the path. "We must hurry."

"If you go, you go alone," Sam warned. "We're here to find the lady's brother, and we're not leaving until we do."

Zayed stopped and violently shook his head. "By now he is dead. It is no use. Even with your guns we are not safe from the Tiger God who protects the jungle."

Fear tore through Kelly. "He's not dead," she snapped.

The native spoke to Kelly for the first time. "Miss, his leg was broken. He was bleeding. That was four days ago, so he is dead."

Kelly, clearly outraged, cried, "You just left him to die?"

"You do not understand," the little man protested.

"We can discuss this later. Right now lead us to him or

go your own way." The obdurate expression on Sam's face told the smaller man he'd better make up his mind or be left behind.

"You need to know, if the tiger springs at you, even if you manage to shoot him a dozen times, you are doomed," Zayed pleaded. "His jaws will clamp shut on you. And even if he dies, he will not let go."

Sam nodded. "That's the way I hear it, but we don't have a choice. We're going on. Are you coming with us, Zayed, or going to the shore alone?"

Shuddering, then finally steadying himself, the smaller man moved carefully around Sam, still shaking his head.

"We must just follow the trail," he said. "But hear me well. The tigers are probably still waiting under his tree, if they have not already eaten him. We should not have come here. It is forbidden. We are allowed to come only once a year to gather wood and honey, and then we bring a priest with us, one who can convince the Tiger God we mean no harm, for he protects the jungle for us all. Without the tigers there would be no jungle."

Kelly wasn't superstitious, but hearing Zayed describe her brother's possible death had her stomach threatening to rebel. It took her a moment to clear her head of the dreadful picture that flared to life in her mind—Jeff being devoured by tigers.

When she could think more clearly, she realized he'd said the tigers were lounging around, waiting for Jeff to come down from the tree. And certainly he couldn't climb down with a broken leg. Therefore, he *could* be alive.

"How did Jeff get up into the tree?" she asked Zayed.

"I tied a rope around him and hauled him up. It not be easy, but I do it."

"I see." She peered up at Sam, a questioning look on her face.

"Tigers aren't tree climbers," he offered helpfully. "They're too damn big and heavy."

"I believe anything of those devils," Zayed whispered.

"Is this man high up in the tree?" Sam asked, wondering how they'd get Jeff down with a broken leg.

"Yes, Mr. Jeff, he is high up in a cage in the tree," Zayed informed them.

"A cage?" Sam raised an eyebrow.

"Yes. There are two cages left by someone else, in two trees close to each other. He is in one of them."

"Who's in the other one?" Sam asked.

Zayed shivered. "No one, now. I, Zayed, and one other were there, but the other man went for help. He never returned."

"So you left, too," Sam growled.

"It is not what you think. I left to bring help. But one of the tigers followed me and I climbed the tree." He indicated the one where they'd found him. "The tiger, he circle the tree and stare. His eyes laugh at me. Then he lie down and wait for two days. I ran out of food and water this morning. It was terrible. I thought he would never go. Then suddenly he leave." The man shuddered again.

Kelly vividly remembered the tiger they'd spotted from the boat, and how his beautiful eyes had shone with wicked intent. To have one sit and stare at you for two days while death shone from his eyes was undoubtedly mind-bending. She couldn't blame Zayed for being terrified. For a brief moment, a self-protective instinct threatened to turn *her* into a tree climber herself. But then she thought of Jeff and what it must feel like to pray for deliverance for days while the tigers waited, licking their chops.

She plucked at Sam's sleeve. "We have to hurry."

Sam eyed Zayed, who appeared about to flee toward the water. "You coming or going?"

137

After gazing longingly down the trail toward the shore, Zayed shook his head, as if sensing doom lay in that direction if he ventured alone.

"I will lead you, but keep your rifle ready. You are a good shot, yes?"

"The best," Sam agreed.

The little man nodded, muttered something malevolent, and finally began the trek with tentative steps. Sam followed, with Kelly tight on his heels.

They'd traveled for just under an hour when Zayed turned and placed a finger against his lips.

He whispered, "Not make noise, please. The wind, she blow our way, so the tigers not scent us, but they hear every little sound. Their eyesight is most keen, as well."

Sam nodded.

Kelly tried to swallow, but her mouth was so dry she nearly choked. Without making a sound, she moistened her lips with her tongue, took a deep steadying breath, and doggedly followed in Sam's footsteps.

They followed Zayed down the trail for what seemed like hours, but was only minutes, when he came to an abrupt halt. Gesturing to Sam and Kelly to hunker down, he took two steps forward and parted a patch of dense foliage to their right. Leaning into the gap, he peered straight ahead. Then, after a few seconds of concentrated attention, he moved his head slightly left and right, twice.

Allowing the foliage to gently fall back in place the way it had been, he returned to Sam and Kelly. "The tigers are no longer under the tree. They are gone, I think," he whispered.

Sam moved around him, parted the foliage, and took a look for himself.

A small clearing lay just ahead. And in the clearing a giant mangrove tree harbored the large bamboo cage Zayed had described. There was something in the cage all right, but from this distance it appeared to be nothing but a bundle of soiled, rumpled clothing. It certainly didn't appear human. Or alive. Sam scanned the clearing for predators. Finding none, he stepped out into the opening. After testing the waters, so to speak, he waved for Kelly and the little native to follow.

Kelly's eyes flew to the cage and her blood seemed to thicken with dread. Jeff, if it was Jeff, lay still as death.

They'd moved directly under the tree when Sam handed the rifle to Kelly. Zayed was undoubtedly still an unknown, in Sam's mind. "Keep watch, while I have a look," he whispered.

He started climbing the strips of wood nailed into one side of the tree. Moving quickly, he vanished for a moment among the leaves of the lower branches.

Kelly's breath stayed a few moments too long in her lungs, only easing out as Sam's head reappeared above the greenery. The same brief disappearing act happened two more times before he reached the man-made platform where the bamboo cage had been secured to a triangle of branches.

Sam crouched in front of the cage and studied what he could see of the man inside, searching for signs of life. There were none, but the sole occupant wasn't a native and his leg was splinted, so Sam figured the guy had to be Kelly's brother, Jeff.

He gave one last glance down at Kelly and shook his head—there was no point in getting her hopes up—before he reached inside the cage to loosen the latch that held the door closed. Sliding back the bolt, he opened the door and, still crouching, began to enter.

"Shhhit!" he hissed a second later.

Chapter Nine

The bamboo hinges of the cage door creaked, waking the injured man who suddenly no longer resembled a pile of dirty rags, but a dangerously ill and frightened human being.

Raising a rifle in quaking hands, he aimed at Sam's chest. "You sons-of-bitches are startin' to look like men now," the injured man swore. "But you don't fool me." He levered a shell into the chamber.

"Hold it! Just hold it right there!" Sam yelled, raising his hands.

The injured man's bloodshot eyes narrowed as he tried to clear his impaired vision. "If you're really a man, don't come any closer," he warned.

Sam nodded. "You got it. Your name is Jeff, right?"

The guy's eyes widened in sudden wonder and he lowered the rifle with trembling hands. "Oh, my God! Jan made it back. He brought help."

"Not exactly," Sam replied. He realized Jeff was burning with fever, but not sweating—a bad sign.

Jeff squinted at him. "What do you mean?" He sounded weak and puzzled.

"How long have you been out of water?" Sam asked, ignoring the other man's question.

Jeff shook his head and sank back against the tree, his limited energy spent. "Don't know . . . maybe a day or two."

"Hell." Sam unclipped his canteen and held it out. "I've got water. May I come in?"

"Please."

Sam crossed the cage, squatted in front of Jeff, and put the canteen to his lips. "Take it slow . . . real slow." He had to pull the canteen from Jeff's lips a couple of times to get him to ease up. "Take it easy. If you don't, it's gonna come right back up."

Jeff nodded, but his wounded gaze followed the canteen when Sam pulled it away, as if it were Alice about to disappear down the rabbit hole.

The rustle of leaves behind him in the tree caught Sam off guard, and he only just managed to draw his holstered weapon and jerk around in time to see Kelly, a mud spot on the middle of her forehead, emerge into the open. Ruefully, he admitted that if Kelly had been a tiger, he'd have been knee deep in doo-doo, since he'd left the cage door wide open; an invitation to a hungry predator.

But, hell, there aren't that many predators around and tigers don't climb trees, he reminded himself, putting the pistol away.

"Dammit! Don't you ever listen?" He snarled at Kelly. With three of them crammed inside the cage, he worried the platform might give way.

Her frantic look swept past Sam, ignoring him. "Jeff . . . Jeff," she cried. "You're alive!"

Squeezing by Sam, she knelt in front of her brother, her gaze running over him. Then, obviously realizing he was in an extremely delicate condition, she gingerly wrapped her arms around his neck and hugged him lightly.

"Sis, you . . . you shouldn't be here. It isn't . . . safe." Jeff's voice faded, as if the effort of speaking had taken the last of his strength.

"I'm fine," she assured him. "It's you we have to worry about. I'm just so grateful you're alive."

Jeff uttered a low sigh and his head abruptly dropped foreword, landing heavily on Kelly's narrow shoulder.

She panicked as he began to slip out of her hand. "Jeff, talk to me!"

Sam quickly eased in beside her. "Let me take him."

He feared all along that they'd find her brother dead, if there was anything left to find. Now he realized the circumstances could be a darn sight worse. They might have found him in time to watch him die. And in her present state, he dreaded that outcome, believing Kelly wouldn't be able to handle that grim situation.

Sam gently maneuvered Jeff onto his back on the floor of the cage, then efficiently took his pulse. "He's okay. Just looks as if the exertion of seeing us wiped him out. We'll let him rest for a while. Then we'll try to get some food into him. The water should have helped." Sam glanced at Kelly's forehead. "What happened?"

She frowned before she appeared to understand that he was referring to the mud spot. "Zayed put it there. He took the mud from one of the paw marks and put it on my forehead to ward off the tigers."

Sam checked Jeff's pulse again. "Not real strong." He frowned.

Kelly babbled, "We have to get him out of here. Get him to a doctor right away."

"It's too late today," Sam cautioned. "Besides, we have to try to get him fit enough to move. If we try to take him like this, he might not make it to the boat."

Kelly's throat felt constricted. She turned a pleading glance toward Sam. "He's not that bad, is he?"

"He's dehydrated, feverish, and obviously hasn't eaten in days. Then there's his leg . . . by now he probably has gangrene. I wouldn't wanna chance moving him until he's stronger."

"He can't die!" Kelly cried, totally distraught.

Raising the wounded man's head, Sam eased more water down his parched throat, taking care that Jeff swallowed before he administered more. Another burst of rustling leaves killed any verbal response Sam might have thought to make. He drew his weapon and waited.

Zayed's head appeared above the leaves. His eyes wild, he sputtered, "It . . . it is not safe down there." He pointed below.

Sam holstered the gun and moved out of the cage. Standing on the platform, he searched the surrounding jungle, but observed no stealthy movement.

"Did you actually see anything?" he asked the overwrought man.

"Not see, no, but it is dangerous to be standing around," Zayed muttered. His gaze bounced from Sam to the floor of the jungle and back.

"Okay. Let's have you keep a lookout from here. You think you can do that?"

"Yes, sahib. I can watch very good." He gave Sam a sheepish smile and peered below.

"Let me know right away if you spot anything bigger than a bird."

"Yes, sahib. I will surely do that."

Sam returned to where Kelly ministered tenderly to her brother, urging him to take small swallows of water at short intervals.

"How's he doing?"

Jeff looked up at Sam as Kelly swiveled around. "Better . . . much better," she replied. Jeff gave Sam a weak but grateful smile.

Nodding, Sam acknowledged the appreciation. "Keep at it. I'm gonna go down and take a good look around."

Instantly swiveling back around, Kelly asked, "Is that wise? Safe?" She wanted to tell him not to go, but she could hardly do that under such dire circumstances. He was the only one capable of getting them safely back to the boat. The one they had to rely on.

"Safe?" He shot her a speculative glance. "Surely you jest."

She grimaced, wondering how he could joke in such a desperate situation. "Just go."

Sam gave a short humorless laugh. Then he left the cage, shooting a last remark over his shoulder as he started down the ladder. "*I'll* be back."

Kelly felt the urge to get hold of his neck, but she went back to helping Jeff get as much liquid down as possible without having it all come back up.

"Are you feeling a little stronger?" She tried to concentrate on her brother and not on the fact that Sam was out there, somewhere, without her. Somewhere he might not return from.

"I'm a lot stronger," Jeff whispered.

Kelly, pretending she actually believed him, smiled. "That's great." Then she helped him sit up and lean back against the trunk of the tree. "I think that should be enough water for a while."

Jeff nodded and promptly fell asleep.

Meanwhile, Kelly worried.

Sam wasn't back.

She glanced at her watch. He'd been gone ten whole minutes. Her stomach tightened.

144

"Do you see anything?" she asked Zayed.

He shook his head, his grip firm on Jeff's rifle. "Nothing," he whispered.

She thanked him and went back to worrying. They were all lost if Sam didn't return.

Suddenly, Zayed waved his hand, drawing her attention. "I see sahib."

Kelly sighed with relief and said a silent prayer of thanks.

Two minutes passed before Sam reentered the cage. "Is your brother any better?"

Blinking rapidly to banish the tears of relief that threatened, she smiled. "Much better."

Sam knelt by the wounded man, took his pulse, and gave Kelly an arched eyebrow. "Much better, huh?"

Quickly on the defensive, Kelly said, "He's taken a lot of water and talked a little. He said he feels stronger. He's just taking a little nap."

Sam's features hardened. "Yeah, a little nap. More like a little coma."

Kelly started to deny Sam's claim, even as Jeff began to raise his head. "Not in a coma, old man. Just took a little nap."

"Let's get some juice down you, then." Sam rummaged in his knapsack and came up with a plastic juice box. Inserting the connected straw, he held it out so Jeff could drink.

After a couple of large swallows, Jeff dropped the straw and grinned. "Hey, that stuff's great."

Sam partially smiled, then Zayed called him.

Handing the carton to Kelly, he returned to Zayed. "See something?" he asked.

"Not see anything, but listen. You hear how the jungle noises have changed?"

After a moment, Sam nodded. The animal sounds held a shriller note, as if they sensed danger.

"Was anything left in the other cage?" he asked Zayed. "Anything to eat or drink?"

"I took only what I could carry. So, yes, there should be food left."

"You think you could get it and bring it back here?" Sam asked, eyeing the native speculatively.

Zayed's pale color faded to an unbecoming sheet-white. "I believe the tigers are on their way back," he whispered. "And I don't want to be down there when they arrive."

Sam squinted. He had the same uncomfortable feeling, but wondered if there was something Zayed knew that he didn't.

"What makes you think they're close?"

Holding a trembling hand out, Zayed murmured, "My body . . . it tells me so."

Sam grunted, stepped back to Jeff and Kelly, then turned to Zayed. "You think you can get a little juice into Mr. Jeff from time to time?"

"I can do that, yes." Zayed sounded relieved. He apparently realized he was being given an easier job than going to retrieve the food from the other oversized mangrove tree.

"Give it a try, then." Sam took the box from Kelly and extended it to Zayed.

Kelly tried to retrieve the box. "Let me. I can give Jeff the juice."

Sam shook his head and reached around her, handing the box to Zayed. He watched closely as Zayed performed the task as gently as Sam had.

"We'll let Zayed do it," he said. He slipped off his backpack and produced a couple more juice boxes. "Let him rest, Zayed. In between, give him a little juice. But not so much it makes him sick. He's been without food or liquid for a couple of days, so his stomach will adjust slowly. We'll be back as soon as we can."

Zayed nodded his understanding. "I do as you say, sahib."

Kelly's mind zoomed in on the words "We'll be back," and she instantly became concerned. Voice tight, she asked, "Who's coming back . . . from where?"

"Someone has to get the food from the other tree. Besides, four people are too many for one cage. Two is a close fit. But two can lie down, sleep. We'll go for the food, and in case we don't get back before dark, we'll all be safe."

"You and Zayed go. I'll stay here with Jeff."

Sam unbolted the cage door and stepped onto the platform. "Zayed can be more protection for Jeff than you can. He obviously knows how to use Jeff's rifle. So we'll do it my way. Come on."

She shook her head. "I'm staying here."

He came back in and latched onto her arm. "This isn't a democracy. Let's move it."

Reluctantly, she went along. When Sam had her outside the cage, he closed the door behind them. "Bolt this, Zayed. And keep a sharp lookout."

"Most certainly," Zayed agreed.

Sam watched as the door was bolted, then turned to Kelly. "I'll go down first. When you hear me whistle, you hustle butt."

Kelly's chin had a stubborn cast. "I can use a rifle, too."

He pointed at the cage. "Like I said, two people can stay comfortably in there for days. Any more and it's too damn crowded."

She nodded and her shoulders slumped in defeat. She said good-bye to Jeff and assured him she'd be right back. He just nodded, his attention on the juice box.

"Like I said, come down when I whistle." Sam began the descent, keenly aware of everything within his restricted line of sight. When he reached the jungle floor, he scrutinized the small clearing for long moments, straining to see if hungry, shining eyes lurked nearby in the dense foliage. Finding nothing untoward, he issued a clear but faint whistle. Then he waited for Kelly to reach him, continually scanning the tangle of vegetation for signs of predators.

When Kelly's feet emerged, Sam tensed and whispered, "Hold it a minute while I take a closer look."

She froze, her heart pounding in her ears, fear stroking her nerves as he moved away. When she finally heard him return and okay the rest of her descent, her watery legs threatened to drop her from the ladder. Persevering, she got close enough to ground level to feel one of his arms wrap around her waist and pry her from the rungs. Then she was on the jungle floor, pressed protectively against his side.

Quietly, he said, "Stick like glue."

Kelly swallowed hard and nodded. That wouldn't be a problem.

Following Zayed's directions, Sam headed for the other giant mangrove tree in the area. It wasn't that far, but the vegetation separating the two trees prevented a clear view of one from the other. Actually, there wasn't a view from ground level at all. The foliage was far too dense.

An unusual hush fell over the jungle as he and Kelly prepared to climb the slats nailed to the side of the mangrove. A hush that made a panicked look appear on her face.

Sam, equally aware, reacted instantly. Leaning his rifle against the mangrove, he grabbed Kelly at the waist and lifted her as high as he could reach, starting her climb to the platform higher on the ladder than ground level.

"Hurry," he whispered.

He didn't have to urge her. As soon as her feet hit the first slat, she pulled herself up as fast as her feet found the next rung. She only stopped when her lungs were on fire from exertion and fright. Reaching the platform supporting the cage, she stumbled across and fumbled with the closed door. Frenzy made her clumsy and it seemed like hours before the door swung open.

A sudden thrashing of the nearby ground-level vegetation, followed by an animal's squeal of fright, sent a chill to her already queasy insides.

Panic rushing her, bone-chilling dread gripping her, she finally managed to open the door. Then, terrified half out of her mind, she turned and watched for Sam to emerge.

"Get the hell inside," Sam ordered sharply, as soon as his head appeared. He seemed to fly the rest of the way to the platform and across to the cage. Slamming the door behind him, bolting it, his gaze glued to where he'd just emerged, he waited as if in suspended animation.

Seconds later, the immense, brilliantly colored head of a tiger emerged from the leaves. It rested its chin on the platform and stared hungrily at them. Up close, the tiger's colors were vivid, breathtaking, the eyes awesome and beautiful.

Kelly might have screamed from fright, but the sheer beauty of the animal transfixed her. She gazed into its eyes, mesmerized once again by the hypnotic effect the predator possessed. She wondered if its kills were partly accomplished by the effective sight of its splendor, rendering its prey defenseless long enough for it to attack. For them to die.

Sam backed away from the door, out of harm's way. When he reached Kelly, he put an arm around her and hauled her with him to the back of the cage, the part that rested against the tree trunk. That side of the cage was safe from predators.

"Tigers don't climb trees," he muttered, more to himself than Kelly.

"So what's he doing up here?" she whispered back.

"Tigers are too *heavy* to climb trees," Sam insisted, shaking his head.

"You said that already," Kelly grumbled, elbowing him in the kidney.

Sam just continued to shake his head. "This beats the hell out of me."

When she could speak again, Kelly whispered, "My God, he's magnificent."

Sam's arm tightened around her waist. "Don't fall in love," he advised dryly. "He'd as soon eat you as look at you."

After his best friend was killed by a tiger, Sam had gone into a rage. He'd wanted to slaughter every tiger on the islands, but had gotten dead drunk instead. And now, after seeing one of the extraordinary creatures up close, he couldn't raise the feelings of hatred he'd harbored at the time of John's death. Couldn't give in to revenge. The tigers were an endangered species, which supposedly protected them, but Sam knew that didn't keep them from being killed by poachers.

Kelly whispered, "I suppose he would kill me, yes, but he's so beautiful." The colors of the cat's fur were extraordinarily sharp and beautifully defined.

"No supposing about it. He'd have you by the throat or scruff of the neck in seconds, if you weren't safely behind bars."

The tiger proceeded to leap gracefully and effortlessly onto the platform, surprising them again.

Kelly, already pressed against the tree trunk, reared back and bumped her head in an effort to meld with the bark and stay out of reach.

The cat padded to the cage just feet away from them, lifted one of its large velvety paws, and pushed against the bars as if testing them.

Kelly's hand flew to her mouth and she half-stifled a terrified scream.

"The bars will hold," Sam said.

He sounded convinced, but Kelly couldn't help but wonder what would happen if the tiger decided to throw his considerable weight against the bamboo. "What if they don't?" she managed in a strangled whisper.

"They will!"

A shiver shimmied up her spine. "But . . . what if?"

"I can shoot over his head and scare him," Sam said.

"What if he doesn't scare?"

"I'll have to kill him," Sam muttered, sounding extremely unhappy.

"Kill him?" Kelly's stomach pinched at the thought of killing such a magnificent animal.

"If it's our lives or his, yes. I'd have no choice."

For long moments they sat in silence. "You think he'll go away when he realizes he can't get to us in here?" Hope gave her voice a marginal lift.

"Hard to say." Sam eased into a sitting position on the floor, the rifle across his knees. Looking up at Kelly, he said, "Take a load off. Sit."

She shook her head. "Are you sure he can't reach your feet?" Worried, she glanced from Sam's feet to the tiger outside the cage.

"His legs aren't that long."

Kelly studied the cat. "I don't know. . . ."

"It's okay," Sam insisted. "Sit."

She sat very carefully, with her knees pulled all the way up to her chest, but she still felt extremely vulnerable. "How will we ever get back to Jeff and Zayed?"

"I don't know," Sam said, "but we will. We'll just have to give it time, wait and see what happens."

151

"You should have left me there."

"Well, I didn't."

They sat in an irritable, huffy silence for several minutes while they watched the tiger watch them.

Then, with elegant, cat-like ease, the feline predator assumed a sphinx-like position. It was painfully apparent that he, too, was going to wait and see.

Sam finally sighed and stood.

The tiger's spectacular eyes followed his every move.

"I guess we'd better let Zayed know we won't be coming right back." Turning in the direction of Jeff and Zayed's tree, Sam called, "Can you hear me, Zayed?"

The answer came back immediately. "Yes, I hear you, sahib. Are you on your way back?"

"No, I'm afraid not. We've got a small problem. We have a tiger keeping us company."

"A tiger . . . he is back under the tree?"

"Not exactly," Sam hedged.

"Then how do you know for sure he is still there?" Zayed asked.

Sam gave Kelly a look, shrugged his shoulders, and said, "It seems he likes to climb ladders."

"Mother of Buddha save us. This tiger, he is a devil. Tigers don't very often climb trees," Zayed shouted in agitation.

"He didn't climb the tree, exactly. He climbed the ladder and is making himself at home on the platform."

"I do not believe *he* is the Tiger God, so you can shoot him!" Zayed shouted.

"How is Jeff?" Sam asked, ignoring Zayed's suggestion.

"He has taken juice and more water. He is awake, but weak."

"Try to get some food into him later. For now, we'll all just have to hang tough."

"You have a rifle, kill the man-eater, he is *not* the Tiger God."

"I don't want to kill him unless I have to. There are too few of them left in the world. Besides, they're on the endangered species list."

"Sahib, are we not endangered, as well?"

"Maybe right now, but things could change. We'll wait a while. Keep a check on Jeff. Let me know if anything happens."

"I will, but I don't know. . . ."

"We'll wait," Sam snapped. "It's too late to start back to the boat today anyway, so we'll just see what we have to do tomorrow."

"It is as you desire," Zayed returned. "Buddha be with you through the long night."

"And with you, my friend," Sam called.

Kelly felt a certain amount of relief at hearing that Jeff was awake and taking liquids, but she still worried about the fever that could indicate a serious infection.

"We can't leave Jeff out here much longer," she warned. "He needs to be in the care of a doctor."

"Look around you. The sun is beginning to set. Even if the tiger leaves, we'd never make it back before full dark. Traveling at night through the jungle isn't just impractical, it's suicidal. We'll wait until morning, then get out no matter what it takes."

Kelly swallowed hard. She'd be spending the night alone in the tree with Sam. Unless she counted the tiger.

A small part of her aligned Sam's ability to seduce right along with the tiger's mesmerizing killing ability. They were both devastatingly handsome, with stunning killer eyes. Both predators. The thought that she might not survive through the night weighed on her. Heavily. Seated once again, Sam removed his backpack and began to assemble an assortment of edibles.

He handed Kelly two oranges. "Here, hold these."

She took the oranges without comment, her mind churning.

Then he produced two wrapped cheese sandwiches and a bag of chips. He handed one of the sandwiches to Kelly.

"Soup's on," he quipped.

Her stomach growled at the sight of the food, and every other thought vanished. Kelly took the sandwich gratefully, unwrapped it, and began to nibble. She helped herself to a handful of chips from the bag Sam held out and ate them along with the sandwich, savoring each bite, while the tiger scrutinized every move she made. She finished up with the juicy orange.

"At least I'll die full," she murmured, finally feeling secure enough to stretch out her legs.

"Worth something, I guess." Sam gave her an encouraging grin.

"What do I do with the peel?" She'd placed the orange peel in her sandwich wrap.

Sam hadn't touched his orange. "Just toss it onto the jungle floor. Something will eat it. Nothing's wasted out here."

"Maybe he'd like some." She indicated the tiger with a nod of her head.

Sam slanted her a raised eyebrow. "He's a carnivore."

"I *know* he eats meat, but doesn't he eat other things once in a while?" Kelly obviously believed in a well-balanced diet.

"I doubt it." Sam's dry remark didn't sound as if he admired her spunk, but he did; the very idea that she'd think to feed the tiger gave him a warm feeling, however foolish it sounded. He added, "You could always toss him one peel and

154

see what he does with it. You never know, he might be so grateful for a new taste treat that he'll decide to let us live."

"I don't think that's very funny," she grumbled.

"Lighten up, blue eyes. It's gonna be a long night."

Perusing the jungle from their tall fortress, Kelly noticed the shadows had already deepened. Glancing up through the branches above, she saw the sun had deserted them. It had dropped, unnoticed, behind the trees.

Spooked by the relentlessly advancing darkness, Kelly tossed the tiger a large section of peel.

It landed a couple of inches from his paw. But, showing total disdain, he ignored the somewhat unusual offering.

"It'll be really dark soon, won't it?" Her voice had a hitch in it as she tossed the rest of the peelings onto the jungle floor.

"Yeah, relatively soon," Sam confirmed, doing his own evaluation. Would he have felt any better if he'd left her behind? he wondered. He quickly decided he'd have felt worse. In fact, he more than likely would have killed the tiger to get back to her, and the thought bothered him more than he could have imagined. There were under a thousand tigers left in the world, and about five hundred of them were within close proximity to them. Just their bad luck.

He and John hadn't come to kill tigers. They'd come to stalk them, but not to kill. They'd wanted to see the elusive man-eaters at close range. Then leave, go home safely, and remember the beauty of the killing machines. And they'd come damn close to doing just that.

They'd come ashore on the back side of the island for the third time—three days in a row—and moved inland. That last day they had spotted several of the big cats from a distance. But the cats had been full of food, and shy, so he and John hadn't been able to get very close. Finally, the two men retreated to the safety of the cruiser to wait out the night, thinking they'd get a fresh start in the morning.

But John was a confirmed challenger. And if he could one-up Sam, he would, every damn time. They kidded often about all the times John had allowed his urges to control him, and using more guts than sense had jumped feet first into one adventure or another. More than once, Sam had to bail him out. But those times never dulled John's adventurous spirit. And this time was no exception.

He'd brought a Polaroid along. He had decided to leave before dawn, get close to one of the cats, take its picture, and bring the photo back to gloat over while he watched Sam eat breakfast.

John had concluded, from their three previous outings, that the reputation the tigers had achieved hadn't been honestly earned. Sure, maybe they ate the dead bodies left like debris on the beach after cyclones, but he and Sam had seen them turn away, had seen them take to the deeper jungle to escape. John had known legends weren't always based on pure fact. Sometimes fiction played a larger role. He had always pointed to the Loch Ness Monster as one of those legends after his trip to Inverness in Scotland, when an extensive cruise of the loch, with a working underwater radar screen, turned up nothing of consequence.

When Sam woke and found John missing, Pele told him what his friend had planned and explained that he'd been unable to stop John. His rationale, Pele explained, had been that he and Sam had seen the tigers run away when they were spotted, just like every other animal John had ever known. Thus, he concluded that all animals were the same; they'd avoid conflict unless cornered. Unfortunately, it was a mistake he wouldn't live to regret.

When Sam had finally found what was left of John, the evidence spoke for itself. It was horrifyingly clear that while John had stalked the tiger, the tiger had also stalked him. And by the time John realized his danger, it was too damn late. John must have died a horrible death. Sam's only ray of hope was that the tiger had killed John outright before devouring him. But there was no way to know for certain, and not knowing would haunt Sam for a lifetime.

The light continued to fade. Kelly shivered. As if sensing Sam's depression, she shared the thought that had preoccupied her.

"We should have waited until morning to come onto the island to search for Jeff."

"No." There wasn't the shadow of a doubt in Sam's one word disclaimer.

Kelly's head snapped around. She stared at Sam. "If we'd waited, we'd have had all day to get here, find Jeff, and get back out."

"Your brother more than likely wouldn't have made it through another night without water." Sam didn't want her regretting the decision they'd made. He knew better than most that regret was a defeating emotion. One that could lead to dangerous consequences.

Some of the tension appeared to ease out of Kelly and she sighed. "Of course, you're right. I hadn't thought of that."

The last rays of sun slipped over the horizon and the night came swiftly, plunging them into a black void, where at first they could see nothing. Then rays of moonlight filtered through the tops of the trees and illuminated the tiger's brilliant eyes, glaring directly at Kelly.

"Ohhh. . . ." She scooted closer to Sam.

He responded by slipping an arm around her. "Give it a little time. Your eyes will adjust to the dark."

Before she could agree, the tiger's gleaming eyes vanished.

"Sam!" Kelly slipped her arms around him and buried her head in his chest. "Where did he go?"

Sam's arm tightened. For the first time in hours he felt pretty damn good. "Probably didn't go anywhere. He could just be looking the other way. We'll know for sure when our eyes adjust."

She shivered, closed her eyes again, and snuggled closer. "Tell me when you can see something."

It was obvious she didn't want to look into that vast blackness and worry about what might be out there waiting to attack them. It was undoubtedly bad enough to know the tiger was there, waiting for a warm-blooded body. Sam grunted, fighting a body that was responding wildly to Kelly's touch. Her hair tickled his chin, and the strands smelled like orange blossoms. The softness of her body pressing against him tightened his groin unmercifully. He damn well knew this was no time to indulge in sexual urges. But anytime he touched her, he stopped thinking normally.

So what's new?

Abruptly, the tiger's eyes reappeared, glowing with their undeniable inner beauty, fierce and all-consuming.

"Look, he's been here all the time," Sam whispered. Lifting Kelly's chin, he turned it toward the front of the cage.

"I should have known he wouldn't give up that easily." She pulled her arms from around Sam's chest and brushed a wayward curl off her forehead. "Do they ever sleep?"

"Sure. In the daytime. Nights are spent hunting."

"Well, darn it. I wish he'd go hunt somewhere else."

"That's not likely to happen. Not when he has two tasty meals just waiting. He gets us and he won't have to search for a kill for a week."

She grimaced. "Boy . . . I can't tell you how much better that makes me feel."

Sam grinned in the dark. A woman who could keep a sense of humor in this kind of situation was one hell of a damn fine woman in his book.

Compulsively, he turned her chin toward him. His vision had adjusted enough to be able to see her fairly clearly. But it didn't take seeing her to want her. He'd wanted her from the minute she'd snuggled against his chest. Actually, that was a lie. He'd wanted her from the minute he laid eyes on her, back in the bar in Kalgola.

The wanting grew to proportions no breathing man could possibly deny, and he lowered his mouth to hers. The first kiss was as soft as a feather tickling her mouth. The second teased at her lips, inviting them to open. The third had his tongue pressing against the seam of her lips, encouraging them to open, finally demanding they do so.

Kelly, a mass of mixed emotions, harbored the desire to escape harsh reality for even a small space in time. Making love with Sam would certainly take her mind off everything else. Sorely tempted, with only the fear that she'd become just another conquest, easily forgotten when they were safely away, she finally allowed her lips to open.

That small surrender seemed to send Sam's passion into overdrive. He couldn't get enough, couldn't delve too deeply. His tongue mimicked his body's desire, stabbing into her tender mouth over and over again.

As always, Sam's sensuality awakened and ignited something Kelly hadn't realized existed within her. A wild need to return his hungry kisses. A desire so strong it couldn't be subdued.

Suddenly, an agonized screech awakened the jungle, jarring Sam and Kelly back to harsh reality. Sam lifted his mouth from hers and squinted into the darkness.

"That *was* an animal, wasn't it?" Kelly asked. The scream

159

hadn't sounded human, but there had been such pain in it she couldn't be certain. She immediately thought of Jeff.

"Yeah. Sounded like a monkey."

"Should we call over to Zayed to make sure?"

"Okay, sure. Zayed, everything okay over there?" he called, raising his voice.

"Yes, sahib. We okay."

"Goodnight, then."

"Goodnight."

Sam's arms tightened once again around Kelly, and he lowered his mouth, prepared to take up where he left off. But Kelly, giving her self-protective instincts full vent, pulled out of his arms.

Sam let her go with nothing more than a grunt of protest.

"I don't think we should take our eye . . . eyes off him." Kelly stuttered, but it wasn't just from fear of the tiger. It shook from fear of her reactions, as well. When Sam had kissed her, she had wanted to hold on and never let go, even knowing it was a bad idea. Knowing it would just complicate matters. She realized if they shared many more of those fiery kisses, it wouldn't be easy to stop with mere kisses. Not that any kiss from Sam could ever be described as mere. On the contrary, they were to die for.

She was still on fire, still inclined to throw caution to the wind, and she knew he was just as ready, probably more so.

"I don't suppose we dare fall asleep." She stared at the tiger, trying to distract herself. Her vision had also adjusted to the dark, and she could see the beast quite clearly. He hadn't moved. She doubted he'd even twitched when hearing the scream. She supposed he was used to the sound because he made frequent kills himself.

"You can try to get some sleep, if you're tired," Sam said, sounding frustrated. And distracted.

Kelly didn't know if his preoccupation was due to the tiger or the kisses they'd just shared. She couldn't blame him if the kisses were the culprit. He had to be confused. One minute she'd be on fire and all over him, and the next she'd be distant and cold. At the very least, her quixotic behavior had to leave him guessing.

Sam knew damn well Kelly would never make love with the kind of guy she thought he was—footloose and uncommitted. Of course, he could set her straight, tell her who he really was, an upright citizen. But he wanted her to want him in spite of the fact that every sense she had warned her off. Wanted her to want him the way he wanted her. Wholeheartedly and without regret. It was that important to him.

Oh, hell! Who was he trying to kid? He'd take her anyway he could get her. Take anything she was willing to give. For as long as she was willing to give it. *Dammit!*

"Holy shit!" he shouted.

Kelly noticed the same phenomenon Sam did, at the very same moment. In response, her legs jerked up as tight as they could to her body. She folded her arms around them protectively. At the same time, the air *whooshed* from her lungs in a strangled, "Noooo. . . ."

Chapter Ten

The sight before Kelly and Sam was tongue-tying, a foreshadowing of future nightmares. For long tense moments neither of them spoke.

Then Sam growled, "Well, looky here."

Kelly didn't really want to look, but she couldn't pull her attention away. Over the back of the prone tiger, another pair of gleaming eyes pierced the darkness. Eyes identical to the first pair.

With effortless ease, the prone tiger rose and swung around to face the intruder.

Kelly held her breath, waiting for all hell to break loose, for fur to fly as the tigers fought over *her*. If she could have freed her hands from around her legs, she'd have covered her ears. The ferocious roars would be deafening this close. But at that moment, prying her arms loose would have been a *really* big chore, even for a strong man.

For an agonizing eternity, nothing happened and the tension mounted. Now she could only see the rear of the tiger on the platform, and she had no way of knowing what would transpire.

Suddenly, the platform tiger swung back around and stared at her, unblinkingly, with some semblance of regret in its irreverent glare. Then, in a flash, he was gone.

162

Sam jumped to his feet and rushed to the door, straining to see through the bars, watching the tiger's descent until it disappeared into the leaves.

"Amazing." His tone held awe.

I'm sure! Kelly said it only in her mind because she wasn't functioning vocally. Not yet. Not after the fright of seeing two of the huge, exotic animals within arm's reach.

How Sam could still be excited by the tigers' maneuverings was beyond her. Sure tigers were beautiful, and she admired them. And they were agile. No doubt about it. But they were man-eaters, for Pete's sake. And they'd wanted to dine on her!

"You missed it," he said.

"Fine by me," she muttered. She wanted to see the last of them, but not literally. In spite of her fright, Kelly didn't want them killed.

"They're gone." Sam actually sounded disappointed.

Now that the immediate danger was over, Kelly struggled to relax the hold she had on her legs, but almost instantly a disturbing thought assailed her. "Do you think they went over to Jeff's tree?"

Sam came back to stand beside her. "I don't know. We'll give it a minute, then call over and see."

Panic seized her by the throat and wouldn't let go. "Call now, Sam. They might have fallen asleep and gotten too near the bars."

"Okay, take it easy." He leaned down and touched her shoulder, trying to calm her, then raised his voice so it could be heard across the divide between the trees.

"Zayed, you awake?"

"Very much so. What is happening?"

"We had a second visitor," Sam advised. "The two tigers just went off together, so keep your eyes open in case they decide to pay you a visit."

"Do not worry. I will not even blink," Zayed assured him.

"How's Jeff doing?" Sam asked.

"He sleeps. His fever is better, I think."

"That's good. Take care and we'll see you in the morning."

"Morning can not come too soon for me."

"I can relate."

But, actually, Sam couldn't. Now that the tigers were gone, all he could think about was Kelly. Kelly and the dark night that artfully surrounded them. They were alike in Sam's mind. Kelly's softness was equal to the velvety night.

Of course, he realized the tigers could be out there patiently waiting for human error, but Sam didn't think so. He believed the second tiger was the first one's mate, and that it had arrived to lead the first tiger to greener pastures, at least for the time being.

He hoped to hell they had good luck. That they got their bellies so full they wouldn't be hungry for a few days. Actually, one day would be all he'd need to get Jeff back to the boat, even if he wound up carrying him all the way.

He hunkered down on the deck beside Kelly. After rummaging in his backpack, he withdrew a clean shirt. Wadding it into a ball, he handed it to Kelly.

"Here, use this for a pillow. See if you can get some sleep." It wasn't his first altruistic act, but it was undoubtedly the toughest. If she slept she'd leave him, at least mentally.

Mutely, she took the shirt, placed it on the cage floor, and curled into a tight ball, her head resting on its softness.

"Goodnight, Kelly." The tone in Sam's voice was intimate, as if they'd been lovers for decades. As if he were familiar with every minute detail of her life. As if she belonged to him.

Disturbed, Kelly managed a shaky, "Goodnight." Then

she closed her eyes as Sam settled onto the floor beside her. She listened as he placed the rifle by his side. Instinctively, she knew he watched her.

She experienced almost as much discomfort as if the tiger was still watching them hungrily. Which, in turn, made her aware that her own breathing had turned irregular. She found she had to swallow repeatedly, a reflex she normally wasn't aware of.

The jungle's nocturnal sounds differed from the daytime. They were more sinister, stealthy, as if, while the predators prowled, the rest of the population held its breath, hoping to be bypassed and spared to live through another night. Left to experience another magical new day. Because, by day, the jungle was indeed magical. Dangerous, but nonetheless enchanting.

The strain of feigning sleep grew too burdensome. Kelly finally gave up and sat up. "I can't sleep."

"Better try. You'll need all your strength tomorrow." Sam had been congratulating himself on his chivalry, ignoring the fact that with Kelly sound asleep he wouldn't be called on to exercise that particular mental muscle.

Now, with her awake, it was another story entirely. His armor lost its luster, his white horse transformed itself into a donkey, and he grew feet of clay.

"It's no use . . . I just can't sleep right now," she muttered.

He sat up, as well. "Are you hungry?"

She thought a moment. "No. Not really."

"Thirsty?" The question was more growl than anything else.

"No."

Well, damn, *he* was thirsty. He wanted to drink in her kisses, crush her to him, and most of all have his way with her. He could envision her legs wrapped around him, her mouth open for endless exploration, her tight moist heat encasing him.

Dammit! Sam lurched to his feet.

"What is it? What's the matter? Are the tigers back?" Kelly quickly stood beside him, and gazed out fearfully at the surrounding darkness. There was no movement directly below them, at least nothing large enough to be seen at this distance.

"This whole damn thing is what's the matter," he said, his voice tight and low.

Kelly didn't need to be told it was an unfair and rotten situation for Sam, but she thought he'd adjusted rather well. At least, until now. Still, she acknowledged, he was here risking his life for a stranger, so she could hardly blame him for being angry.

"I'm really sorry to have gotten you into all this," she murmured.

Sam jammed his hands deep into his pockets and stared down at her. "Yeah, well, it's a little late for sorry, isn't it?"

Her conscience assailing her, she blew out an unsteady breath. "Yes. I guess it is. But I'm afraid there's nothing I can do about it at this late date."

"Oh, there's something you could do all right," he whispered, his tone of voice sensual.

His meaning became instantly clear to Kelly. Heat filtered into her cheeks, she stiffened, and her guard went up.

"I'm not sure what you mean by that," she said, "but I don't think I like the inference."

He laughed, a rough humorless sound. Then he reached out, pulled her to him, and planted the longest, hottest kiss she'd ever experienced in her life on her, leaving her gasping when he finally let go.

"Sleep on that," he muttered. Then he sat with his back against the tree, and shut his eyes, closing her out.

The kiss continued to sift through her, warming every last little inch of her body. And, suddenly, Kelly felt like a tigress. She wanted to pounce on Sam and have her way with him. She wanted him so badly she burned as with a fever.

But dammit, this isn't the time or place. They were literally up a tree, for heaven's sake. Of course, they had a ladder, so it wasn't quite as bad as being up a creek without a paddle. But close, *darn* close.

Get a grip. Kelly became aware of the moon as a cloud slowly floated west, uncovering its ghostly surface, illuminating their bamboo platform.

As if he could read her thoughts, Sam's eyes popped open. They stared at each other.

He reached up, begging her to take his hand, the hunger on his face etched in every line.

Like a spineless fool, Kelly slipped her hand in his and allowed him to pull her down onto his lap, prompting him to bury his face in her neck. He nibbled the tender flesh beneath her ear, then moved over her face with hungry kisses. When he got to her mouth, he plundered its sweetness, growing bolder with every thrust of his tongue.

But when his hot, roving mouth moved on to the top of one breast, Kelly experienced a moment's panic.

"Wait . . . no. . . ." She pulled out of his arms, keeping him at a distance with extended arms.

Sam reluctantly let her go, plowed his hands through his hair, shot to his feet, and moved to the far side of the cage. She was gonna kill him. *For damn sure.*

"I didn't mean. . . ."

Close to exploding, Sam snapped, "I warned you about pushing a man too far. You're close to disaster right now, blue eyes. So, if I were you, I'd watch what I said and did *real* close. You get my drift?"

167

"Uh-huh." He'd let her off the hook again.

The dear man.

Suddenly, there were no doubts. Some indefinable sense of the rightness of things told her that, whatever the consequences, she wanted Sam. Here. Now.

Kelly rose and moved toward him. She slipped her arms around his waist. Nuzzled her nose against his back. Stood on tiptoe to press kisses on his nape.

Turning on her, breaking her grip, Sam grabbed her head in his big hands and got in her face. "Did you hear what I just said? Or have you suddenly gone deaf?"

She managed a nod in spite of his firm grip. "I heard."

"Well, dammit, keep your distance."

"No."

"No?" His eyebrows lifted. A pulse beat a wild tattoo in his temple. "I kiss you again, I don't stop. *Period!*"

"Okay." It took her breath to say that one word, but she meant it.

It was more than okay.

It was necessary!

Sam's squint disappeared. Doubting his hearing for a heartbeat, his head canted to the side as he studied her. "You do comprehend what I just told you?"

This couldn't be happening. Not to him. Good things didn't come his way that often. At least not anything *this* good.

"Uh-huh." Taunting him, she pursed her lips and kissed air in his general direction.

Sam latched onto Kelly with a growl, prepared to devour her. But the minute his lips took hers, gentleness overtook him. She was giving him his dream, his fantasy, everything he wanted. Unless he'd fallen asleep and was right that moment having one hell of a dream. *Please, no!*

Her mouth was all honeyed warmth. And when she returned his kisses, her small pointed tongue dueling with his, it sent enough heat to his groin to start a four-alarm fire. Finally her tongue dipped deep into his mouth to explore with the finesse of a hummingbird on a nectar run, undoing him.

Sam's shaft hardened to the consistency of an iron rod and threatened to rip through his jeans with its latent strength. He'd never been so hard in his whole damn life.

Lifting Kelly into his arms, he carried her to the back of the cage, safely out of the reach of any marauder but himself.

She'd never be safe from him now. She'd given consent. And he'd have her or die trying.

He knelt and placed her on the floor of the cage, following her down. He heard her whisper something, but took her mouth with his, not letting her repeat it, afraid of what he'd hear. While his mouth ravaged hers, he unbuttoned her shirt as fast as his clumsy, shaking fingers would permit.

Sam knew that his caresses, accompanied by his kisses, heated her sensitive skin, brought her nipples almost painfully erect, and fueled a raging passion that could only be extinguished by Sam himself.

The rounds of her breasts above her bra shone like alabaster in the moonlight. When he finally disengaged his mouth from hers and trailed kisses down her neck to those soft mounds, he paused, struck by the softness of her skin.

Reverent now, he reached under her and released her bra, discarded it, then struggled to keep breath in his lungs.

She was perfect.

She was *his*.

Suddenly shy, Kelly tried to cover herself with splayed fingers. Sam took her hands in his and brought them to his lips, kissing one palm and then the other. Then, unable to resist for one more moment, he trapped one breast in each hand

169

and lowered his head to plunder. Like a thief in the night, he suckled one erect pink nipple until it was fully extended, then kissed his way to the other, giving it the same rapt attention. His hands held her breasts up from the bottom like an offering for the gods.

He was no god. More sinner than most. But his reverence for her body knew no bounds. She was the most exquisite female he'd ever seen.

Soon it wasn't enough to ravage those tender thrusting mounds. He needed more. The rest of her.

Her zipper came down easily. The jeans took a little more effort, but were no deterrent to Sam's determination.

A ribbon ran around her waist, holding a tiny triangle of lace that barely covered her. The rest of her lay bare.

Sam sat back on his heels and just plain stared. "Thong underwear," he whispered.

He sounded so choked, Kelly worried. "Don't you like thong underwear?"

"Hell, yes . . . I *love* it."

With one finger Sam traced the triangle of material ending with the part that ran between her legs, then lowered his mouth to kiss the same line. When he reached the point that disappeared between her thighs, her legs opened automatically.

Sam planted a hand on the inside of each thigh, making certain they wouldn't close and deny him what he had sought for so long.

A sigh of pleasure escaped Kelly as Sam kissed the lace between her thighs. And when his hands went to the elasticized ribbon waistband and began to pull it down over her hips, she lifted her buttocks to accommodate him.

With her body freed from the microscopic bit of clothing, Sam ran his finger where his mouth had been, his heart hammering against his rib cage hard enough to break through his chest.

She was wet, slick. *His.*

He wanted to howl at the moon. Wanted every animal in the jungle to know how it felt to have its heart's desire. But, more than that, he wanted Kelly.

She moaned and sudden fear invaded him. Dropping his mouth over hers, feeding his hunger and silencing her at the same time, he ran a callused hand up her thigh and over her mound and down the other leg almost to her knee. Then back up. But this time, when he reached her center, one finger dipped into her moist heat.

He probed that secret place with wicked, delicious results. She surrendered, completely opened to him, and to his stunned delight hungrily raised her hips to meet him.

The carnal invitation had Sam surging dangerously, made him fight for control. He couldn't afford to lose it now, not when heaven lay within reach.

Needing both hands, he reluctantly removed his hand to unbutton his jeans. All the while, he continued to kiss her.

This sure as hell was no time to have her come to her senses.

Kelly moaned again, and her hips rose, searching, needing.

Jeans dispensed with, Sam sprang free. And like a homing pigeon, his shaft found her center. All thought fled. Now there was nothing but heat and the need to bury himself in her.

She was so tight he penetrated her a sensitive half-inch at a time, pounding a little deeper with each new thrust, until completely imbedded. Engulfed by radiant heat, he settled between her thighs for a blissful moment.

He belonged here. This was his. This velvet glove that fit like no other was meant just for him.

And then he moved because he had to. Because she urged him with murmurs. Because lust overcame him.

He drove into her over and over again, slowly, teasingly at first, then roughly, holding off the final ecstasy, giving them both every ounce of pleasure possible. She climaxed first, and spasmed around him. Then, and only then, he gave in to overwhelming need and the rapture of release, pulsing into her until he was completely spent.

The enormity of what she'd caused to happen hit Kelly while Sam was still inside. While she could still feel the hammering of his heart against her breasts, feel the warmth of his seed invade her body. They'd made love without a thought about protection. They'd rutted like two driven beasts, unable to think about the consequences, or anything but coupling. The need to take and be taken. To own and be owned.

Unfortunately, reality crept in and she began to wonder what he must think of her? Yet even while she worried, a part of her glowed. Another part wanted even more.

I've turned into a slut! She stifled a giggle. What was the matter with her?

Sam recovered enough to rise on his elbows, but he couldn't bring himself to pull away. Gazing lovingly down at Kelly, he whispered, "Are you okay?"

Shy now, she said, "I'm not sure."

"I'd like to stay a little longer," he admitted.

"Ummmm . . . well . . . okay." She couldn't quite meet his gaze.

"Is it?" He watched her eyes darken as he began to grow.

"Are you?" she whispered.

"Yeah," he growled.

Demure, she murmured, "We probably shouldn't."

He pulled out halfway and slid back with velvety smoothness.

She caught a breath. "I don't think. . . ."

He withdrew nearly all the way, then plunged home roughly.

"You don't think what?" he rasped.

She whimpered, then wrapped her legs around him. "I don't think you should stop."

His grunt was more a release of tension than anything else.

They had more than sex. They had all the world's pleasures wrapped into one night, tied up by the magic of love that both had difficulty acknowledging.

The end of a perfect night started with the first rays of light that glimmered through the trees as it scaled the horizon. Then, while Kelly and Sam were still naked, a light rain fell, cleansing them.

Reality raised its head with the first few bug bites and they took turns covering each other with bug spray.

Dressed in damp clothing, they shared fruit and protein bars for breakfast. Just like Tarzan and Jane, Kelly thought. Except for the protein bars. Then, quite naturally, as more light crept into the day, shyness overcame her. She couldn't directly look at Sam for fear of what she'd see—disdain. And the acknowledgment that she was easy, that he'd known it all along. Her cheeks turned crimson and stayed that way.

It was a relief when she heard the soft call from the other tree. A distraction that meant she didn't have to think about Sam and what the night meant, even as a small voice in her head told her it meant nothing. Warned her to expect nothing. Informed her she'd be sorely disappointed if she counted on anything permanent with Sam.

"Any sign of our furry friends?" Sam called back over to Zayed.

"No. But I believe we had better hurry and leave."

"We'll be over as soon as we pack up," Sam said. He helped organize Kelly's pack and adjusted it on her back, feeling his love for her ooze from every pore. Lowering his head, he kissed the back of her neck.

Kelly jerked away.

Sam wasn't certain what her moodiness meant, but the knot in his gut returned. In his mind, they'd made a commitment during the night. But, like most men, Sam wasn't much of a talker. He let actions speak for him, and he'd made love to Kelly with all the tenderness, passion, and love he'd been capable of giving. He thought it had been enough. But this morning she seemed more embarrassed than anything else, and he just sort of figured that came from shame.

He sure as hell wasn't ashamed of anything he'd done during the night. He had loved her to the fullest. He had felt ten feet tall, until he'd gotten a look at Kelly's downcast face with first light. One glimpse and he'd been reduced to feeling about two feet tall. *Damn!*

With no time to explore her feelings, he swung the cage door open, walked to the end of the platform above the ladder, and searched the jungle floor. No sign of the tigers. Instinct told him they weren't around at that moment.

Turning his head, he whispered, "You ready to roll?"

Kelly swallowed sudden fear and nodded. "As ready as I'll ever be."

Sam sent her a reassuring smile, but didn't hug her the way he'd have liked. The vibrations she was emitting weren't cuddle-me vibes. "We'll be okay. We made it here and got through the night. Hang tough and before you know it, we'll have Jeff safe on the boat."

174

What he didn't say was that the tigers could be out there, just biding their time, waiting for breakfast.

"I'll go down first and if it's safe, I'll whistle low. When I do, you get down as fast as you can." He stared at her, as if he wanted to say more, then abruptly turned and left. This was no time for injured feelings.

In under a minute Kelly heard the whistle and started down the ladder. But even though Sam had gone first and given an all-clear, she felt exposed, vulnerable, and open to attack. The tigers were huge.

When she cleared the last camouflaging leaves, she stopped and looked down. Sam stood under the tree, his head always moving, surveying the dense, vibrant, green foliage. His rifle was held in both hands, ready to fire. She hurried down the last ten feet or so. Then she dropped softly to the ground behind him.

"Stick close," Sam murmured. He led her quickly to the other tree. When they reached it, he called softly, "Everything okay up there?"

"No tigers," Zayed answered.

Sam gestured with his head. "Climb."

Kelly placed a foot on the first rung and started up. When she reached the platform, Sam was close behind. Zayed quickly opened the cage door and let them in. Kelly saw Jeff sitting up against the tree trunk and smiling at her. She ran to him and gave him a big, tender hug.

When she buried her face in his neck, his arms slid around her. "Hey, baby sister, I'm all right. Don't cry."

Kelly pushed back far enough to get a good look at his face. She ran a hand lovingly through his dark hair, and she murmured something Sam couldn't catch.

It jarred Sam to see Kelly in Jeff's arms after their night of lovemaking. The exchange rattled him, even though he knew there was no reason for his strong reaction. This was his first brush with what he feared was a major case of irrational jealousy, and it didn't help that Kelly had totally ignored him this morning. More than ignored—she'd jerked away from him as if she couldn't bear his touch. That was what hurt the most.

"He cannot walk." Zayed drew Sam's attention away from Jeff and Kelly. "How will we get him down and to the boat if he cannot walk?"

Sam pulled his mind back to the problem at hand. "I'll carry him. But first, I need to check him out." He stepped behind Kelly. "Move over," he said.

Kelly gave Jeff a tender kiss on the cheek, then allowed Sam to help her to stand. She wiped a tear off her cheek as she backed away.

"How do you feel?" Sam asked.

"A hell of a lot better than yesterday," Jeff responded, managing a smile for Sam.

"Great. You think you can stand?"

"If it'll get me out of this damn tree, I'll sure as hell try."

Kelly grabbed Sam's arm in protest. "He shouldn't. Don't let him."

Sam's patience snapped. "Back off. We have to know what he's capable of."

She dropped his arm as if it burned her. "Please," she begged, "don't let him stand on his own."

Sam thrust his rifle at her. "Hold this."

She took the weapon, holding it carefully, obviously understanding how much damage it could do with the twitch of a careless finger.

Sam addressed Zayed. "Go down, check around, and let me know if it's all clear."

Zayed nodded, then quickly started his descent, Jeff's rifle slung over one shoulder. A minute or two later, they heard a soft, "Okay."

"Now you, blue eyes." Sam jerked a thumb at Kelly. "Take my rifle with you. Put it over your shoulder."

Sam scowled when she didn't move quickly enough.

Kelly sent Jeff a teary-eyed smile and started her descent.

"Don't be too hard on Kelly," Jeff said. "She's just worried about me."

"Yeah, well, maybe you should try staying home so she doesn't have to worry."

"Kelly wouldn't want me to do that. She's always been supportive about my work. Truthfully, I don't know what I'd do without her."

Sam stared down at Jeff, wanting to tell him he'd better start adjusting to being without her. But he didn't, because a sudden tension in his midsection warned him he might be the one who'd have to do without in the end.

Chapter Eleven

"Hurry!" Kelly's urgent plea from below pulled Sam back to the immediate problem of getting Jeff out of the tree before the tigers returned.

He leaned down and lifted the other man, placing him as gently as possible over one broad shoulder. When Jeff grunted from the pain, Sam managed an apology in spite of his inner turmoil. "Sorry, but this is the only way to get you down."

Teeth gritted against the pain, Jeff grunted an acknowledgment. "I know. Don't pay any attention to me."

"If you can hold on, it'll help steady you," Sam advised. He made his way slowly down the ladder, and since he needed both hands for the descent, did a balancing act while Jeff held on to his belt in the back.

"Not much longer now," Sam offered, aware of the pain Jeff must be enduring with every jolt he received as they descended rung by rung. "Hang in there for another minute."

They were about six feet from the ground when Jeff's hold on Sam's belt loosened and he went limp. Sam descended the last section of ladder with great care. Stepping to the jungle floor, he swiveled anxiously around, noting that both Kelly and Zayed were scanning the dense, encroaching foliage, their weapons raised.

"Any sign of 'em?" Sam asked.

"Nothing," Zayed assured him.

"I think he passed out." Sam eased Jeff onto a patch of long, springy grass directly under the sheltering tree.

Kelly knelt and dropped the rifle carelessly by her side. "Oh, no. What have you done? Let me see him."

Sam grabbed her by the shoulders and pulled her away.

"Take it easy," Sam said. "It won't do him any good if you fall apart now."

She tried to wiggle out of his grasp, but he held her firmly. "I won't fall apart, dammit. I just want to see him."

Sam released her with a shake of his head, his heart thudding painfully. She was back to treating him like hired help.

While Kelly stroked Jeff's deathly pale forehead, Sam unsnapped the canteen from his belt. Lifting Jeff's head, he dribbled water along his lips, then sprinkled his face.

The wounded man blinked, opened his eyes, and gazed up at them. "Sorry about that. Guess I must have conked out on you for a few minutes."

"No problem," Sam muttered. "But as soon as you feel up to it, we better move on." He clipped the canteen back onto his belt, avoiding eye contact with Kelly. He feared his irrational jealousy would show, and he knew damn well he wouldn't win any points with her if it did.

Jeff shivered and took a deep bracing breath. "Give me a minute and I'm all yours."

Sam struggled to control his emotions. "Take two," he growled. Then, reaching down, he retrieved the rifle and checked the chamber to make certain it was ready to fire.

Kelly smiled encouragingly at her brother, although her eyes remained sad. "I'm so sorry, Jeff. This must be excruciating for you."

"Don't worry, sis. I'll be okay." He tried to sit up to prove it to her, but fell back down with a groan. "Guess I'm not as macho as I thought I was, huh?"

"You're wonderful." She patted his arm, then turned with a frown as Sam crouched down beside them.

"Ready to go?" he asked.

"Give him a few more minutes," Kelly pleaded.

Ignoring Kelly, Sam spoke to Jeff. "We need to get out of here as soon as possible. It's a long way back to the beach."

Jeff took a shuddering breath. "I'm up for it when you are."

Kelly quickly said, "Please, you can see it's too soon to move him. He's still deathly pale."

It was difficult as hell for Sam to ignore Kelly as he bent over, preparing to lift Jeff and place him over his shoulder again. "Sorry, but we'll have to do this thing the same way. It's the only position that will work for long."

"Don't apologize, just do it." Jeff's face tightened as he braced for the pain, drawing into himself, calling forth every resource he possessed.

Sam surged to his feet with Jeff over one shoulder, the rifle in its sling over the other. Then, gesturing with his head, his expression cool, he indicated that Kelly should walk ahead of him.

"Let's go, Zayed. You lead. Kelly, you go next. We'll follow."

"I'll go last. You go second." She wanted to help and thought she'd have a better chance to protect them if a tiger came from the rear.

"Don't piss me off!" Sam growled. "Haul ass outta here."

"I think we'd have a better chance if I covered the rear."

"I don't care what you think. Move out!"

The venom in Sam's voice moved Kelly as nothing else

could. She eased carefully around him, suddenly as leery of him as if *he'd* been a hungry predator. Then she hurried after Zayed.

Progress was slow, but for the first hour they proceeded without incident. Jeff, however, needed frequent breathers, and it was during one of their rest stops in the second hour that the first sign of trouble appeared.

Sam propped Jeff up against a tree and saw that he drank enough water and juice to keep dehydration at bay. Kelly succeeded in getting him to eat part of a protein bar. But they all noted how much paler he'd turned, and this time, even after a longer rest, his color didn't improve.

"Sam, could I speak to you a moment?" Kelly asked as she moved a short distance down the trail, out of earshot of the others.

Sam grunted an affirmation and followed. "What is it?"

"He can't take much more. You saw him. He'll die if we keep up this pace."

The muscles in Sam's jaw hardened. Every time she looked at him, as if he meant nothing to her, he had the urge to kill. Unfortunately, there was no one around on which to vent his frustration except Kelly herself. His words came out slow, with a hard edge. "And just what do you expect me to do about that?"

Kelly had a difficult time believing this was the same man who had made tender love to her during the night. She wanted to ask what had happened to change him so drastically, but fearing the answer, didn't go there.

"I thought maybe we could construct a litter and carry him that way," she offered. Surely Sam could see value in the idea, even if it *was* hers.

"That would take time and equipment we don't have. Any other bright ideas?"

"We could use bamboo for the handles," she continued, unwilling to give up so quickly.

"And what in hell do we stretch between the handles?"

"We have extra clothing. That would work."

He gave her an evil-eyed squint. "And just how long do you think a couple of shirts would hold a man his size?"

She dropped her head. He had a valid point, even though it galled her to admit it to someone as obnoxious as he'd turned out to be. How could she have ever thought him gentle?

"Well, if that won't work," she said, "maybe something else would."

"Like what?" The words were ground out in a clenched whisper.

She raised her head and there were tears shimmering in her eyes. And they weren't tears strictly born of Jeff's condition. They were there because Sam's attitude wounded her. She should have known better than to fall for a guy like Sam.

"I don't know. I thought maybe *you* could think of something."

The tears weren't for him, but they touched Sam more than he would have liked. His manner softened. "Look, I've tried to come up with another plan, but there just isn't any other way. Sure, we could probably make a stretcher out of wood, but that would take time we don't have, and make way too much noise. Which, as you know, isn't advisable. We'll just have to let him rest more often. That's the best I can do."

Sam adjusted the rifle on his shoulder. He knew that his success in the construction business partially came from his ability to get directly to the root of the problem and fix it.

Kelly sighed and nodded, giving in.

Sam's arms twitched with the desire to pick her up and

hold her. But he knew better than to indulge himself, especially in front of the others. He just naturally figured she'd hate him for sure if he caused the others to suspect they'd been intimate, especially now that it was something she obviously regretted.

"You think you're ready to take another shot at this?" Sam asked. He returned to Jeff and eyed him with ill-disguised concern.

"I thought you'd never ask."

Jeff's quip solicited a grudging smile out of Sam. "Here we go." He bent over, getting in position to hoist Jeff onto his shoulder.

Kelly aided them by helping Jeff get a grip on Sam's belt and placing the broken leg in the best possible position. Quietly, she asked, "Are you okay?"

"Never better," Jeff whispered, giving his sister a smile that was more a grimace.

"You poor thing. I wish there was something I could do."

"You've already done it. You came out here after me."

His temper short, Sam muttered, "If you two are done yakking, I'd like to get this show on the road."

Kelly quickly darted around Sam, having decided the best thing she could do was to not give him a reason to become more hostile. Zayed started down the trail and she followed, occasionally glancing over her shoulder to see how the two behind were faring. On one of those occasions, where the jungle was especially dense, Zayed moved out of sight. However, with Sam and Jeff directly behind her, Kelly wasn't worried. At least, not until she heard a strangled cry of terror.

Halting in her tracks, blood-chilling dread overwhelming her, she wheeled around to Sam. "Did you hear that?" she whispered.

He had already lowered Jeff to the trail and beckoned her to his side. "Stay here with Jeff."

Before Sam had taken a step, Kelly screamed, horrified by the apparition moving toward her.

Zayed could barely stagger. Encased in the muscled grip of a huge python, his movements were feeble at best. Seconds later, immobilized completely before he could reach Kelly, he collapsed onto the jungle floor.

The twenty-foot snake, wrapped around him from neck to below the knees, had applied so much pressure that Zayed's face was tinged a deep purple. The python was literally and slowly squeezing the life from him. Beyond speech, the suffocating man's eyes pleaded for help.

Sam dropped the rifle, grabbed his pistol from its holster, and sprinted to Zayed's aid. After a struggle, he managed to pry the snake's head up and away from Zayed's chest. All the while, the python's tongue flickered wildly. When Sam felt he had the snake's head far enough away, he fired several shots, killing it. Even then, uncoiling the dead beast wasn't an easy exercise.

As the python's body finally fell to the jungle floor, Zayed gasped. Shaking from fear and shock, he crawled a foot or two away from the creature and collapsed.

Stepping over the snake, Sam knelt beside the fallen man. "Don't move until I check you out."

Zayed nodded, shuddered, and closed his eyes.

"Does it hurt when you breathe?" Sam applied pressure, testing Zayed's ribs, one at a time.

"Hurts very much, sahib."

"Did you hear anything crack, feel anything break?"

"I do not think so, but who knows? I could not breathe. He was a *very* big snake." Zayed shuddered again.

Sam nodded. "Never seen bigger," he agreed. He continued to pressure-check Zayed's ribs. "I don't feel anything give, so maybe he didn't have time to break anything. How do you feel? Do you think you can sit up?"

"I . . . I will try."

"Good man, let me help." Sam eased the injured man into a sitting position. He then stepped back, hefted the dead python, took a few steps off the trail, and dumped the carcass into the dense foliage, out of sight. That accomplished, he turned to check on Kelly and Jeff.

Reaction had set in and Kelly was trembling uncontrollably. She slumped to the ground. By the time Sam got to her, she resembled a crumpled doll. Although Jeff attempted to reach her, he failed. Willingly, Sam cradled her in his arms and started to rub circulation back into her limbs.

"This is no place for her," Jeff muttered to no one in particular.

Sam ground his teeth to stop from lashing out. He wasn't the one at fault, as Jeff seemed to imply. If the damn fool had stayed home and taken care of himself, Kelly wouldn't have been here now.

Kelly opened her eyes, blinked a couple of times, and asked, "What happened?"

"You *really* don't like snakes," Sam whispered. And, in spite of everything, he had a twinkle in his eyes.

"Ugh!" Remembering the terrible vision, she buried her face in Sam's shirt and shuddered.

He held her close and ran a soothing hand over her hair with one hand, not giving a damn what the other two thought, relishing her dependence, her touch. And he wished with all his heart that things were different. That he meant something to her. That he meant *everything* to her.

Partially recovered, Kelly became acutely aware of who was holding her, whose arms were giving comfort. If she

185

could just snuggle closer and shut out the world around them, she would. But that wasn't possible, not in the midst of the jungle with miles to go before they reached safety. Still, the horrible facts didn't stop her from wanting to any less. It was the first time Sam had touched her in hours, and it made her realize just how much she'd hungered for the contact. She deeply regretted that he'd turned into someone she barely recognized, but there was nothing she could do about it now. Some mistakes couldn't be rectified. She couldn't go back to the time before they'd made love. And, deep down, she didn't want to. At least she had those memories to cherish.

But now there were others to think of—Jeff and Zayed. Pulling her face away from the comfort of Sam's chest, she turned to search for her brother and found him beside her, worry etched in every line on his face. She took an unstable breath and said, "I'm all right, Jeff. It was just the snake and the nasty way it wrapped itself around Zayed."

Sam didn't miss the fact that the first thing out of Kelly's mouth was reassurance for Jeff. And not a word to him, of course, even though she was still being held tightly in his arms. Hell, no, he was just the hired help.

Disappointment made his voice sound tight. "Can you stand on your own?"

"Sure, I'm okay. Well . . . maybe a little wobbly."

Kelly looked over at the wiry native and concern crossed her face. "Is Zayed badly injured? Can he walk?" The questions drained her, and she looked back at Sam as if pleading for reassurance.

The fact that Sam was fast becoming the only able-bodied person in the group wasn't lost on him. "He's not seriously injured, but I can guarantee he'll have major bruises."

Sam started back to the seated man. *And I sure as hell hope he can walk,* he thought. "How you doing?"

"If you would help me stand, we can once more be on our way," Zayed murmured.

Sam complied, but watched anxiously as the injured man took a few slow, unsteady steps. *Hell!* "I think maybe we better get you up into a tree while I take the others to the boat. After I get them safely aboard, I can come back for you."

"No, no, please, I can walk." Sudden panic deepened Zayed's voice. "Do not leave me behind. I beg you."

Leaving Zayed behind was the last thing Sam wanted to do. Another trek into the jungle later in the day would be asking for trouble, but there was no way he could carry two men.

"Look, my friend. In your condition, I don't think you can make it all the way to the shore. Let me go ahead with the others, then come back for you."

"Please . . . let me go with you. I hurt, but I will not slow you down . . . not that much. Please."

Sam gauged their chances of getting safely to the boat with two injured men, and he didn't like the odds. Still, he felt he had to give Zayed at least a shot at keeping up.

"We'll try it." He glanced at Kelly. "But the lady's safety comes first, so we may have to reconsider down the line. Are you sure you don't want to stay here for a few hours of recovery time?"

"I am most sure," Zayed stated flatly. He straightened his shoulders with a grimace and turned toward the shore.

"Okay," Sam said. "I'll give you a head start while I get Jeff situated."

"Thank you."

Zayed's first steps down the trail appeared stiff and painful, confirming Sam's concern, but he decided to give the man a chance to keep up, so he didn't let his reaction show.

"You ready to go?" He advanced on Kelly.

She nodded. "Is he going to be all right?" She flicked a worried gaze toward Zayed, then back to Sam.

He shrugged. "Wish I knew. But we've got to give him the opportunity to try to make it on his own." He turned to Jeff. "You ready?"

"Absolutely."

The word was uttered firmly. Jeff had to know their position had been dangerously compromised by Zayed's injury. Perhaps he thought to reassure both Kelly and Sam, for he seemed more alert now, in less pain.

Sam hoisted Jeff into position and gestured for Kelly to lead the way. "Let's move out. Keep a sharp lookout."

Kelly hadn't the strength to argue. Her legs were still feeling like limp pasta, but even so, when she neared the spot where Sam had discarded the snake, they seemed to firm up, helping her move faster. It wasn't long before she caught sight of Zayed. He, too, seemed to be moving with more fluidity, which brought Kelly a sense of relief. She didn't want anything to happen to Zayed and she certainly didn't want Sam to make another trip back into the jungle to retrieve him. It didn't seem to matter that he'd turned as cold as an Arctic wind, because she cared more than she could bear to think about.

She realized full well why Sam had turned cold. He'd sated himself in her body and no longer lusted after her. Which, unhappily, proved she'd been right all along. Things had turned out exactly as she'd feared. Still, a part of her wanted to deny that he'd actually turned from blazing hot to solid ice so quickly. After one night! It boggled her mind.

Unfortunately, as was the case in most lopsided love-affairs, their night of lovemaking had caused a reaction directly the opposite for Kelly. She still wanted him. Desperately. His slightest touch still ignited her, making the coldness all the more devastating.

I love him—that's the God's awful truth.

Well, I'll get over him.

If only I could believe that. . . .

Her scrambled thoughts were interrupted by Sam's ragged voice behind her. "Hold up. I think Jeff's passed out again."

Zayed and Kelly turned as one. But as Zayed sat down gratefully, Kelly rushed to Jeff's side. "Let me help you with him." She eased Jeff's head to the ground as Sam lowered him.

"He's out," Sam grunted. He lifted one of Jeff's eyelids. Unclipping his canteen, he sprinkled water over Jeff's lips and face while Kelly held his head upright.

"It's too much for him," she said. "If we just had pain pills, something to ease the agony."

"There's a medical kit on the boat, but nothing out here. I just didn't think to bring anything along, so the sooner we get him back the better," Sam responded.

"I can't stand it. I just can't bear to see him suffering this way," she whispered.

Sam ached for the injured man, too, but he had to stay strong for Jeff's sake, as well as Kelly's. "You're gonna have to bear it and so is he," Sam said, his voice gruff.

How could I have ever believed I loved this ruthless man, Kelly wondered, as Sam's seemingly uncaring response pierced a stab of pain through her heart.

Jeff's eyes slowly opened and took in the faces of the two people hovering over him. "Damn. Did it to you again, huh?"

"Yeah," Sam said, his voice grave from fatigue, worry, and loss.

"It's all right, Jeff. Take your time. We'll wait until you're rested," Kelly assured her brother. "We all needed a rest anyway." She shot Sam a furious look, daring him to contradict her.

His back teeth clenched. "Sorry, we don't have the luxury of waiting around until we're all nice and rested."

"How can you be so unfeeling?" she blurted. "I want to stay right here until Jeff's up to moving."

"I have no interest whatsoever in what you want or *think* you want at the moment," Sam said, his words stinging like a whip. "I'm going to go about getting us back to the boat in one piece, the best way I know how."

Kelly stood, backed away from Jeff, and gaped at Sam. She couldn't possibly love this man. She didn't even know him.

I know him. This is the uncouth lout from the bar in Kalgola. Remember?

She closed her eyes for the briefest of moments and experienced a flash of memory—the two of them making love during the long velvety night. When she opened her eyes again, she wanted to sob with regret.

Sam had Jeff over his shoulder and Zayed was on his feet. "Let's move out," Sam growled.

Wordlessly, Kelly followed Zayed, but her world had turned dark and chaotic. Not too surprisingly, it took her several minutes to realize the jungle actually had turned darker and more forbidding during the time they'd been resting. Gazing up, she found she couldn't distinguish the sky through the canopy of trees, and she wondered, dully, if they were in for another shower.

Earlier Sam had noted the subtle change in the air. He worried, not about a light rain, but about the monsoon-like downpours that could flatten the jungle's ground vegetation, effectively wiping out visible signs of the trail they'd followed into the interior. If that happened, he knew they'd be in deeper trouble. As if they didn't have enough to contend with already.

He hadn't vocalized his fears because he didn't want to give Kelly more to fret over, even when he knew he'd probably pay for his reticence later. But hell, she hated him now anyway, so what did it matter?

Damnation, it compressed his guts to see her look at him with open condemnation and deep-seated regret. It constricted his heart even more to realize the regret was for the intimate night they'd shared just hours before.

He should have known better. He had suspected all along that there was no way he'd get more than he'd already gotten. Knew he was damn lucky to have had that. But hell, he wanted to believe. Wanted her too much to think. Too much to do anything but take what she offered. And what she offered had been everything—everything he'd ever dreamed of having.

Now *all* he'd have to do for the rest of his life was forget. Forget how it had felt to touch her intimately. To hold her. To feel himself deep inside of her. To have her with him whatever the circumstances.

Sam knew damn well a roughneck, hired hand could never hope to win a fair lady, no matter how much wealth he accumulated. He'd never be suave, or be considered a gentleman. He was just too damn rough around the edges. He'd had to fight for everything he owned.

He had grown up dirt poor. His childhood taught him that nothing was permanent. His father could never hold a job for long, so the family had grown used to being evicted from their home every few months. Moving wasn't a problem because they'd just rent a house a couple of blocks away. And the kids—there were four, three older brothers and Sam—would carry the furniture from one dump to the next.

Then there was the parade of cars. Always a different car. They'd have one for a few months, and then one morning they'd come out and it would have vanished. But they never called the cops because they knew the vehicle's fate. The car had been repossessed. Dad would make the initial down payment and keep the car as long as he could without paying monthly payments. Then, *poof,* one day the car would be gone and they'd be walking again. Until the next time.

Sam had also learned to fend for himself early on. He'd worked his way through college, saved his money after graduating, and finally opened a construction business. The company flourished, making Sam a wealthy man, but he never forgot where he came from. And he knew, damn well, he'd never be considered a gentleman. Like Jeff.

Chapter Twelve

The rain hit hard. It came down in drenching, windswept sheets.

Shoved violently around by the punishing gale, the jungle's foliage lashed them unmercifully. The worst part of it wasn't that they were immediately soaked to the skin. No, the worst was the noise itself. Deafening in its intensity, it drowned out any and all jungle sounds. A nightmarish experience for the four people being pummeled from all sides.

They couldn't even hear each other when they yelled from a few feet away. Sam had to grab Kelly by the shoulder before he could capture her attention. In turn, that was how she stopped Zayed.

Sam gestured for them to follow as he plowed his way through a stand of bamboo to another large mangrove tree a dozen yards off the trail. Escaping most of the pounding rain, he unburdened himself, making Jeff as comfortable as possible by bracing his back against the tree trunk.

"You okay?" Sam asked Jeff, shouting over the torrential downpour.

Jeff nodded, too spent to speak. Then he leaned his head against the mangrove, and after giving Kelly a half-hearted smile, closed his eyes. Zayed, already seated next to Jeff, followed suit.

Sam helped Kelly out of her pack and positioned her, without words, on the other side of Jeff. Then, rifle over his shoulder, machete in hand, he worked his way slowly around the tree, thrashing the jungle down a foot or two all the way around. It wasn't much, but they'd have a little warning if a tiger sought the same shelter. Then, nearly exhausted himself, Sam sat next to Kelly and rested his head against the tree for a few blissful seconds.

When he opened his eyes again, the dense rain, a foot or two from the sheltering tree, resembled a waterfall of staggering proportions.

There was nothing for them to do but to wait out the worst of the storm. The hell of it was, the large trees in the jungle, theirs included, were the preferred sanctuary for most, if not all, of the animals.

The downpour continued unabated for fifteen long minutes.

For one tense moment, early on, Sam thought they were going to be attacked as a presence began to emerge from the waterfall at the edge of the tree directly in front of them.

He raised the rifle, then lowered it, as a painted stork waddled into the shelter of the tree. The stork hunkered down almost immediately, its neck disappearing as it ruffled feathers protectively around its head.

"Looks as if birds hate to have their necks wet, too," Kelly shouted.

Sam barely nodded. Any other time he'd have appreciated Kelly's comment—at least she was talking to him—but he had a lot to occupy his mind. Getting them safely back to the boat was foremost. And then there was last night, when the intimacy had been complete and so satisfying he'd held the hope that it would overcome any other obstacles to their union for the long haul.

The thought of marriage hadn't even been a bleep on his horizon. Until last night. Then, it had begun to consume him. During the night, while she slept, he had tried to decide how best to go about raising the subject. How he could convince her it was the right thing. The only thing.

And then, the world had given him another slap in the face.

When daylight arrived, everything changed. Kelly cringed when he touched her, proving just how wrong a guy could be. Reminding him that he was no more than the hired help. Someone she'd dump as soon as she got her precious brother to safety. Shattering his dreams.

Rescuing her brother was all she was interested in—come hell or high water, earthquake or Sam Tanner. And fool that he was, he'd done the job for her, at risk to himself and Pele. He'd handed Jeff to her on a silver platter. And was still idiot enough to break his back carrying the guy to safety. *All for her!*

Well, hell, he'd learned a long time ago that life wasn't fair. But it still tore at his heart to think he'd finally found the one woman he'd give his life for and then discovered she'd just been using him.

Suddenly, the rain ceased the same way it had begun, with startling abruptness. One moment it was roaring loudly, the next it was over. And the jungle was so silent you could hear individual drops of rainwater falling from the trees onto broad leaves or muddy puddles here and there. Slowly, the inhabitants came to life as well, the normal chirps and chatters returning. The stork hobbled up awkwardly and gave the four humans a bright-eyed glance. On its spindly legs, it moved into the dense surroundings and vanished in seconds.

"I've never seen anything like that," Kelly said, shaking her head in wonder. "Does it rain like that very often?" she asked Sam.

He'd already risen and begun to ready himself for the trek ahead. "I haven't been here that long," he answered, sounding distant. "Zayed? Ms. Griffin would like to know if it rains like that often out here."

Ms. Griffin? Kelly felt as if she'd been sucked into a black hole. Certainly the world as she thought she knew it was no more. Although she hadn't expected a commitment from Sam, she'd expected *something*. Warmth, an acknowledgment, or maybe even a thank you for the intimacy. But no, it was business as usual, only colder.

From the moment they'd met, she knew he wanted her. She couldn't help but see the hunger in his every glance. And now there was nothing. The horrible fact was, he didn't even glance her way. He seemed intent on avoiding all eye contact.

Was he afraid she'd demand something of him? They hadn't used protection. Was that what he was afraid of? That he'd gotten her pregnant? If so, would he vehemently deny they'd even been together? Was he one of *those* men? A man who avoided responsibility at every turn? Probably. Early on she'd figured him for a loner. A man who didn't believe in commitment.

So why had she fallen under his spell and given herself to him? *Given myself?* Hah! She'd thrown herself at him. And he'd taken everything she had. But he'd given, too, she reminded herself. She thought of all the intimate ways he'd aroused her. It made her blush when she remembered how he'd buried his mouth hotly in the triangle of curls between her thighs and driven her mad with desire. It embarrassed her to remember how she'd begged him to take her shortly thereafter.

Humiliated by her memories and Sam's continued coolness, she stood up and shouldered her pack. The sooner they got back to the boat, the quicker she could distance herself and avoid more emotional injury.

For the rest of the trek, Kelly concentrated on Jeff and his welfare. Whenever possible, she ignored Sam.

Following the trail wasn't easy now, for all the low-lying vegetation had more or less been beaten flat by the punishing downpour. There was nothing to do now but let Sam lead and Zayed follow up the rear, with Kelly holding down the middle position. That placement was fine with her because she could keep a close eye on Jeff and be out of Sam's view. *Apparently, I'm already out of mind,* she thought, feeling dull and stupid.

"See any sign of tigers?" Jeff managed to ask Kelly.

"No, but I feel they're always there . . . just out of sight. What do you think?"

"I think they're damned elusive, until they decide to attack."

"I think you two should save your breath and strength." Sam's voice had taken on a rough edge that put an end to the conversation between brother and sister.

Finally, after several more tense rest stops, they burst through the edge of a particularly dense stand of shrubbery and stepped out of the jungle into mud. Mud filled with strange looking fish that seemed to be slithering through the muck.

Stepping to avoid them, Kelly said, "Are they stuck?"

Zayed shook his head. "Not stuck, no. They are mudskippers. See how they wiggle their way toward the water?"

"Boy, I wish we could skip over the darn stuff." Just then, she sank into the mud up to her ankle and cringed, almost afraid to move on. Pulling her foot out, she found solid ground again.

Sam glanced back in time to observe her struggle. "Stay right there until I load Jeff into the dinghy."

The last thing Kelly wanted to do was ask Sam for help. As soon as he turned his attention away, she took another tentative step.

The dinghy was right where they'd left it. And when she looked up at the cruiser, Pele was visible, waving wildly, so excited to see them that he nearly took a header over the side.

Sam loaded Jeff and swung around to go back for Kelly, but she'd nearly reached him. Scowling at her, he snapped, "Some people just like to ask for trouble."

When she opened her mouth to protest, he said, "Zayed, you row Jeff over to the boat, then come back for Kelly."

Sam would have liked to get Kelly safely aboard first, but knowing she'd object because of Jeff's injury, he didn't bother to try. There seemed no point in wasting his breath, not when they were all on the edge of exhaustion. Besides, he felt confident he could protect her at the water's edge. If they were attacked and he couldn't scare a predator off with gunfire, he'd kill their attacker without hesitation to save her life. But, damn, could she ever piss him off.

With the dinghy shoved off, Sam swiveled around to keep watch for any danger that might be lurking behind them.

Once Jeff was safely on board the cruiser, Pele, seeing the bruises on Zayed, handed him the rifle and quickly returned in the dinghy for Kelly. As Sam pushed them off, he and Kelly's eyes met for a heartbeat and then skidded away, each fearing what they'd see. Yet by the time the dinghy had made it halfway to the boat, Sam had noted a hint of concern in her expression, and he believed it was for him. She might not love him, but she cared what happened to him. It was small comfort, but far better than the hate he feared she might feel because of a night in which passion had been allowed to rule. He understood why she might blame him for exploiting her vulnerability. But still, he wondered why she had responded so hotly. Because the sex had been hotter and heavier than anything he'd ever experienced?

Or had she just been out of her head with fear?

Can fear do that to a woman?

He didn't want to believe that was possible.

She loved it, dammit!

And she was as far from a slut as you could get.

So why *did* it happen?

In spite of everything, the bigger question in his mind was: could he make it happen again?

Because he had to try. He could *not* let her walk away from him without a fight. No matter what kind of heel that made him.

Far from hating Sam, Kelly was terrified by the fact that she had to leave him alone on the island. The journey to the cruiser seemed to take forever and Pele's trip back took even longer. Only when Sam and Pele were both on their way back in the dinghy, did she feel some small sense of relief. No matter what Sam's feelings were for her, hers were loving, and she could not bear it if anything happened to him. Especially not on her account. She'd only feel guilt-free after they parted company in Kalgola. Then, what she'd feel would be pain. The pain of shattering loss.

She stood by the railing, watching until the dinghy hit the side of the boat, and then, breathing a sigh of relief, she escaped to the cabin where Pele had placed Jeff. She cleaned him up as well as she could, without jarring his injured leg, and gave him pain pills and an antibiotic she found in the medicine kit. After taking his temperature, she encouraged him to rest. There was nothing else she could do. Unless it was to pray for his recovery, which she did. It was only when she heard the engines fire and felt the motion as the cruiser got underway that she realized Jeff had dozed off. Only then, did she leave him to go to her own cabin.

After a shower and a change of clothes, she returned to check on her brother. Finding him sleeping, she ventured into the galley, allowing her nose to lead the way.

Pele, busy manning the stove, acknowledged her with a nod and a wave.

"What *is* that wonderful smell?" she asked.

Pele gave her his impish grin. "That Pele's special soup. You sit. I get you some."

In seconds he placed a steaming bowl of soup in front of her. "You eat. Make you strong."

It didn't take more urging. With every spoonful of the nourishing fare, Kelly did feel stronger. When she'd first arrived in the galley, overcome by fatigue, her stomach growling, she wasn't certain she was strong enough to eat.

"Biscuit?" Pele waved a plateful of tempting baking powder biscuits under her nose.

"Oh, yes. Thank you." She snatched two and coated them liberally with butter, then closed her eyes in contentment as she inhaled the first one. "Ummm, that's so good."

"Missy like?" Pele sounded pleased by the idea.

"Missy love. Pele, you are a wonderful cook."

The little man nodded. "Yes, wonderful." Grinning, he settled onto the bench across from her.

When he ventured to speak again, however, the grin was not evident. "You see tigers . . . yes?"

Kelly sent him a big-eyed look. "Two. And you won't believe how close they were. So close I could have reached out and touched one." She shook her head. "They're just awesome."

"Awesome?" His small face puckered. "That mean good?"

"Yes . . . I guess it does." She nodded. "And bad, too. They're just so beautiful and dangerous, all at the same time."

Inadvertently, she thought of Sam. To her, he was beautiful. Dangerous, as well. She'd given him her heart and he'd broken it. And now she'd have to go on and make a life for herself without him. That task felt daunting at the moment, but maybe after they parted company it wouldn't be as terrible as she anticipated.

Sam stayed at the helm for hours, avoiding Kelly and ignoring his mounting fatigue, as he guided the boat safely back toward the small devastated town. He wouldn't be able to dock the cruiser where he'd tied it up earlier, but would have to take it directly to the dock in the village in order to get Jeff safely onto shore.

Then, abruptly, before he realized the lateness of the hour, the sun set. Total darkness swiftly followed. They wouldn't reach their destination that night. The water was too dangerous to navigate in the gloom.

Concerned that Jeff would have to spend another night without good medical care, Sam reluctantly dropped anchor in a small inlet and went below. Pele had carried soup and biscuits to him earlier, when he was at the wheel, so now all he wanted was a snack before hitting the sack.

"I had a long nap," Zayed said, greeting him in the galley, "so I can stand watch for a few hours, if that is good for you?"

"More than good. I appreciate it, Zayed. I'm really beat." He glanced around. "Where's everyone else?"

"Jeff, he sleep. Kelly and Pele, too, I think."

"Are you sure you're up to standing watch?" Sam asked. "You must be sore as hell from the snake."

"I am most certainly sore, but I will be okay." He sent Sam a reassuring smile.

Sam ran a hand wearily across his eyes. "Okay, then, but call me or Pele when you get tired."

"You can be sure of that, sahib."

On the way to his cabin, Sam passed Kelly's door. Hesitating for a few moments, he forced himself to move on.

When he reached his cabin, he hit the bed and was sleeping soundly within seconds.

Zayed took one of the rifles with him on deck and for the first hour or two made regular painful sojourns around the cruiser, checking for anything that might pose a threat. But the water stayed calm, the night quiet, and he made fewer trips. Ultimately, he gave up walking his watch in favor of a deck chair aft. Finally, thanks to the gentle, lulling rocking motion of the cruiser and his less than excellent physical shape, sleep overtook him.

The last of the rain clouds high above disappeared, allowing the full moon to rise into a clear night sky, one displaying a multitude of touchable-appearing, bright, twinkling stars.

Perhaps it was the moonlight shining in through her porthole, or a bad dream, but Kelly woke with a start. Opening her eyes almost fearfully, she half expected something to jump out of the stateroom shadows and attack. Slowly swiveling her head, she took in the small cabin's every detail. Nothing moved.

The cruiser continued to rock silently.

It should have felt peaceful, lulling, but, for some inexplicable reason it didn't. She felt uneasy—threatened.

She rose to her feet and padded to the porthole. Silver moonbeams caressed the water. Still, she felt strangely on edge and restless. Realizing, regretfully, that she'd never get back to sleep while harboring such feelings, she turned from the porthole.

"Maybe I'm hungry."

She had gone to bed wearing one of Sam's shirts. It swallowed her, covering her to her calves. Knowing she'd appear decently clad, even with nothing under the shirt, even if she ran into anyone, which seemed unlikely in the dead of night, she left the cabin.

After making her way to the galley, she searched the refrigerator and found a small bowl of Pele's leftover soup. Delighted, she popped the bowl into the microwave oven and set the timer for four minutes. But even the prospect of the tasty soup couldn't keep a chill from creeping down her spine.

Uncertain why she felt so unsettled, she wondered if Sam was standing watch. Since she had time to check before the soup heated, she decided to go on deck and ask if he wanted something to eat. She might even offer to share the soup. Of course, she'd have to see him to ask and that might be a problem for both of them.

Is that what's bugging me? she wondered. *The fear of what I'll see in his eyes?*

Certainly that's a possibility.

Oh, hell . . . don't be such a wimp.

Defiantly, she marched out of the galley, though the lounge to the ladder, and was halfway up the ladder when she felt the boat rock.

Seconds earlier, the view from her porthole had displayed a river of shimmering water with a surface flat as glass.

Could the wind have come up suddenly? she wondered. *Or have we been boarded?*

The hairs on her neck did a slow dance upward. She'd noticed a rifle in the lounge when she passed, but there were only four more steps to the deck. Kelly decided to take a look outside before she leapt to an erroneous conclusion. Sam could have boarded after an early morning swim. It seemed likely he'd enjoy the exertion of a brisk swim, even in dangerous waters.

Are there crocodiles? she wondered. *Or deadly snakes?*

Probably snakes. They'd sure been plentiful in the jungle.

She thought of the green tree snake Sam had saved her from. Remembered how it felt to be held in his arms. And would never forget how she'd lost herself in his devastating kisses.

She *really* needed to talk to him, to clear the air, even if it meant irritating the man.

Two steps from the deck, Kelly's head cleared enough for her to be able to gaze out into the night. At that exact moment, a terrible shriek of fear and agony rent the humid night air, filling her with blood-chilling dread.

Sam?

Almost immediately the tail, then hindquarters of an enormous tiger moved across her field of vision, not four feet away, followed by the rest of the awesome animal. He had Zayed by one leg, tightly clamped between his teeth, dragging him relentlessly along. As he passed Kelly, the tiger locked gazes with her for a terrifying split second, in which it crossed her mind that he might decide to change the menu. Then he continued to the rail, with Zayed struggling and screaming for his life.

Kelly's pulse raced. Her blood ran cold.

When her muscles recovered from frozen shock, she knew she had to act quickly. Diving back down the ladder, she dashed for the rifle. She felt wicked as she thanked God that it wasn't Sam caught in the tiger's clutches. She scrambled back onto the deck. Quickly loading a shell into the chamber, she aimed and fired at the tiger just as he went over the side, Zayed in tow, still screaming in terror and pain.

"It's too late!" Her mind reeled. Her heartbeat escalated to warp speed.

Do something!

Breathless, she reached the side of the cruiser just as the tiger and Zayed resurfaced, still connected. Panicked—it might already be too late to save Zayed—she commenced firing over the tiger's head, pain from the rifle's recoil repeatedly jarring her shoulder. She aimed high, not wanting to risk coming too close to the tiger for fear she'd hit Zayed. The tiger was much smaller in the water, where only its head and shoulders appeared above the surface.

For whatever reason, the earsplitting gunshots or Zayed's desperate struggles, the tiger relinquished its hold and made for the shore, minus his reluctant, now floundering meal.

The rifle was suddenly wrenched from Kelly's grasp by Sam, who took in the scene in a split second, then abruptly handed the weapon back. Before she could speak, he dove over the side and she watched as he swam to Zayed and started to haul him back to the ladder.

Please don't let the tiger change his mind and come back. Don't let him get Sam, Kelly prayed.

By the time Sam reached the ladder, Kelly was white as fresh untrammeled snow and rigid with fear. Pele had to gently move her aside to help Sam get Zayed on board.

Once on board, Sam slipped off his belt and used it as a tourniquet to stop the bleeding from a leg full of deep tooth punctures. Even though he worked quickly, the deck turned slick with the injured man's blood.

"Pele, help me get him below," Sam urged. "Kelly, you go down first." He hadn't had time to notice her condition. He just knew he didn't want her on deck in case the hungry predator changed its mind and returned to try its luck again. The big cats were persistent. And deadly.

Sam and Pele carried Zayed into Sam's cabin and worked over him until they were satisfied the blood had begun to coagulate. Then they bandaged the leg carefully, after padding it with thick layers of gauze. Kelly held Zayed's head up while he downed a couple of the pain pills she'd been doling out to Jeff. Then Sam gave Zayed a precautionary shot of antibiotics.

"That's all we can do for you tonight, my friend. Try to get some rest. As soon as it's light we'll get you to a doctor," Sam assured him.

Zayed gazed gratefully up at Sam. "You saved me from the tiger. I do not know how to thank you. I will be happy to be your humble servant for as long as I shall be fortunate enough to live."

Sam shook his head. "I just pulled you out of the water. You have Kelly here to thank." He pulled her forward. "She saw what was happening, got the rifle, and scared the hell out of that damn cat by firing at him."

Kelly blushed. Praise from Sam was a heady thing.

Zayed stared at her in wonder. "It was you who saved me, Missy?"

She shrugged. "I just fired the rifle because I didn't know what else to do. I didn't even come close to hitting the tiger, but maybe the idea of a woman with a firearm terrified him." She grinned. With Sam standing right beside her, observing, Kelly wasn't about to admit that she'd been frightened out of her wits and had acted on nothing more than instinct.

"Then I will forever be in your debt, Missy, and will be *your* humble servant if you will allow me to do so."

"Thank you, Zayed. I appreciate your offer, but you see, I don't need a servant. I live very quietly in a small apartment in Los Angeles."

"If I can ever do anything for you . . . you need only ask," Zayed persisted.

"Don't worry. If I need you, I will call on you immediately," Kelly replied, sounding solemn, giving Zayed's offer the respect it deserved.

"Try to rest," Sam advised. "We'll check on you often, but the best thing you can do is get some healing sleep."

Zayed nodded. "I am very tired, sahib."

When the others were back in the lounge, Kelly vocalized her worries. "He lost a lot of blood. Do you think he'll really be all right?"

Appearing just as concerned, Sam shook his head. "It isn't the blood loss that will get him. He can recover from that in time. It's infection we have to worry about."

"You gave him a shot of antibiotics," Kelly reminded Sam.

"That doesn't mean it will keep him from developing some damn deadly infection. There's no medication that will kill all germs, especially in an area teeming with insects the way this one does."

"Are you saying that applies to Jeff, as well?" Kelly turned paler at the thought.

"We need to get them both to a doctor as soon as possible. A hospital would be even better. There's one in Calcutta, if it's still standing after the earthquake."

Kelly sank into an overstuffed swivel chair and lowered her head to her hands. "If we're careful, couldn't we travel tonight?"

"There's no way to be careful enough. We hit a floating log and put a hole in the hull and we'll all be in trouble." He glanced at his watch. "It'll be light in a couple of hours. Go back to bed and get some sleep. We might need you later."

Kelly wanted to hear loving words and feel tenderly cared for. But Sam's orders were issued in the same vein as those he'd given to Jeff earlier and Zayed moments ago. The words contained sound advice, but were devoid of any real feelings. It was as if he'd completely forgotten their night of love.

To him it wasn't love, she reminded herself. It was sex.

Get that through your thick skull and you'll see things the way they really are.

No matter how much it pained her to admit it, how deeply

it cut to acknowledge the truth, she gave up on Sam right there and then. If she'd entertained the idea of him belonging to her earlier, hoping it would come true, it hadn't changed anything. It was past time to move on. Any delay in accepting the truth and she might spill her guts and humiliate herself. Not to mention embarrass Sam. Because he wasn't a bad man, he just wasn't a man looking to settle down anytime soon. Certainly not with her.

Forcing herself to rise, she made her way back to her cabin, closed the door, and crawled into bed. And even though it was still hot, she pulled the covers over her body for comfort. Surprisingly, she escaped into sleep rather quickly.

Sam wiped the sweat from his forehead, and tried to relax muscles that were tensed to the max. He knew he couldn't blame Kelly for her appearance. It was obvious she'd jumped out of bed, without a thought to what she had on when she went to help Zayed. But *he* knew. Dammit, did he ever.

She had nothing on under that shirt.

He could have pulled her into his arms and had her naked in a second. Could have been inside her in even less time. That knowledge had him hard as a spike and aching for relief. Never mind that now wasn't the time. His body just flat didn't give a damn.

For a minute or two he let his imagination run wild. He'd get her somewhere alone and screw her brains out until she forgot who he was. Until he convinced her to marry him and he got her name on the dotted line. Then he'd have time to show her he could be everything she needed. And then some.

Sam had a hell of a time forcing himself to walk in the opposite direction, away from Kelly's cabin, to climb the ladder and go on deck to relieve Pele.

"See any sign of him?" Sam whispered, meaning the tiger.

"No." Pele's teeth flashed white in the dark. "Missy run him off good."

"That she did," Sam agreed, sharing a grin.

"She not afraid," Pele marveled.

"Probably 'cause she's got the heart of a tiger," Sam muttered.

Pele cut Sam a look out of the side of his eye. "Man can conquer woman . . . just needs courage."

Sam blew out a breath. "I wish it were that simple."

"Some women not easy, but they worth more." Pele nodded sagely.

"Can't argue with that one," Sam agreed. "You have a woman of your own?"

Pele shook his head. "No. But there is one I want and when we get back I going to tell her."

"She doesn't know?"

The little man laughed self-consciously. "I always afraid to tell her before."

"But now you're not afraid?"

"This trip show me life is short. *Now* I tell her."

"Damn good idea," Sam agreed.

They sat in silence each presumably with his own thoughts. Finally Sam said, "You better go below and get some rest. I'll stand watch the rest of the night."

Like a small spirit, Pele disappeared below, leaving Sam to watch for tigers and worry about what he'd do with the rest of *his* life.

Chapter Thirteen

When Sam lifted anchor, dawn was a crack of light through the porthole.

For a few tense moments, Kelly couldn't decide what woke her. Then she acknowledged motion as the cruiser cut through the water. She heard the hum of the engines. They were on the move.

Still exhausted, she hadn't the will to pull herself out of the bunk. In seconds, she fell back asleep. An hour later, when they tied up at the dock in Kalgola, the silence woke her once again. And this time she pried herself out of the bunk, showered, dressed, and made her way to Jeff's cabin to check on his progress.

"You're awake." She smiled and placed a gentle hand on his forehead. He heated her hand and the smile vanished. "How do you feel?"

"Better than I have any right to expect." He returned a faint smile. "How are you? Pele told me about your confrontation with the tiger."

Kelly shivered and shook her head. "I surprised myself. I was trying to scare him off, not kill him, and I'll tell you, it was just dumb luck I didn't hit Zayed in the process."

"I think you're being far too modest." Jeff took her hand in both of his.

Before Kelly could reply, Sam stepped into the cabin. "We need to talk." He eyed Kelly coolly. "How's your patient this morning?"

"I think he has a fever," she responded, worried abut Jeff and wishing her temperature didn't soar every time Sam came near. She wondered why he thought he had to sound so cold and distant. Didn't he know she'd already gotten the message that he wanted nothing more to do with her?

"That's not good." Sam sounded distracted. "Zayed's looking better, though. I sent Pele into the village to see what medical help is available. We spotted a Red Cross flag flying over a building in the center of town. With any kind of luck we can get help there."

"We're docked close to town?" Kelly lifted an inquiring eyebrow. Hadn't Sam told her he didn't dock close to town so he'd avoid possible trouble?

"There was no other choice, not with two injured men aboard." He headed for the door. "I need to get back up on deck. We'll talk more when Pele returns."

Kelly watched Sam leave, sighed, and turned back to her brother. He was watching her with a sympathetic expression.

His voice soft, he asked, "You're hooked big time, aren't you?"

Kelly shook her head, trying to deny the depth of her feelings. "He's way too difficult."

"You avoided my question," Jeff gently chided her.

Her lashes fluttered down over her eyes, and this time the sigh came from her toes. "Yes . . . I'm hooked. Really big time."

"I thought as much. So come clean, what's the problem?"

She inspected her tennis shoe tops.

"Kelly?"

Her head came up, exposing pink cheeks. "I think it's a

case of . . . I think once he's acquired something, it's no longer desirable."

It took Jeff a moment to register what he'd just heard, and then he cursed low in his throat. "That bastard!"

"He saved your life, you know," Kelly reminded her brother, her voice dropping an octave.

"Maybe you should have left me out there."

Jeff rubbed his unshaven cheeks, obviously fretting over his weakness at a time when he'd like to be able to help her. Kelly knew that he would beat Sam to a pulp, if that's what it took to protect her.

"Never! I'd never leave you out there!" Kelly bent down and gave Jeff a hug. "You're more precious to me than anything in this world."

It was Jeff's turn to shake his head. "Maybe to you, sweetheart, but I have a lot to make up for. I lost men out there, men who died because I wanted to make a film. It sounds damned trivial now . . . nobody should lose their life over the production of a TV show."

Her brother's despondency made Kelly realize, in comparison, how small her own problems really were. Sam didn't love her, but she could go on with her life. The lost men where gone forever.

"We'll try to find out what happened to them. See that the families are compensated as much as that's possible," she promised, wanting to ease his conscience.

"How can you replace a son or husband?" Jeff asked morosely, plucking idly at the sheet that covered his broken leg.

"You can't, but that doesn't mean we can't do something to help out. Right now, though. . . ."

The cabin door opened after a quick tap. This time it was Pele who entered. Behind him was a small, whip-thin man, wearing wire-framed glasses and dressed in surgical-green.

The man entered with a black bag in his hand. He introduced himself as Dr. Maratoc.

Pele eased back out of the room as the French-accented doctor took charge of the patient, displaying an air of competence that reassured both Kelly and her injured brother.

"Let's have a look at you, young man." Dr. Maratoc slipped a thermometer from a plastic case, inserted it under Jeff's tongue, then took his patient's pulse. "A bit too rapid." He withdrew the thermometer and studied the mercury reading. "High. Not a good sign. Let's have a look at that leg." He eased the sheet down and began to unwrap the dressing around the injured limb. When he had the dressing completely off, he began probing the leg with a gloved hand, testing for swelling and checking for infection. Finally, he wrapped the leg with fresh bandages and sat on a chair beside the bed.

"You must go directly to the hospital in Calcutta. There they can x-ray the leg and see what has to be done. Our arrangements here are far too primitive. You will need surgery and perhaps need to be airlifted to yet another hospital to save that leg."

Kelly paled. "How bad is it?"

"He has gangrene. I will give him an antibiotic shot, but he needs surgery."

Blinking rapidly, she asked, "What about Zayed? How is he?"

"We can treat Zayed here. Since that is his wish, he is being taken to the camp hospital in town, even as we speak. The antibiotics you administered have already started working and we'll see that the dose is continued." He smiled at Kelly. "You're a good nurse, young lady."

"Oh, it . . . it wasn't me. Sam Tanner, the captain, was the one who knew what to do."

"Well, the antibiotic was the ticket. If Zayed's luck continues, he'll be getting around in a day or two. Must have been one *big* tiger, though, from the tooth marks."

Kelly's mind jumped back to the horrifying scene of the night before, the huge beast with Zayed's leg clamped tightly in its mouth. She nodded. "Yes, big."

The doctor rummaged in his medical bag and came up with a syringe and small bottle. He prepared the syringe and gave Jeff a shot in his good hip. He rummaged again and came up with a bottle of pills. Shaking a few out into an envelope, he handed the lot to Kelly. "These are excellent pain pills. I know you have some, but we don't want him to run out before you get him to Calcutta."

"Thank you, Doctor." Kelly accepted the pills, tried to smile, and failed.

Doctor Maratoc shook hands with Kelly and Jeff, wished them Godspeed, and let himself out.

Minutes later, Sam reappeared, his expression unreadable. "The Doc says you need to be taken to Calcutta, so as soon as Pele returns with supplies we'll head back. Unless you'd rather try the ferry?"

Kelly's stomach went into squeeze mode. *Did Sam want out?* Glancing at Jeff, who looked worn out from the doctor's probing and didn't appear to notice Sam's mood, she gave a slight gesture with her head toward the door.

"Excuse me for a minute, Jeff. I'll be right back."

Jeff, eyes already closed, nodded and gave a slight sigh. "Take your time. No hurry. Think I'll doze a little."

Kelly caught Sam before he could go topside. "If it isn't too much of an imposition, we'd both appreciate it if you could take us to Calcutta. The doctor said Jeff should get to the hospital as soon as possible. He has gangrene."

Sam gave a curt nod and turned to go.

Before he made it into the hallway, she hesitantly asked, "You were going to Calcutta, weren't you?"

He turned, a muscle beating rapidly, emphasizing his square jaw. "I was, yes."

Their gazes locked for a long, probing moment.

Sam ultimately broke the connection. He departed through the open door, leaving Kelly to exhale a relieved sigh. She knew, from the intensity of his stare, there was more Sam wanted to say. But she was glad he'd kept it to himself, especially in front of Jeff. Eventually, she'd have to find out exactly what was on his mind, but she hoped to put the reckoning off until they were well on their way back to Calcutta. She couldn't take a chance he would get so riled up, he'd dump them ashore at the makeshift hospital and leave without them.

After Sam left her standing alone in the narrow corridor, it didn't take Kelly long to admit the fear that Sam would dump them belonged in the category of least likely to happen. He wasn't that kind of man. He'd risked his life to rescue Jeff for *her*. If things went wrong between them personally, it hadn't made Sam any less heroic. He'd protected her, her brother, and Zayed, a virtual stranger, with his life. She was the one at fault. She'd initiated the intimacy when she should have been strong enough to resist. If she *had* resisted, there would undoubtedly have been no repercussions. Sam, she decided, was just showing normal male confusion and worry that she might try to pin him down to something he didn't want. Commitment. The dirty word most men avoided at all cost.

Pain in her shoulder had been a continuous dull ache. But until she reached her cabin, she hadn't given it any attention or thought. It was only after removing her shirt and getting a look at the large bruise developing there that she realized the injury was from the pounding she'd received from the rifle butt as she'd fired above the tiger.

"A small price to pay," she whispered. Remembering the agony in Zayed's cries, she felt extremely grateful she'd been able to help save his life. Of course, without Sam diving into dangerous waters after him, she wasn't convinced they'd have won in the battle with the tiger. In her mind's eye, she could envision the tiger seeing Zayed flounder, could envision the tiger turning back and snapping his jaws over Zayed again. And this time he'd be too weak to fight and she'd be too afraid to open fire.

Shaken, Kelly slipped the shirt back on and waited impatiently for the cruiser to leave the dock. Until that happened, she didn't want to have to deal with anything more difficult than brushing her hair.

When the boat finally backed out of its slip and turned toward Calcutta, Kelly's tensions eased.

She wasn't ready to face Sam again, however. Not yet.

Maybe she'd never be ready.

Sam's relief at having Kelly aboard was tempered by the worry over Jeff's injuries. Sam wished he was well and somewhere else right now, even though he'd done everything he could to see that Jeff was properly cared for. He'd been worried that the doctor would want to keep Jeff in Kalgola. He knew, if that had happened, Kelly wouldn't be on the cruiser now. Wherever Jeff was, she'd be. Of that Sam hadn't the slightest doubt.

If the doctor had kept Jeff, Sam would have had no reason to hang around the hospital. No excuse to stay close to Kelly. He'd have been out in the cold.

This way she was fairly well trapped on the boat, just a few feet away. Close enough to have a chance with her.

It made him feel like all kinds of a black-hearted bastard, but he wanted one last chance to convince Kelly she belonged

to him. And if that meant using every cunning wile he possessed, so be it.

The cruiser cut though the water with the grace of a swan,
leaving a wake of ruffled swells behind to wash onto the shore
with lacy bubbles.

Sam manned the wheel while Pele stood on the bow,
watching for debris large enough to damage the hull. The
earthquake had significantly added to the amount of floating
objects in the water, making it crucial they keep a sharp
watch. A floating log could pierce the hull and send them
quickly to the bottom.

They were never far from the beach on the Kalgola side,
but that isolated area wasn't conducive to spending a great
deal of time ashore, especially with an injured man aboard.
Not to speak of the tigers.

Late in the afternoon, a squall streaked out of the east and
released monsoon-like rain on everything in the vicinity, re-
ducing visibility too damn close to zero for Sam's comfort.
He was forced to drop anchor in a shallow cove to wait out the
storm.

Kelly checked on Jeff, found him sound asleep, and ventured into the galley in hopes of finding Pele. She wanted to
know why they'd stopped short of their destination.

Instead of Pele, she encountered Sam, who was busy
fixing a sandwich. Her heart rate accelerated.

"I presume we dropped anchor because of the rain." She
vividly remembered the dense rain that had drenched them
on the island; rain that had cut visibility to mere inches. Not
too long after, they'd made love in the tree.

Forget that.

How?

Don't ask me . . . I'm not in charge here.

Kelly had Sam's attention from the moment she stepped into the galley.

"Yeah," he said. "It would be suicide to try to navigate the river in a torrent like this." He raised a questioning brow. "You hungry?"

Her stomach always reacted as if she were falling great distances around Sam, so it wasn't immediately clear whether she was hungry or not. After a pause, she said, "Yes, I guess I am hungry."

"How about a ham sandwich?" He reached for the bread.

"Sounds great, but I can make my own."

He shot her a stunningly sexy smile. "Let me," he said, "I'm a wizard at ham sandwiches."

"Okay . . . sure." Seated at the tiny eating bar, she watched him slice the bread and ham, spread one side of the bread with mayonnaise, slap on the ham, and add some sliced tomatoes.

"Chips?" He held up a bag of Fritos.

"Yes, please." She realized, to her mingled surprise and disgust, she'd probably say yes to anything he suggested. *Anything* at all.

Sam shook some chips onto the plate that held her sandwich, then brought his plate along with hers to the bar. "Want a beer?" he asked.

"I'll just have coffee." Anything stronger and she'd beg him to make love to her again. Fortunately, she'd noticed the pot on the stove and still had enough strength to get up to pour a cupful. "You?"

"I've got a beer. Thanks, anyway."

An air of politeness surrounded them, isolating them from each other like a wall, and although Kelly realized he probably hadn't meant such a reaction to occur, it set her nerves on edge. The first couple of bites of her sandwich threatened to stick in her throat. Thankfully, the hot coffee saved her from choking.

Thoughts of Sam's arms around her, performing the Heimlich, weren't all bad, though. For seconds she even considered the possibilities, but finally decided it might not be all that romantic to have Sam see her spitting out pieces of partially chewed bread and ham. *Scratch that one.* A sigh she wasn't aware of sounded as if it came from her toes.

Immediately concerned, Sam's head swiveled toward her. "What is it? What's the matter?"

Kelly turned a puzzled gaze his way. "What do you mean?"

"You just gave a sigh that sounded as if your best friend died." His voice sounded tight.

She blinked, then realized how the sigh would have sounded to him. "Oh, that . . . that was nothing."

"Nothing?" He frowned at her. "Sounded like a hell of a lot more than nothing."

How could she possibly explain? How could she tell him she wanted him, while she sat here with a ham sandwich in her hand? How would it look, for heaven's sake?

Kelly placed the half-eaten sandwich on her plate and pushed the plate away. "I guess I'm not very hungry, after all."

"I think you'd better tell me what's bothering you," he muttered. "We've done everything we can for Jeff for now." His fingers tightened on his sandwich.

She shook her head. "It's not about Jeff. It's about what happened between us in the jungle."

Sam swallowed hard. "And you regret it, right?"

Her head snapped up. "Do you?"

"Now why in hell would I regret making love to the most beautiful woman I've ever met?"

219

She stared at him. "So that's all it was to you? An opportunity?"

"Shit! Did I say that?"

He looked totally frustrated. Apparently, talking about feelings wasn't his thing. She stood up, ready to flee. Then, perhaps because she was so disconcerted, her feet tangled, pitching her toward Sam.

Sam launched into action, dropping his sandwich and catching her in his arms.

Held firmly in his embrace, Kelly froze. All she could manage to do was gaze mutely up into his face. Their gazes caught and held for a slow take.

Unable to resist, Sam lowered his head until his mouth was level with hers. When she didn't try to jerk away, he stamped her mouth with a kiss that was almost chaste—for two whole seconds. By the third second her lips parted and Sam took advantage of the situation, using his tongue like a sword to destroy all resistance, even though, if he'd been of sound mind, he'd have realized there was none.

Kelly clung, content to let the situation progress to whatever level Sam initiated. She hoped the kisses would lead to bed, without her having to suggest it, so she gave him all the encouragement she could.

When she pushed her small tongue into his mouth, she felt him surge against her. Then he sucked her tongue deeper, giving it a thorough going-over.

Her knees began to noticeably tremble. Sam picked her up in his arms and carried her through the lounge. When he reached the narrow hallway that led to the cabins, he was forced to move down it sideways until he reached his door. Once inside the cabin, he half expected her to wake up and realize his intent. But she remained silent when he closed the door, moved to the bunk, and sat down with her on his lap.

She spoke not a word while he bared her breasts to his hungry mouth and hands, but only moaned slightly when he tenderly caressed and sucked each swollen nipple. The only movement she made was to lace her hands into his hair and latch on, anchoring him in place.

When he ultimately lowered his mouth, following the indentation down to her navel, she coaxed him back with gentle tugs on his hair. He complied twice, while deft fingers worked to relieve her of her jeans. Sam was delighted to see she wore the same tiny scrap of material she so blithely called underwear.

His arousal, trapped inside jeans, throbbed painfully, until he finally managed to shuck them.

They were lying on the bunk when he eased off the thong, lowered his head, and spread her legs. One flick of his questing tongue and her knees came up to accommodate him. She offered herself without reserve, moaning and writhing as he brought her to fulfillment.

She was still open for him, all honey-sweet and sleek heat, and he couldn't wait another moment. Knowing what waited for him, he took her with one long thrust, then lifted her buttocks to push deeper. Realizing this might be his last opportunity to claim her, he stroked her long and hard, willing her body to remember if her mind should somehow forget. Needing her to know that she was his as much as he was hers and that, even if someone else claimed her, she'd always belong to him.

Chapter Fourteen

Before meeting Sam, Kelly had no knowledge that love-making could be so overwhelming. Had not believed it possible for a woman to have several climaxes in one session. But with Sam it seemed most anything was possible. He used his hands, mouth, and sex to turn her mindless over and over again. And she loved it. Absolutely loved it. Because she loved him.

After the third climax she was toast—milquetoast. She couldn't have risen from the bunk to save herself, even if the cruiser went down. She'd just have to go down with the ship. How Sam managed to rise, shower, and dress, she'd never know. It was *way* beyond her. All she wanted to do was snuggle down and float away on wonderful dreams that couldn't quite match what she'd just experienced. Sam. In all his glory.

He bent over her, gazed into her eyes, and her mouth just naturally turned up at the corners. In the back of her mind she remembered Scarlett's smile the morning after Rhett carried her up a flight of stairs and ravished her, and she believed her smile must have been very similar because Sam chuckled low.

Then he lowered his head and gave her one last mind-stopping kiss. "I'll be back . . . don't go away," he whispered.

She managed to nod her head.

By the time he reached the door, she'd stretched and yawned.

As he opened it, her eyes were drooping.

She didn't even hear him lock her in. If she had, at that moment it might not have mattered. She was his love slave for as long as he wanted her. All she hoped was that he'd want her for a long, long time.

Forever would be good, she thought, just as she dropped off to sleep.

The sex had been so fantastic, Sam was euphoric for hours after he left Kelly locked in her cabin. It was only after he began to wonder what she'd do when she found out she was locked in, unable to leave unless he let her, that he began to think. And when that happened, the euphoria dissolved quickly. In his heart of hearts, Sam knew sex wouldn't hold Kelly, no matter how good it was. Not if she felt there was no future for them.

He could lock her away, but that wouldn't stop her from wanting to be free to pursue a life that didn't include him. One she felt he wasn't qualified to deal with. From the way she looked, talked, and behaved, he felt certain she was too high up on the social ladder for the likes of Sam Tanner.

The rain had ceased and they were moving again, gliding across the water slowly and carefully, making their way to Calcutta.

Turning over the wheel to Pele, Sam hurried below to unlock the cabin door before she woke and tried to get out. There'd undoubtedly be hell to pay if he didn't beat her to the punch. What *had* he been thinking? Cursing under his breath, he reached the door as she started to pound on it.

"Son-of-a-bitch," he whispered. *Too late!*

"Let me out!" Kelly's voice was low and tense, and he detected panic just under the surface. He assumed she was afraid to shout because that would wake Jeff, and disturbing him would cause her even more concern than being locked in her cabin.

"Take it easy." Sam put his mouth close to the door so she could hear and, hopefully, Jeff couldn't. "I'll have you out in a second."

He unhooked the latch fastening, slid the door open, and stepped back, wanting to appear as non-threatening as possible. "I'm sorry. I don't know what happened."

Kelly swept by him and fled into the lounge, where she turned on him with an expression of pure outrage. "How could you? How could you lock me in that way?"

"Don't look at me like that, sweetheart. It wasn't intentional." He held out his hands, palms up. "It was just some sort of reflex action I can't explain."

Yeah, right, he thought.

Kelly had awakened with a delicious sense of well-being. She had showered, dressed, and fussed with her hair. She had even put on a little makeup, wanting to look her best for Sam. Then, anxious to see him, she had hurried to the door and found it locked.

Her stomach had plummeted. Sam had locked her in.

Her Sam.

Her love.

At first she had tried to rationalize the ugly fact away, wanting to believe it was a mistake. But that wasn't possible. You didn't subconsciously lock doors with people inside. Especially on a boat, which you might suddenly need to evacuate.

Now she stared at him, as if seeing him for the first time. "What if we'd hit something and the ship went down?"

"I'd have gotten you out."

"What if you couldn't? What if you were hurt or killed?" Even now, the thought of his being injured in any way squeezed something in her chest and made her want to cry through her anger.

On his way to let her out, Sam had had time to imagine the disaster that could have befallen them and the terrible scenario would probably haunt him forever. How in hell could he explain the rush of possessiveness that had turned him into a nut case?

"I can't explain what happened," he answered roughly, "because I don't know. I guess I just must have lost it for a moment. But I was coming back to let you out, just as you knocked."

She eyed him uncertainly, then glanced at her watch. "You didn't come back until three hours later," she accused.

"Guilty, but with extenuating circumstances," he said. giving her a lopsided smile. "I've never been in love before, so please forgive me if I don't act the way you think I should."

She just stared at him. "You expect me to believe that?"

"I sure as hell hope you do."

She shook her head. "Well, I *don't!*"

He sighed. Defeated, hating himself, he dropped to one of the lounge benches and snarled, "You're right. I'm a bastard who just wanted to keep you locked away so I could get into your pants anytime I wanted. Does that make you feel better?"

He'd feared all along that a relationship between them wouldn't work. Apparently, that's why he'd wanted to hold on as long as he could. That's why he'd locked her away, and that was the God's awful truth. He really was a bastard, he decided.

Kelly turned and rushed towards Jeff's cabin. Talk about

confused. Her emotions were running wild. Just hearing him say he'd kept her locked away so he could get into her pants ignited her, turning her hot all over. It made her want him again. Right there. In spite of what he'd done. So, what was *her* problem?

Sam Tanner. Her sassy little inner voice tweaked her—*he* was what was the matter with her. She was in love and in lust with him. And, truthfully, she couldn't blame him that much. The fact that he'd told her he wanted her right where he could get to her made her want to jump his bones. So she ran, because he needed to be taught a lesson. If they were to have a relationship, it had to be freely given. She'd be no man's love slave.

Hah! Her inner voice was laughing its fool head off.

Sam watched Kelly run away with a pained expression on his face.

Kelly found Jeff fast asleep. Not wanting to disturb him, she tiptoed backward out of his cabin. Then, because the last thing she wanted to do was go back into her cabin, she made her way as quietly as a cat to where she could see into the lounge.

Sam was gone, the lounge empty.

Breathing easier, she made her way into the galley. It, too, was empty. Without a second's hesitation, she dashed up the ladder to the deck. She needed fresh air. She also needed a large dose of reality that the jungle surrounding them had a plentiful supply of every day in the week. Nights even more so. As harsh a reality as one could find.

She settled aft, on the cushion that covered the back end of the cruiser, and watched the passing scenery. Sam was in the wheelhouse and so far hadn't noticed her, leaving her free to observe life on the banks of the water. Helping her free her mind and senses of him.

People were scattered sparsely across the sand, some doing laundry, some watering livestock, and a few just standing and watching the boat pass. Occasionally, one of the villagers would wave, and she waved back, smiling, feeling lighter for that brief moment.

She heard Sam before she saw him. Heard him descend the ladder from the wheelhouse and advance on her. She didn't turn to greet him.

"Looks like people are taking advantage of the good weather. Guess they've had enough of the rain."

He was some conversationalist, she thought. All he could come up with to talk about was the weather. *How lame.*

She nodded. "Yes."

They passed a native boat that seemed to be stationary, with the men on board holding ropes. As they moved beyond it, Kelly was fascinated to see that the ropes were tied around otters.

"What are they doing?"

"That's the way they fish around here, if they can afford the otters." Sam pointed. "See the net the men are holding?"

"Yes."

"Well, the otters will herd the fish into the net."

"Are the otters expensive?" she asked.

"About a hundred bucks a piece. Darned expensive for the natives, but it's the only way to go."

Kelly nodded. "I suppose so." At least they were talking, no matter how stiffly.

Shortly afterwards, they passed a native gathering something from the sand and depositing it in a burlap sack that hung over his back like a knapsack.

"What's he collecting?" she asked.

"Probably crabs or shrimp . . . part of the main food supply for the people who live close to the water."

"I see." She lapsed into silence.

Sam knew damn well he wasn't going to get much more out of her. Feeling lucky she hadn't swung at him, he decided to retreat.

"Guess I'll get a cup of coffee," he said. "Could I bring you anything?"

"No, thank you." Her tone was cool.

Shit! He'd really blown it by locking her in.

Halfway to the ladder, he heard a strangled cry.

Expecting to hear a splash and see an empty bench, he spun quickly around. She was still on board, but standing at the rail, a hand over her mouth. He reached her in seconds, and grabbed her arm.

"What is it? What's the matter?"

She pointed back to the beach where the native had been collecting clams. He was in the water now, swimming for his life. A tiger, showing amazing speed, quickly closed the distance between them.

It was over in seconds.

The tiger caught the man by the nape, broke his neck, turned, and calmly paddled back toward shore. When the big cat emerged from the water, the man hung limp in his teeth.

Sam pulled Kelly into his arms. Feeling her tremors, he tried to soothe her.

"This probably won't help, but the natives believe the Tiger God guards their world. They think the tigers are necessary, that they protect the forest, and without them the land would die. As hard as it is for us to understand, they accept that a price must be paid, that they will lose some of their own for the greater good."

"It's horrible," Kelly cried.

"It's a way of life. We're just damned lucky it isn't our way."

"It's too hard." Pushing away from Sam, she whispered, "I'm going below to be with Jeff. I won't be back on deck until we reach Calcutta."

With no clue what to say to change her mind, Sam let her go. He couldn't really blame her, even though, if she thought about it, her world was just as violent. Maybe even more so. Drive-by shootings were nearly an everyday occurrence in the Los Angeles area. Still, this killing had unfolded in front of her in seconds and she'd probably never actually seen a shooting.

When they tied up at Calcutta, Sam sent Pele, who knew the city well because he lived there, to the bustling hospital, to see if he could get the ambulance to come out and pick up Jeff. Sam knew that when the paramedics picked him up, Kelly would leave as well. She'd been by Jeff's side for the last few hours of the trip, even going so far as to eat her meals in his cabin. That, and her joyful response when they docked, told Sam everything he needed to know. She'd talked Sam into finding her brother and now that Sam had gotten Jeff to safety, it was over.

Sam figured it would damn near be the end of him, as well. Somewhere in his chest he had developed an ache so sharp that it hurt like the devil. The rest of him felt empty, numb.

Pele boarded under Sam's ever watchful eye. "The ambulance come, sahib. Real soon." The little man, sensitive to Sam's unhappiness, withheld his usual toothy grin while giving Sam the good news.

"Good job." Sam acknowledged Pele's accomplishment. It wasn't easy to get one of the area's ambulances out, unless a doctor sent in the order.

"You turn the boat in today?" Pele asked.

Sam blew out a breath, then shook his head. "I think I'll

stay aboard for a day or two, until Jeff is well enough to travel home."

Now Pele exhibited his full set of bright, shining teeth. "Okay if I stay aboard, too, sahib?"

"Thought you had other fish to fry." Sam was referring to the woman Pele had decided to pursue.

"Fish, sahib?"

Sam smiled down at the other man. "You know . . . the woman you told me about."

"Ahhh yes, need to fry that fish, but first need to buy new clothes and get haircut." He gazed down at himself.

"Well, let me pay you then, and you can start doing some of those errands." Sam reached for his wallet and extracted a sheaf of the local tender. He counted out what he owed Pele and added a handsome tip.

"Will that do it?" he asked.

"Yes, sahib, that more than enough. I will have new clothes and much money to impress the woman. That is a good thing." He grinned, then sobered. "Does sahib not have enough money to get his woman?"

"I'm afraid it's not a question of money."

The ambulance arrived, its siren shrieking.

"Not money?" Pele appeared perplexed. In Calcutta a man who had money had a nearly one hundred percent chance of gaining the wife he wanted.

Sam just shook his head. "No."

"That too bad, sahib." Pele gazed at his feet and shook his head. Then his head jerked up and his eyes brightened. "One other way work when man wants woman and has no money."

"Yeah, what's that?" Sam was desperate enough to try anything.

Pele beamed. "Man take woman far away with him, where no one can find them. He make baby, then she is his."

"Sounds like one hell of a fine idea, but in this case I don't think that would work."

"You know best, sahib." Pele sounded downright depressed.

"You take off now and find those clothes. Have that haircut, see the woman. Then come back and tell me how it all turned out."

"I will surely do so, sahib."

Hours later, the little man returned with a wide grin and a thumbs up. Mission accomplished.

That was the last time Sam had anything to smile about.

When Sam went to the hospital and found that Jeff and Kelly had left and flown home without a word to him, his guts felt as if they had been ripped out by a tiger while he was still alive.

She had left a handsome check and a note at the admissions desk. She'd thanked him profusely and explained that she and Jeff had been advised to get to the States as quickly as possible. They'd been presented with an immediate chance to leave and had taken it with a moment's notice. The flight was a direct flight to Los Angeles, and she mentioned the hospital that was expecting them.

Kelly's heart ached as the small airplane took off and she spotted Sam's boat below, rocking gently at the dock. It was for the best, she told herself, as tears tried to form. They'd never understand each other. Besides, Jeff's health had to be her first priority. Getting him to the States quickly could save his leg, or at least that's what the doctor at Calcutta's hospital thought. And she wasn't about to second-guess the doctor.

Still, leaving Sam left her feeling as if she had a hole in her heart the size of the valley on the moon. But what could she do? There hadn't been time to say good-bye, and if there had been, she might have lost her head and begged him to love her. And that would have been downright humiliating, under the circumstances. Sure, he'd made love to her. He had said he loved her after he'd locked her in the cabin, but she wouldn't delude herself. That didn't mean a damn thing. Not to a man like Sam. He didn't need a woman for anything but warming his bed.

Sam flew to the States as soon as he could arrange a flight. Even knowing he pursued a hopeless cause didn't stop him from going directly to the hospital in Los Angeles where Jeff was being treated. There, he learned that Jeff wouldn't be ready for discharge for at least a week.

With an agony of doubt dogging his heels, he stopped outside Jeff's room, and took a deep, steadying breath. If Kelly wasn't there, he'd have to somehow persuade Jeff to tell him where she could be found.

How do you bend the arm of a guy with a broken leg? he wondered. If Kelly had told Jeff what a bastard Sam had been, why would Jeff help?

Gearing up for a battle, Sam pushed the door part way open . . . and froze.

Jeff's voice floated to him through the partially open door, and Sam overheard a conversation between Kelly and Jeff that changed his life forever.

"I think it's time you admitted the truth, sis," Jeff said.

"And just what good do you think that would do?" Kelly asked, sounding peeved and unhappy.

"You've been depressed for days. I just think it would do you a world of good if you admit you miss him."

"I *hate* him!"

"You *love* him," Jeff accused.

"I'll get over him."

"Sis. . . ."

Kelly sighed. "Okay, I admit it. I miss Sam. But I don't want to talk about it anymore. Besides, I should go so you can rest." She kissed Jeff on the cheek and said good-bye.

The minute the door closed behind her, she froze in shock. Sam, as big as life, stood directly in front of her.

He went into action, pulling her into the empty room next to Jeff's.

Kelly had ached for Sam every minute of every day. Now that he was here and she could move, she wasn't sure what to do. Throw her arms around him? Or back away in fear? Something in his eyes warned her that he was highly charged.

"Look at me!" he commanded. He held her gaze with an intensity that made her catch her breath.

"What is it?" she whispered. Her heart beat like a wild thing in her chest.

He breathed deeply to ease the constricting tightness in *his* chest. "Were you telling the truth in there?" He inclined his head toward Jeff's room.

"What do you mean?" She hedged. It was clear he'd overheard something of her conversation with Jeff, but what part?

"I heard you say something about me," he said, watching her for the smallest sign of encouragement.

Her stomach fluttered. She'd said a lot of angry things before she'd admitted to Jeff that she missed Sam.

"You're making a mistake," she said.

"I don't think so. I heard my name."

She winced and struggled to stay detached. "Did you?"

His insides quivered. Maybe he'd just imagined she'd said she'd get over him and that she missed him.

233

"It was something about missing me," he said roughly. Her face flooded with color. "People who eavesdrop don't always hear good things about themselves."

"It wasn't intentional," he murmured, suddenly afraid his hearing had deceived him. Maybe she'd been talking about someone else, another man, and he'd just imagined she'd spoken his name and missing him in the same sentence.

Desperation drove him. His hands tightened on her arms. He couldn't let her walk away. Not again.

"What did you say in there?" He inclined his head toward Jeff's room.

A cleaning lady pushed through the door with her well-equipped cart and gave them a quizzical glance.

"If you want to talk, let's go outside," she whispered. If he'd heard her telling Jeff about wanting him, he'd also heard her explain why it would never work between them. So at least she'd be left with a smidgen of self-respect.

Somehow she made it outside, into the brisk air, without breaking down and declaring her love.

He stopped her with a hand on her shoulder. "We're outside. Now talk."

"I said a lot of things. What, specifically, did you have in mind?"

She was driving him nuts. Deciding he'd never pin her down, Sam, being Sam, picked her up and tried his best to devour her with his mouth.

Kelly melted, just like every other time when he'd kissed her.

Apparently, he'd been wasting a hell of a lot of time. He continued to kiss her until horns started blaring and catcalls erupted behind them. Then he reluctantly put her down.

"Gonna tell me now?" he asked in a voice deep with need.

"I might have said something about missing you," she whispered, hanging her head.

He stared down at the top of her head, his heart hammering so loud he felt sure she could hear every beat.

"I know I'm not exactly what you had in mind, sweetheart, but I love you. And if you want me to beg, I'll get down on my knees and grovel. Just say you'll marry me."

In a hushed voice, she asked, "Is that a definite proposal?" She could barely believe her ears.

"They don't come any more definite, blue eyes. When we leave here today, we hop a plane for Las Vegas and get married at the wedding chapel closest to the airport . . . if you're willing."

He watched her like a drowning man.

She felt faint. "Married? Today?"

"Uh-huh."

"I couldn't possibly. Not today."

She looked around her helplessly. Things were moving way too fast for her to assimilate.

"Why not?" His face muscles tightened from tension. *She didn't say no!*

She appeared dazed. "I don't have a dress, anything. . . ."

He leaned back and glanced down at her. "What do you call that thing you're wearing?" She wore a flowered silk dress and sweater with matching trim.

Her eyes followed his. "Well . . . it's not a wedding dress."

Sam lowered his head and took her mouth in a gentle kiss that turned urgent almost immediately.

When he finally managed to pull away, his voice sounded hoarse. "It's the perfect wedding dress, sweetheart. Can we go now?"

With her body on fire, Kelly couldn't think of a single reason why they *shouldn't* get married.

"How long is the flight to Vegas?" she whispered.

"Too damn long," Sam growled, as he lifted her into his arms and headed for his rental car.

Placing her gently on the seat, he lingered, studying her. "There's just one thing I need to know. . . ."

His gaze had gone all squinty-eyed, and a flutter hit her insides. Almost afraid to ask, she finally whispered, "What?"

Sounding almost harsh, he asked, "You said you'd get over me. Does that mean you love me?"

For the first time since she'd known Sam, she saw a chink in his armor, a tiny vulnerable spot. "Yes, darling Sam, I've loved you from the moment you rushed back to the boat, pale as a ghost, because you thought something had happened to me. And I know I'll always love you."

He appeared stunned. "Even before we made love?"

"That's why we made love." She smiled up at him.

"Well, I'll be damned." He shook his head, then sent her a puzzled look. "Why didn't you tell me? It would have saved me a hell of a lot of grief."

She stared at him, silent for a moment, then asked softly, "When did you know you loved *me*, Sam?"

Comprehension dawned. He whistled low, then sighed. "The moment I heard those shots when I was deep in the jungle and thought I'd lost you."

Warm all over, Kelly asked, "Why didn't you tell *me*, Sam?"

He leaned back in and bussed her again. "I tried to tell you on the platform, but I guess you didn't get the message."

Her eyes refocused. "I get it now, darling. Can we go to the airport soon, please?"

He slid behind the wheel and gave her a squinty-eyed, deeply sexy warning. "Don't even think about trying to change your mind."

She just grinned.

About the Author

Marlys Rold has traveled extensively throughout Western Europe, many Mediterranean islands, including Sicily and Crete, and has also visited Turkey, Canada, South America, China, Finland, Poland, Estonia and Russia.